Praise for the
Magical Dressmaking Mystery Series

A Fitting End

"A fun family affair.... Fans will enjoy Harlow Jane's amateur sleuthing with advice from her late great-grandma and the Texas posse."   —The Best Reviews

"Bliss is a wonderfully Southern town, with all its charms and foibles, traditions and society.... This enchanting mystery with down-home charm is as comfortable as slipping into your favorite dress and sitting down and drinking sweet tea with engaging characters who quickly become old friends."   —The Mystery Reader

"Harlow is a delight.... There's something a bit magical about this series. Ms. Bourbon has taken a premise, characters, and a setting that may not have worked with anyone else at the keyboard, and created a fab-tastic series."
      —Once Upon a Romance

"A fun book, with the wide assortment of characters filling the page."   —Fresh Fiction

"The perfect blend of dressmaking and intrigue."
      —Sew Daily

Pleating for Mercy

"Enchanting! Prepare to be spellbound from page one by this well-written and deftly plotted cozy. It's charming, clever, and completely captivating! Fantasy, fashion, and foul play—all sewn together by a wise and witty heroine you'll instantly want as a best friend. Loved it!"
      —Hank Phillippi Ryan, Agatha, Anthony, and
      Macavity Award–winning author

continued . . .

Other Magical Dressmaking Mysteries

A Custom-Fit Crime

A MAGICAL DRESSMAKING MYSTERY

Melissa Bourbon

AN OBSIDIAN MYSTERY

OBSIDIAN
Published by the Penguin Group
Penguin Group (USA) Inc., 375 Hudson Street,
New York, New York 10014, USA

USA | Canada | UK | Ireland | Australia | New Zealand | India | South Africa | China

Penguin Books Ltd., Registered Offices: 80 Strand, London WC2R 0RL, England
For more information about the Penguin Group visit penguin.com.

First published by Obsidian, an imprint of New American Library,
a division of Penguin Group (USA) Inc.

First Printing, July 2013

Copyright © Melissa Bourbon, 2013

OBSIDIAN and logo are trademarks of Penguin Group (USA) Inc.

ISBN 978-0-451-41719-0

Printed in the United States of America
10 9 8 7 6 5 4 3 2 1

ALWAYS LEARNING   PEARSON

For Aunt Sarah,
and for my own best friend, Marilyn.

Acknowledgments

A special thanks to Gretchen (Gertie) Hirsch and her blog, Gertie's Blog for Better Sewing, to Ann Athey for inspiring Harlow's rag quilt, to Diedre Johnson for introducing me to the story of Cynthia Ann Parker, to Carol Loo for inspiring me with her wool beads, and to Carolyn Klein Lagattuta and her spiderweb pictures.

Chapter 1

When I'd first returned home to Bliss, Texas, I thought my hometown would be just as peaceful as it was when I was a little girl. It was still sweet and Southern, sure, but lately death had found a way of creeping in between the seams, and too often, I'd been in the mix.

In New York, a knock on the door in the middle of the night would have been enough to send my heart into a frenzied patter. But I was in Texas now, and a *tap-tap-tap* on the front door of my little yellow farmhouse with the redbrick trim wasn't cause for alarm.

"Meemaw?" I rolled to my side, my voice sleepy. My great-grandmother, Loretta Mae Cassidy, had passed on before I'd come back home, but I'd learned that the Cassidy women didn't always cross right over to the other side. Not something that had filled me with joy when I'd found out.

Meemaw hung around the farmhouse her daddy had built, trying to communicate with me. Or playing jokes, depending on how you looked at it.

If Loretta Mae was tapping on the door downstairs, she wasn't letting on. "Meemaw, I'm sleeping," I murmured, but the sounds continued.

And then, through my bleary eyes, I saw the red and gold curtains on either side of the window rustle followed by a louder tap-tap-tap from downstairs. If Meemaw was up here with me, then who . . .

I lay still in my bed, listening for a repeat, wondering for a second if I had imagined the sound.

But then it came again. *Tap. Tap. Tap.*

I peered at the clock. Two a.m. Surely the Dallas fashion brigade, which was supposed to show up in the morning for part two of an interview and photo shoot, hadn't arrived eight hours too early. I was suddenly wide awake, my pulse zipping along like a sewing machine whose foot pedal was stuck. I jumped out of bed, stepped over Earl Grey, the sweet little potbelly pig Will Flores and his daughter, Gracie, had given me at Christmas, and padded, barefoot, across the cold wooden floor and out to the landing, stopping to listen.

Tap. Tap. Tap.

Mama wouldn't knock. She'd just come on in. Same with Nana and Granddaddy, and *they'd* come in to the kitchen through the Dutch door off the back porch.

It could be Will. We'd been dating for months now, and every day we grew closer and closer, but he didn't just show up on my stoop in the middle of the night. He wasn't that kind of man, and I wasn't that kind of woman. Which led me to— "Oh no, Gracie?" She'd run here, to me, once before when she'd learned the truth about her mother leaving her when she was just a baby. We'd formed a close bond since I'd come back to Bliss, too, and I certainly didn't want her out alone in the middle of the night.

The sound at the door changed, becoming more of a scraping. It seemed to move off to the window. Surely it wasn't Gracie, I reasoned, darting a quick look around for a weapon. Just in case. An antique sidebar stood against the wall in the landing, a decorative metal dress form on one side, a bowl filled with handmade felt beads on the other. I could pelt the intruder with the little round balls of wool, but that wouldn't ward off whoever it was for very long. If at all. The magical Cassidy family charm wouldn't help, either. I could make people's wishes and dreams come true when I made clothing for them, but I couldn't conjure up a spell to protect myself from strangers at my front door.

With nothing but my wits, I descended the stairs. They were even colder against my bare feet, but I made it down, turned left into the part of the house that doubled as my shop, Buttons & Bows, and stooped to snatch up one of my red Frye harness cowboy boots. Not much in the way of defense, but better than felt beads, and definitely better than empty hands.

The scraping turned back to a knocking and I had another thought. Nana's goats! Maybe it wasn't an intruder at all. Nana and Granddaddy's property was directly behind mine, and Thelma Louise, the grand dam of Nana's herd of dairy goats, managed to escape the farm more frequently than not. She was as mischievous as all get out, and she liked to pick on me.

"Harlow?"

I froze, my elbow bent, the boot cocked behind my head. Nana's goats didn't speak. Neither did Meemaw's ghost, for that matter.

With my ear up to the door, I held my breath and listened.

"Harlow, are you there?"

The voice was familiar. It was a woman. Low, as if she didn't want anyone to hear her calling my name, which was silly since it was the middle of the night and she'd already wakened the entire neighborhood with her ruckus at my door.

The doorknob jiggled and I jumped back. "Who's there?"

The doorknob jiggled again. "Harlow, it's Orphie."

Orphie! I dropped the boot, turned the lock, and pulled open the door.

Black, curly, shoulder-length hair. Tall and thin like a model. Bronzed skin. It really *was* Orphie Cates. "You're early!" She wasn't set to arrive for two more days. If I had to be rousted from my sleep in the middle of the night by anyone, Orphie would be in the top three on that list.

I squealed, rushing onto the porch, wrapping her in a bear hug. "I can't believe it! Orphie? Is it really you?" I pushed her back, stared at her, and then drew her in for another embrace. I hadn't seen her in a year and a half, although we'd talked on the phone and had a constant stream of e-mails back and forth.

"In the flesh," she said after I finally let her go. A wry smile graced her perfect lips. We'd worked at Maximilian together, a top New York designer, but really, Orphie should have been on the runway. She was *that* beautiful.

And she was right about the flesh part, too. The dress she wore had a low-cut scoop neck that draped at her cleavage. Two thin spaghetti straps went over her shoulders and crisscrossed in the back. The pattern had been cut on the bias and hung in silky waves over her body. It was her own design, I knew, utterly sexy, and absolutely out of place in a down-home town like Bliss.

But Orphie was Orphie. She had style in spades and she wasn't afraid to show it. I was the same way, but my style was a little less revealing.

As she looked over my shoulder at the shop, I grabbed her by the wrist and yanked her into the house, shutting and locking the door behind her.

"So, this is where the magic happens, eh?" she said, a playful grin on her face.

That one little sentence made me gasp. Only a handful of people knew about the Cassidy charm. My family, of course, since they were all charmed, too. Madelyn Brighton, the town photographer and a good friend, and Will Flores, the man Meemaw had set me up with from the great beyond. His daughter was charmed, too, but didn't know it yet. The little town was bursting at the seams with secrets.

But Orphie didn't know, and she wasn't referring to my magic. She was talking about my dressmaking. "This is it," I said, spreading my arms wide.

She wandered around, looking at the antique armoire that held stacks of fabric, the custom designs hanging on a freestanding rack against the back wall, a bulletin board with favorite sketches pinned to it, oohing and aahing the whole time. Finally she made her way to the French doors dividing the front room of the shop and what had once been Meemaw's dining room. I'd turned it into my workroom. Her gaze took in the cutting table that sat in the middle, a wooden pulley contraption for fancy gowns that was affixed to the ceiling thanks to Will's handyman skills, Meemaw's old Singer sewing machine and my PFAFF, my Baby Lock serger, dress forms, and a shelf unit with Mason jars of buttons, baskets filled with trim, and every other sewing supply I might need as I developed Cassidy Designs.

"It's really great, Harlow," she said, stopping at my newest purchase, a commercial sewing machine. "And look at this!" She lovingly brushed her fingers over the top.

"Business has been getting better," I said. I'd made custom designs for a few of Bliss's most prominent matrons, including Zinnia James, wife to a local senator. I'd worked on several festivals, including the local debutante pageant and ball, and the town's holiday extravaganza. Word was getting around about my designs and how they made people feel.

No one knew it was thanks to my ancestor Butch Cassidy wishing upon an Argentinian fountain. That magic charm had bestowed gifts on all of Butch's female descendants—Loretta Mae was able to get whatever she wanted, Nana had turned into a goat whisperer, and my mother, Tessa Cassidy, had a thumb greener than the Jolly Green Giant's.

"And you're sewing for your mother's wedding now?" She looked around, searching for a wedding dress.

The gown, if you could call it that, was on a dress form in the seating area of Buttons & Bows. It was anything but a typical wedding dress, but I was quite sure the design fit Mama to a tee. From the lace sleeves to the slight ruffle at the neckline, it was Southern sass that fit her age and temperament.

"That, and I'm just finishing my fall collection for the feature in *D Magazine*." I'd recently spent two days in the Dallas Design Center to meet with the journalist who was writing the article, and the two other designers who'd be featured. A day in an artsy showroom and another in the warehouse that housed an atelier had been exciting and new, but by the end of the trip, I missed my quaint little shop in my little yellow farmhouse.

Now it was their turn to see how the other half lived . . . the half outside Dallas.

Orphie went back to wandering the room, as if she were absorbing every last detail. "You said they're coming here tomorrow for the photo shoot?"

"Right. The journalist wants to see both sides of the fashion world. Designers in the Design District, and"—I spread my arms wide—"my little outfit here in Bliss. Tomorrow, the models and designers will come here and they'll shoot pictures to showcase my so-called country sewing space. Big contrast to where the others work and live. I just hope they don't make me seem all Green Acres compared to the new-money bling of Dallas."

"They won't." She trailed her hand across the cutting table, looking longingly at the length of fabric stretched out and ready to be cut first thing in the morning. "It's about up-and-comers, right?"

"Right." I notched my thumbs toward myself, smiling. "And I'm one."

The exact words of the journalist who'd contacted me, Lindy Reece, were committed to memory. *We'd like to do an article featuring Dallas-area fashion designers who offer a unique perspective in the industry, both in and out of their own workspaces. You'll spend a few days in Dal-*

las. The other designers will spend some time in Bliss. Your work has a distinct perspective that's vastly different from what I normally see. It's an aesthetic worth sharing with our readership. I'd like to feature you, Ms. Cassidy.

My newest collection was entitled "Country Girl in the City" and I'd been working round the clock to flesh out the collection, finalize my lookbook, and make sure every piece had a cohesiveness, both in textiles and presentation, but also with my voice and what I brought to the fashion world. "Midori's bringing her models—"

Orphie gaped. "I love Midori! What she does with pattern and cut is amazing."

I did, too, and to have my designs featured next to hers made my skin prickle with nerves and excitement. The Japanese cultural influence she brought to her designs made her unique around these parts. I thought Midori's perspective could steal the show, and I wanted my clothes to show well in comparison.

"The third designer is Michel Ralph—"

"Beaulieu," she finished. "You mentioned that. He's . . . interesting. His aesthetic is a little muddied."

Temperamental was a better word. He got plenty of play on fashion blogs and was plenty popular—if not well liked. "You know what they say."

"Yeah. He *borrows* from other designers," she said, invisible quotations around the word "borrows." "Wonder how true that is." She collapsed onto the red velvet settee in the seating area of Buttons & Bows. "I can't believe he ended up in Dallas."

He'd been there for a long time. "For about ten years now." We both knew Michel Ralph Beaulieu from our days at Maximilian. Back then he'd been everywhere, making the rounds and ingratiating himself with every designer he could. When he'd gone off on his own, we'd seen his success as a sign of what could happen for each of us. Our own lines. A show at Fashion Week. A real future as a designer.

I was developing my own line, and I saw myself as a designer. I no longer cared about showing at Fashion Week. I was content right where I was.

She frowned, but not even that marred the perfect, Botox-free silk of her skin. "Don't you think a lot of his stuff is imitation?"

I'd definitely seen similarities between Beaulieu and Jean Paul Gaultier, whose brilliance was drawn from the world around him, from different cultures, cinema, and rock music, for starters. His designs were worn by icons like Madonna and Lady Gaga, and he brought something utterly new to the fashion world.

"Beaulieu's stuff seems more Prêt-à-Porter." Orphie stretched her long legs out on the settee, stifling a yawn. I hid my own, suddenly reminded that it was now nearly two thirty in the morning.

"I do some ready-to-wear pieces, too, Orphie," I said. She'd glanced at some of the clothing on the portable rack. I preferred couture, like any designer, but Bliss didn't have much use for stagelike costuming or artistic statements through clothing. My Country Girl in the City collection was unique, practical, and truly represented my hybrid perspective. It wasn't boudoir or urban jungle or mishmash like Beaulieu, and it wasn't Japanese punk or metropolis like Midori, but it was *me*, and I was proud of it. Everything I created was a combination of body, heart, and soul. Like with most designers, what I created always expressed who I was as a person. Emotions, complications, layers ... it was all woven into every seam, every cut, every tuck and pleat. I had an appreciation for sewing with care, for reenvisioning couture. Intricately crafting a garment from the design stage to the last seam was all part of what made sewing such an enjoyable experience for me.

"Orphie," I said, sinking down on the love seat opposite her, the coffee table that had been repurposed from an old door between us. My lookbook and another bowl of felt beads I'd been working on for my collection's accessories sat in the middle of it. Another yawn came. I plumped a pillow under my head, and it suddenly felt as if we were back in Manhattan in our minuscule loft apartment. "What's going on?" She'd called out of the blue, telling me she was coming for a visit, but she hadn't said why. Now it was time for her to fess up.

"You said your mom's getting married to that cowboy sheriff," she said drowsily.

I tried to follow her lead, but I could feel sleep slip over me like a veil. "Right." My mother and Hoss McClaine were getting hitched, and it was going to be a really eclectic Southern wedding. I'd been charged with making her dress, which I had done, and my sister-in-law Darcie's bridesmaid dress, which was mostly done. I was maid of honor and hadn't even started on *that* design. On my list of things to do was something for Will Flores's daughter, Gracie. After that I'd be done, but I hadn't come up with the right design for either dress yet. And I only had a matter of days.

Orphie's eyes had begun to drift closed, but she pried them open again, her gaze falling on the red and black suitcase she'd set by the steps to the little dining area. "And you have the photo shoot. I haven't seen you in ages, and I figured you could use a little help with all of it."

She was a true friend, and she sounded sincere, but there was a tenseness in her expression and I knew there was something she wasn't telling me. Southern women had several rules they lived by, one of which was being well versed in doublespeak. True, Orphie wasn't Southern—she was as Midwestern as they came—but she'd picked up some tricks from me over the years, and I suspected there was a little subtext under her statement that she'd come to help. "Orphie?" I said, stretching out her name, my voice lilting on the last syllable.

"Harlow?" she replied.

"What's going on? You did not drive ten hours and arrive in the middle of the night to help me with my sewing, although, don't get me wrong, I'm glad you're here."

She sighed, sitting up and propping her elbows on her knees. I mirrored her, but then she got up and trudged, as much as a five-foot-ten-inch lithe woman can trudge, over to her suitcase. She plopped it down flat, unzipped it, and lifted a book off the top of the neatly folded clothes.

I recognized that book. Hard black cover. Crisp white interior pages. Maximilian logo embossed on the front. I jumped up and backed away as if it were a coiled snake. "Orphie, what are you doing with that?"

"I never told you the reason I left Maximilian," she said, her voice slow and tired.

I didn't like the sound of that simple statement. The fact was, she'd just up and quit. Packed up one day and left, with no explanation. "Family," she'd said later when I'd pressed her.

"Why'd you leave?" I asked, not entirely sure I wanted to hear the answer.

She strode to me, book outstretched in her arms. "This is why," she said solemnly. "You're one of my closest friends, Harlow. And . . . and I need your help."

Oh Lord. So Orphie hadn't come to help me with Mama's wedding to the sheriff, and she hadn't come to be my assistant for the *D Magazine* photo shoot. Which left only one possibility. Had she come here because . . . was it possible that . . . oh no. Could she have stolen one of Maximilian's prized design books, the thing that held his ideas and sketches? I stared at her, trying to make sense of that absurd thought and wondering just how on earth she thought I could help her.

Chapter 2

Orphie and I had lived together for almost two years, which meant I had a good take on how she operated. Or at least I thought I had. I never would have pegged her as the kind of girl to steal a design book from her boss, so maybe I didn't know her at all. In which case, I just needed to be up front.

"What in tarnation are you doing with Maximilian's design book?"

Her lower lip quivered and her eyes teared up. "It . . . it was a horrible mistake," she finally blurted. "I . . . I was so frustrated with everything we were doing for him. All the long hours and endless sewing, and for what? We never got any credit."

"But look at us now," I said, cupping my hand over hers.

"Look at us now? You are barely making ends meet, and I'm nowhere close to doing what I'm meant to be doing."

"Orphie, I'm being featured in a pretty big magazine, and you? You've got your own line and it's fantastic! We're both doing great. It's not New York, but neither of us liked New York all that much."

My words had been meant to cheer her up, but a tear slipped down her cheek and she lost what little control she had over her emotions. Her chest heaved and she dropped her head to her hands. "You d-don't understand, Harlow," she said through her sobs.

I sucked in a deep breath, steadying my mounting anxiety. "Then tell me."

Instead of launching into some sort of explanation, she got up again, made another trip across the room to her suitcase, but this time, she came back with a dress. It was a halter design with a full skirt, full of playfulness, yet the fabric and cut held a subtle hint of seduction. She draped it over the arm of the love seat, the skirt fanning out to show the full design of the crepe de chine.

I fingered the hem. "It's gorgeous," I said. It had a familiar look to it. Similar to . . . My gaze strayed to Maximilian's book. "Oh no."

"Oh yes," she said. She flipped open the book, licking her middle finger and dragging it across the lower right-hand corner, turning the pages. She stopped, turning the book around on the table to face me.

The pencil sketches on the page showed angular models, legs crossed, tiny pointed toes, and a dress from different angles, almost identical—my eyes slid back to the garment she'd brought from her suitcase—to the one lying across my couch.

"Orphie, tell me you didn't."

"I can't," she said, her voice scarcely more than a whisper. "It's one of his older books," she said, as if that made a difference. She paused, swallowed, and seemed to realize how ridiculous that statement had been. "I took it without thinking, and once I had it, I panicked and—"

"And that's why you left," I finished.

"Part of me wanted to return it, but . . . but . . ."

I understood. She'd been at war with herself over doing what was right and doing what she thought might get her some success. Even if it wasn't earned.

"It's not too late, you know."

Her eyes opened wider as she looked at me. "I think it is."

"It's not." My mind raced through the possibilities. "We can just mail it back. Anonymously."

But she shook her head. "Believe me, I thought of that. But if we mail it from here, or anywhere near Texas, they could blame you. If I mailed it from Missouri, they'd blame me. Anywhere in between, they'd figure out I'd driven from there to here and that would be that. No. I can't just mail it back."

"Who's *they*, Orphie? It's not like there are fashion police out there waiting to apprehend . . ."

I trailed off, not sure how to end the sentence. She did it for me, her eyes welling with tears. "Waiting to apprehend thieves? What if they are? Maximilian is a big name in fashion, even if the book is a few years old. I haven't even had a chance to try to make it as a designer and I could lose everything."

"People make mistakes," I said. "You had a lapse of

judgment, but you want to make it right. That counts for something, Orphie."

"Does it?" she asked, more to herself than to me. She cast a sorrowful gaze down. The bones of her shoulders curved in as her back hunched before she added, "I'm not so sure and it might be too late for that."

Chapter 3

The next morning came all too soon. Orphie was keeping something from me. I knew it in my bones. But she wouldn't spill whatever it was, and we'd eventually fallen into a sleepy silence and drifted off—me on the couch and her on the settee. We were awakened when Mama showed up, plowing through the front door and dropping an oversized shopping bag on the floor by my red cowboy boots.

My eyes flew open, sleep instantly leaving and adrenaline rushing in. "What time is it?"

"Time for you to be up and at 'em," Mama said. "What in heaven's name are you doing on the couch?" she asked, but then she laid eyes on Orphie and her furrowed brow smoothed. "Well, bless my soul. Is this—?"

Orphie had pushed herself to a seated position, grinning sheepishly at my mother. "Orphie Cates, Ms. Cassidy. I showed up a little early."

"It's Tessa," Mama corrected, and before Orphie knew what was happening, my mother caught her up in a big ol' Southern hug. "You're every bit as beautiful as Harlow said you are. Even sleepy-eyed, isn't she, Harlow Jane?"

I nodded, padding toward the kitchen. Orphie could be wearing a tattered bathrobe and have an avocado face mask smeared all over her skin and she'd still look like a million dollars. "Yes, ma'am," I said, wishing I could look half as good when I rolled out of bed. I could feel my hair standing on end and the puffiness beneath my eyes. Good Lord, it was nine o'clock. Time really was a-wastin'.

Nana came in through the Dutch door in the kitchen just as I pressed the brew button on my single-cup coffee machine. She kicked off her shoes to pad around in her pristine white socks, which was her habit. "Mornin', darlin'," she said.

As if in response, the gingham-checked drape on the coil rod beneath the sink rustled. Loretta Mae was in the house whispering her own form of good mornin' to us.

A moment later, Nana was in the front room throwing her arms around Orphie, too. "As I live and breathe, we've heard so much about you over the years. I don't know how Harlow would have survived Manhattan without you," she drawled.

"Didn't take her long to hightail it home after you left," Mama added. "So I reckon we should thank you for that."

It was true, Orphie had suddenly quit Maximilian, packed up her belongings, and vacated the little loft we'd shared, and I'd come home to Bliss not long after. The truth was, though, that Meemaw had passed and I'd found out that she'd deeded me her little farmhouse the very hour I'd been born. It felt right to come home to Texas.

"It's a pleasure to meet you both," Orphie said, pulling free from the Cassidy clan. She gathered up issues of *Vogue* and *Marie Claire* that had ended up on the coffee table the night before, slipping them back in the magazine rack near the sitting area, finally turning back to face my mother and grandmother. Mama and Nana looked like two peas in a pod. They stood in front of Orphie, their arms folded in front of them, skeptical looks on their faces. They were small-town women, but were savvy enough to know that a long-lost friend showing up in the middle of the night was cause for suspicion. "What brings you to Bliss?" Mama asked.

Cut to the chase, that was my mama's modus operandi.

Orphie lowered her gaze to mine and I felt as if she were sending me silent pleas to help her somehow. "I haven't seen Harlow in ages, is all, and she told me about your wedding—congratulations, by the way! And the big magazine story? That's beyond exciting for a designer. I just had to be here."

I knew the truth, and I'd known Orphie long enough to know that the zip and enthusiasm in her voice were sincere but also laced with her worry. They did the trick with Mama and Nana, though, softening their expressions instantly. They both dropped their arms to their sides, nodding and letting their skepticism slip off their faces and allowing smiles to slide on. "Isn't that sweet of you?" Mama said. She looked at me. "Isn't that sweet of her, sugar? Came all the way from—" She turned back to Orphie. "Where do you live now?"

"Springfield. Missouri," she added, in case we didn't know our geography.

"All the way from Missouri. That's a good friend."

I nodded, smiling, but my gaze was pulled to her suitcase still sitting undone in the corner by the French doors. Maximilian's book might as well have been a beacon. I wanted to snatch it up, wiggle my nose, and have it disappear from here and end up back in Maximilian's hands.

But that wasn't going to happen.

Nana walked into the workroom, picked up the garment on top of my work pile, and held it up. It was a straight skirt with a scalloped edge. She looked at me, a silent question passing from her to me as she said, "Harlow tells us these two designers she's with in the magazine article are some highfalutin bigwigs."

"They are," I said as I picked up a length of lace and handed it to her, along with the pincushion and a spool of thread. "Midori brings in specialty fabrics from Japan and puts design elements together that are . . ." I was speechless for a second. "She's in a class by herself, that's all. And Michel Ralph Beaulieu? People just love his clothes—"

"Regardless of how good they actually are," Orphie said, and I knew she was referring to his derivative nature.

"He's a little abrasive," I added, "but he does quality work."

"I hear he refused to use models from the DFW Metroplex," Orphie said.

I'd heard the same thing, and the modeling community in Dallas, such as it was, wasn't happy about that.

"True. But Midori's the same way. She has her go-to girls and no one else can wear her clothes."

"At least she chooses locals," Orphie said. "Beaulieu's a New York snob. I heard he won't work with anyone who hasn't walked a major runway."

"He doesn't sound like my kind of people," Nana said as she dragged a stool from the cutting table to the threshold of the workroom and perched on the edge of it. She draped the skirt over her lap, threaded the needle, and expertly stitched the lace behind the hemline.

"He wasn't all that bad when I met him in Dallas." I pointed to a scallop on the skirt. "Gather it at each point."

She nodded. "Lovely design, ladybug," she said.

Orphie grinned, her tired eyes lighting up. "Ladybug," she said, her voice reminiscent.

She and I knew almost everything about each other, including childhood nicknames. The only thing she didn't know was the reason behind the ladybug nickname—namely that the Cassidy women tended to hang around after they'd passed. Family legend said that my great-great-grandmother, Cressida, had fluttered around as a ladybug, sticking close to me when I'd been a child learning to sew with Meemaw.

"Did you make your dress yet?" Mama asked me. Her wedding was just days away, and the devil was in the details. Rehearsal dinner at Babe's Chicken House, ceremony at the Baptist church, and reception at the new bed-and-breakfast opened by sisters Hattie Barnett and Raylene Lewis.

"Not yet, Mama, but I will."

She sent me a scolding look. It wasn't that I was procrastinating; I just hadn't figured out what to make quite yet. Somehow designing for myself was overly challenging. I didn't think I could make my own dreams come true, and I wasn't entirely sure what I wanted beyond what I already had. Maybe that was what held me back. Regardless, my mind was blank in regards to my own dress.

Thankfully, like any supercharged bride-to-be, Tessa Cassidy was on to the next task on her list. "I've decided that I don't want a traditional veil."

Uh-oh. Mama making fashion decisions meant I'd been coerced into designing a cowgirl wedding gown that she'd be wearing with embellished cowboy boots. All of which, I knew, Hoss McClaine, her fiancé, would adore, but which fashion bloggers everywhere would eschew.

"What do you want instead?" I asked, afraid of the answer.

She reached for the shopping bag she'd left by the front door and took out a bundle wrapped in tissue paper. I knew what it was before she had all the paper undone.

Orphie gasped.

Nana grinned.

My heart dropped.

Mama held a brand-spanking-new white suede cowboy hat, smiling from ear to ear. "This is my veil," she announced.

"But, Mama—"

"Bling," she interrupted. "Lots of bling, just like the boots. And I want a short length of tulle attached from the back." She placed the hat on her head, smashing

down the loose curls of her short hair, completely covering the streak of blond sprouting from her temple.

I frowned. My collection for the *D Magazine* shoot
showcased my Southern aesthetic, but it didn't include
white suede, tulle, and sequin-covered cowboy hats.
"Good grief, Mama, are you sure?"

"Are you kidding?" Orphie clasped her hands together. "It's fantastic!"

I tilted my head and squinted to see if I could visualize it.

I couldn't.

But I could visualize the clock, and I knew time was
running out. I directed Orphie to the spare bathroom
upstairs, and we split up to get ready, reuniting a short
while later back downstairs. And just in the nick of time.
As I took the last step and turned to walk back into the
front room, the bells attached to a wide strip of grosgrain
ribbon hanging from the doorknob jingled and the door
flung open. A man with a camera on a wide shoulder
strap waltzed in, followed by a woman toting an oversized bag—the journalist Lindy Reece.

The *D Magazine* people had arrived. "Great to see
you again, Harlow," Lindy said, stretching her arm
toward me. I gripped it in a firm handshake. No Southern
belle limp hand from me.

"Quite a trek out here to Bliss," I said.

"But worth it. Lovely town."

"We think so," Mama said, sidling forward, her cowboy hat veil still cradled in her hands.

The photographer, Quinton, raised his camera, adjusted the focus on his lens, and snapped a picture. For
the magazine or his personal collection, I didn't know,

but I could see why he'd taken it. Mama was adorable. A blushing country bride.

I introduced everyone all around. "I worked in New York with Harlow," Orphie said, stepping forward.

Lindy gave a faint smile. "Friends forever, eh? And you came to be here for the shoot?"

"That, and for her mother's wedding."

Lindy nodded as Quinton pointed his camera toward the workroom, focusing on something in the distance, depressing a button with his index finger. "We'll get some test shots," he said, "do the photo shoot when everyone else settles in and the models are ready, and we'll be on our way."

"Perfect."

Lindy waved to Orphie and said, "Nice meeting you," before following me and Quinton, who apparently only went by the one name, around as I showed them my little farmhouse. It didn't take long. We ended in the kitchen, where I poured them each a glass of lemonade from the pitcher my mother had made, stepping aside as Mama carried the tray with the rest of the glasses out to the front room. To Mama, Southern hospitality meant lemonade all around, whether a person wanted it or not.

We followed her back to the front room. A moment later, just as she set her tray on the repurposed coffee table in the sitting area, a thin Japanese woman wearing a color-blocked dress in black, red, and white came in. She carried a long bolt of fabric wrapped around a heavy cardboard cylinder. It was a Japanese print, and beautiful. Just like her. Midori. Before I could step forward and greet her, Michel Ralph Beaulieu blew through the door looking as though he owned the place—and with a disdainful puckered upper lip. The very beginnings of crow's-feet around his eyes and a slight wearing of his skin put him well into his thirties. His bright yellow scarf, a black rhinestone-adorned vest over a white shirt, unbuttoned halfway down his front, skinny forest green pants, and pointy-toed brown leather shoes made him look more suited for Project Runway than a little Podunk town in Texas. He tossed a white disposable coffee cup into the trash and then lowered his chin, raising his eyes at us for the briefest of glances around the room. "Fashion takes place here?" he said.

From his tone, Michel Ralph Beaulieu might as well have asked if he was going to be made to lick the floor. I bit back the response teetering on the edge of my tongue—just barely. I'd been nothing but respectful when visiting his showroom. I'd hoped for the same from him. I kept a clean house and shop, and fashion could be defined in a lot of different ways, and it could be created anywhere. Including Bliss, Texas.

The air in the room grew tense. Nana bristled. Mama threw her shoulders back. A whirl of agitated air circled around me. Even Meemaw was fighting her anger. The V of Orphie's eyebrows and her deep frown showed her disappointment in this well-known designer. I'd lost a lot of my starry-eyed perspective working in Manhattan, and after she'd shown me Maximilian's prized book last night, I knew that she had, too. But despite her lapse in judgment in taking Maximilian's book—and his designs— she was still a dreamer and I knew she wanted to believe the best of people. Herself and Beaulieu included.

I could see in her eyes that she was realizing the truth. The tales about Beaulieu hadn't been exaggerated. One more dream dashed.

Quinton continued to peer through the viewfinder of his camera, snapping more test shots. Lindy Reece, and *D Magazine*, had insisted on getting both the Dallas Design District version of fashion, as well as my small-town perspective. "It will show dichotomy in fashion," Lindy had said, "and make it accessible for everyone, not just the models, the runway crowd, and the rich and famous."

I hoped she was right, or I might come off looking like a homespun hick compared to the Midori and Beaulieu side of high fashion.

"Good light. Good color," Quinton said to no one in particular. "No clutter. This'll work just fine."

Midori leaned her fabric against the wall and strode forward, her arm outstretched. "It is nice to see you once again, Harlow. What a quaint shop." She offered up a smile before flashing a glance back at Beaulieu.

"Nice to see you, too. And thank you," I said, my accent thickening instantly, as if it were a barrier against any disdain that might be launched my way. I met her smile, but Beaulieu didn't look convinced by either of us.

"It's so . . . bourgeois," he said, not bothering to hide the sneer curling his lips. He sucked in a deep breath through his nose, swallowing heavily as he adjusted the front of his shirt under the waistband of his pants. "Even more so than that chain coffee shop we stopped at outside Dallas."

Mama and Nana looked at him, at each other, then at me. I just shrugged. Bourgeois wasn't a bad thing in my opinion. The high life wasn't all it was cracked up to be.

But I was beginning to doubt Lindy Reece's stipulation that Midori—and especially Beaulieu—do the photo shoot with the models here in Bliss. From Beaulieu's re-action, it just seemed like a bad idea. But I pasted a smile on my face and buried my building frustration.

His grimace deepened as he looked around, taking in every last detail. "Does this place have a decent loo?" he finally asked.

I ignored his tone and his affected British vocabulary and directed him to the half bath off the kitchen. He hur-ried past Orphie as she zippered up her suitcase, frown-ing at her as she started to drag it. It was as if he couldn't get away from my pedestrian sewing space quickly enough. Lord almighty, it was going to be a long day. The models were due to arrive after lunch for the fashion shoot, and who knew how long that would take? I got the feeling nothing went smoothly with Beaulieu.

Midori disappeared outside, returning a minute later with a second bolt of fabric. She smiled sheepishly as we watched her haul it into the shop. "I bring this with me everywhere," she said, her fingers lightly brushing the fabric. It was a reprint of what looked to be a girls' ki-mono fabric from half a century ago. "It's hand-printed," she said. "There is a Yuzen factory in Kyoto that hand-prints all of these fabrics with stencils. I have them ship to me occasionally and usually I see the pattern and know just what I'm going to design. But not this one. It stumps me, so I bring it with me hoping inspiration will strike."

"I've never seen anything like it," I said. The chirimen crepe was rayon and looked almost wrinkle free. Differ-ent flowers, all stenciled, lay on top of one another on the rose-colored background. "Lovely." I looked more closely, noticing something I hadn't at the first quick glance. Hummingbirds hid behind the flowers, playing peekaboo, lending a playfulness to the pattern.

"I will figure it out," she said, nodding. She set it aside as Orphie returned from depositing her suitcase upstairs and Beaulieu returned from the bathroom. Another woman, who I immediately recognized as Beaulieu's assistant, stumbled inside, an overloaded garment bag in her arms. She headed for the love seat, ready to drop her heavy load.

"No, Jeanette," Beaulieu snapped, and pointed. "Over there." He paused and his eyes strayed to the kitchen. Then he said to her, "Water. Get me some water."

From under her burden, Jeanette nodded. She detoured around the love seat and set the bag on the red settee and headed to the kitchen, but Mama beat her to it, pouring a glass of water and handing it to Beaulieu.

She and Nana disappeared again into the kitchen, leaving the chaos behind. I wanted to go with them, but this was my shop, my photo shoot, and my chance to show off Buttons & Bows. I wasn't going anywhere.

Beaulieu stood off to one side, tapping his foot, his arms crossed over his chest, while Jeanette lifted garments from the bags and Midori carried in a modern-looking dress form and arranged a strapless tiered ruffled dress in a floral print. They'd each brought samples for their models to wear. Quinton had said he wanted to do a series of outside shots, again, to show the dichotomy of fashion in the country, and he wanted his photographs to represent each of us and the Texas perspective.

I still had to bring out my collection, but I'd seen both Beaulieu and Midori shoot wayward glances at my mother's wedding dress. Next to their upscale designs, the quirky lacy white dress looked like a throwback from *The Beverly Hillbillies*.

I quickly grabbed the dress form with the wedding dress on it and hauled it from the front room through the French doors and into the workroom. I pushed it against the wall, out of sight, and took a quick moment to stand still and breathe. "Don't let them get to you," I muttered to myself. I could hold my own against Midori and Michel Ralph Beaulieu. I was proud of my designs, and that was all that mattered

The hemline of Mama's dress fluttered and from somewhere in the house, pipes suddenly creaked, sounding an awful lot to my mind like someone saying, "It's all good, it's all good, it's all good."

Meemaw. My great-grandmother always knew how to make me feel a little better, even from the hereafter.

I grabbed the three garment bags that stored my new collection, bringing them into the front room and draping them over the back of the green paisley couch, trying to block out the annoying chatter. Michel muttered to the still shell-shocked Jeanette. His gaze darted around my shop. "The whole town is straight out of an old western movie. All that's missing is John Wayne."

Hoss McClaine was more Sam Shepard than the Duke, but he was as country as a country sheriff could get. Somehow I didn't think mentioning any of this would ease Beaulieu's mind.

I turned to Midori, but she was intent on setting up her headless mannequins, draping silk red, black, and cream-colored scarves around the stubbed necks, straightening the bust of the first dress, standing back to survey the look, then moving forward again to make another adjustment.

Her designs had a sleek, polished look to them, plus unusual design elements like enormously wide hems and exceptional closures, and I wanted to get a better look. "It's good to see you again," I said, coming up beside her. "I studied your work when I was in school." She'd been held up as a designer with a unique perspective, and with a singular compassion for the ordinary person. She sold her runway designs to everyday people for pennies on the dollar. *Everyone should have a chance to experience high fashion,* she'd been known to say.

She looked up at me. "I guess I have been around too long to be an up-and-comer, then," she said. A twinge of self-doubt flitted over me. Did that mean that I was too young? Too green? Too country?

No, I was being overly dramatic. I was good at what I did, and what I did was fashion for the everyday woman.

Orphie seemed to sense my doubt. "Soon everyone will know Harlow's name," she crooned, gliding up beside me and slinging her arm around my shoulders. "We were both on Maximilian's premiere design team."

Beaulieu's head snapped up, his stare burning holes right through us both. Looked as though there was no love lost between him and Maximilian. "Maybe so. We should talk," he said. Or more accurately, he ordered. "We have some things to discuss."

Orphie continued, looking right at Beaulieu as she said, "She learned from the best, but developed her *own* style. Harlow's designs are unique. No one has an aesthetic like hers. She has a special gift."

This time *my* head snapped up. There it was again. Orphie's reference to my gift made my heart stutter. Only a handful of people knew—and that's how I planned to keep it.

I laughed, waving away Orphie's praise—and my suspicion that she might know more about my charm than she was letting on. "I work hard, that's all," I said.

Beaulieu scoffed as he plucked an issue of *Vogue* from the magazine rack and absently flipped through it, flashing a look at each of us in turn, ending with Midori and then with me. "We all work hard, sweetheart. There's nothing new about that."

"Some more than others," I said, not letting his dismissive comment get to me. "I've built my shop from the ground up—"

"In Bliss. Go to New York. Better yet, go to Europe. At least you'll do something more than . . . than that," he said, gesturing toward my work room.

"I'm right where I belong," I said. "Bliss is my home."

"You'll never amount to anything if you stay here," he said.

"I'm doing what I want to do." I hadn't thought about it in such clear terms before this moment. I'd chosen to leave Manhattan, I'd set up shop in Meemaw's house, I knew she'd brought me here for a reason, but I hadn't questioned it too hard. I'd fallen into life in Bliss just as surely as my little teacup pig, Earl Grey, rooted in the mud outside when I let him. We sought out what felt good and right, and Bliss fit the bill for me.

Lindy Reece stepped between us, looking as if she were ready to break up a fight. "Like I said, it'll make for a great story."

"Every Texas tale needs a hillbilly element," he said, not even bothering to play off his comment like a joke.

The journalist looked tongue-tied. She clearly didn't want to offend me, but Beaulieu was a bigger name. More important to keep him happy. "You each have something different to offer our readership," she said.

"If you say so," he said, but his snide smile made it pretty clear he didn't agree. Jeanette dropped one of the garments she'd been unpacking from her boss's collection. Like a predator tracking its prey, Beaulieu seemed to sense the disturbance. He whipped around, zeroing in on his assistant. "Be careful with that," he snapped. He shoved the copy of *Vogue* back into my magazine rack, and he moved to her in three long strides. "How many times have I told you to never ... *never* ... crumple the garments in your sweaty little hands? It needs to be pressed. Now."

Red splotches appeared on Jeanette's cheeks, and the same color crept up her neck. Poor girl. From where I stood, it hadn't looked as though she'd done anything to the fabric, but she seemed to know how to handle her boss. She drew in a bolstering breath, gently took the dress back—which, I realized, looked familiar—and turned to me. "Do you have a steamer?"

Did I have a steamer? That was akin to asking a cowboy if he had Skoal in his back pocket and packed in his cheeks. I smiled widely at her. "I sure do. Follow me."

Jeanette and I went into the workroom. I spread my arm as if I were selling a product on an infomercial, grinning at the steamer in the far corner. It had been my first major purchase, after my commercial-grade sewing machine, since being back in Bliss.

Jeanette just nodded. She didn't seem overly impressed, which meant Michel Ralph Beaulieu probably had a higher-end steamer. I turned it on so it could warm up, and made idle chitchat. "How long have you worked for Beaulieu?"

"Almost a year," she said. She bit her lower lip and darted a quick glance over her shoulder. "I'm sorry about what he said out there. He forgets his manners sometimes. He's usually not this bad."

Forgets? I wasn't sure his mama ever taught him any in the first place. "It's fine," I said. It was a lie, but I was a good Southern woman and wasn't about to bad-talk Jeanette's boss no matter how much of a numbskull he happened to be.

"You really worked with Maximilian?" she asked as she hung the dress on the steamer's hanger. "Beaulieu is determined to surpass his success one day."

I just nodded. If Beaulieu's dreams were based solely on one-upping Maximilian, then I felt sorry for him. He could dis me all he wanted, but I liked who I was and what I created. I didn't need to one-up anyone.

I left Jeanette to her steaming and went back to the front room. Beaulieu had been riffling through my designs on the portable clothing rack while Midori had been flipping through my lookbook. When I reappeared, they joined me at the dress forms. "Ready," I said to Lindy and Quinton. It was high time to get this show on the road and get back to the wedding plans, which, now that I thought about it, was all I really wanted to do.

Chapter 4

Meemaw made her presence known by clanking the pipes, making them moan and creak during the photo shoot. It was a response, I suspected, to Beaulieu's under-his-breath mutterings as he poked around my shop, shaking his head and wiping his hands on a handkerchief. "How can you live here?" he asked me, staring at the ceiling after a particularly loud reverberation.

"Family and history," I said. "Being in my great-grandmother's home makes me feel closer to her."

He smirked, as if family were the worst possible reason to do anything. Clearly it was a fundamental difference between us. I'd come to realize that family was the best reason to do anything, and that being back at 2112 Mockingbird Lane meant that Loretta Mae wasn't gone from my life.

I was dotted with sweat by the time Quinton was done snapping me sitting at Loretta Mae's old Singer, by one of my garments, and standing, arms folded across my chest, in front of the privacy screen that doubled as a changing room. The screen resembled oversized window shutters connected by antique hinges. I'd taken down some of the fabric I normally kept draped over the side, and positioned just one hanger with a dress that perfectly represented my country girl design perspective, from one of the upper slats.

He ended the shoot by having the three of us—Midori, Beaulieu, and me—in front of our dress forms, one of each of our pieces showcased behind us. I snuck a glance on either side of me. Neither one of the other designers smiled, but me? I was giddy. I stood next to two of the top designers of our time—inside Buttons & Bows—and I was going to be in *D Magazine*. I couldn't help it. One side of my mouth lifted. This was a proud moment.

"We're good," Quinton finally said. He kept his camera handy but wandered to the sitting area and the tray of glasses Mama had set out, hemming and hawing as he picked up first one, then another, and a third canning jar from the array. Finally he settled on one and poured himself a tall drink of sweet tea from the pitcher next to the lemonade. He settled back while Midori stretched out on the red velvet settee and Beaulieu sat on the love seat, absently flipping through a home decor magazine, scowling as if he could hardly stand the feel of the paisley fabric.

Lindy Reece stood by the rack of ready-to-wear clothes just outside the little area. "Thanks for making the trip out here for the shoot," she began, addressing Midori and Beaulieu.

"It was a mistake. I feel ill," Beaulieu said under his breath, but loudly enough to make sure we all heard.

Unbidden, a line from a Taylor Swift song flitted into my head. *Why'd you have to be so mean?* It was a good question, but one I couldn't answer. I gave up trying to figure him out. I had to get through the rest of today. Gracie and her friend Holly would be wearing my garments. As long as I focused on them, I could keep Beaulieu and his ornery attitude at bay.

"Yes, well, it'll be worth it in the end," the journalist said. "Concessions must often be made for the sake of a story."

Mama came into the room just in time to hear this snippet of conversation, fresh pitchers of sweet tea and lemonade in her hands. She stopped short just behind where Beaulieu sat. She raised her arms and my heart seized.

She lifted the pitchers higher.

I started. She wouldn't dare

The pitcher tilted forward, the amber liquid sloshing.

Oh Lord. She couldn't. She wouldn't! "Mama . . . ," I said with a hiss.

She blinked, caught my eye, and instantly pulled her arm back. Instead of splashing onto Beaulieu, the tea sloshed over the spout of the pitcher and onto the floor.

Beaulieu must have sensed what had almost happened. He whipped around, gently patting his hand over the gelled hairs of his faux hawk. "What the hell's the matter with you people?"

"You people?" Nana said, venom dripping from her heavy Southern accent. She'd been hanging back, sitting on the steps of the staircase, the scallop-edged skirt in her lap, a threaded needle gripped between a rubber-encased index finger and thumb, but now she surged forward. I threw my arm out, stopping her from plowing straight into Beaulieu.

"Nana, don't," I said. The last thing I wanted was for Lindy Reece to get a bunch of ammunition to write about the crazy Cassidy family from Bliss. It might sell magazines, but not for the right reasons.

It didn't take a genius to figure out what Mama might have done with that pitcher of tea, and Beaulieu wasn't about to let it go. "You're all hillbillies," he spit. He was laying it on thick.

My arm still held Nana back. She tensed, but stayed put.

"Michel—"

He cut me off and his attention cut back to me like a guard dog suddenly training his attention on a new sound. "This place . . ." He gestured to the room at large. "You're a disgrace to the fashion industry."

And like a worn length of elastic stretched too thin, I snapped. My open palm flew to my chest and I felt heat rise to the surface of my skin. "You're in *my* hometown," I said, my voice raw and edgy. "This is my home . . . and my business. How dare you come in here and call us hillbillies and . . . and . . . ?"

"And a disgrace to fashion," Nana whispered in my ear, as if I could forget.

"Right, and a disgrace. My designs are . . . are . . ." I saw the dress Jeanette had taken from the garment bag and pressed, registered somewhere in the back of my mind that it was familiar, and remembered what Orphie had said about Beaulieu. She wasn't the only one who'd borrowed a design from someone else. "They are original," I said.

A collective gasp went up all around. Jeanette lost her grip on her oversized shoulder bag. It fell with a thud, her wallet, lip gloss, and other personal items spilling onto the floor. Orphie pressed her fingers to her mouth. Midori, Mama, Nana, and even Beaulieu himself stared at me. It had been a veiled accusation, and one that I couldn't take back now that it had been spoken aloud, much as I wished I could.

"You must be the only virtuous one left in this room," he said, looking around, pausing on each person as if he knew some big secret about each and every one of them. He ended on Jeanette, holding out the magazine he'd been perusing. I stared, flabbergasted, as she stood from collecting her things, hurriedly taking the glossy from him and setting it back on the table. As if he couldn't have reached the table himself. Diva. It was the only word that came to mind. And Jeanette was his lackey.

The scratching of Lindy's pen against her notepad sounded magnified, but my blood pounded in my ears and drowned it out, the sound louder than a thunderous summer storm. "Not virtuous, but honest." Orphie had experienced a blip in that virtue, but I bet that deep down she wished she could turn back the clock and take back her momentary lapse of judgment.

Beaulieu just kept talking. "All of you think you deserve success more than I do, is that it? Why? Because I didn't grow up poor? Because I'm a man?"

"Michel—"

He held up a hand, stopping the rest of his name from slipping off my tongue. "My work will stand on its own. My designs will blow your mind, and anyone who reads the article and sees what I do will know that you"—he pointed at me—"and you"—he pointed at Midori—"are outclassed. Neither one of you should be here."

I could picture him sitting on a stool, ranting to some television producer about his sob story, going for the sympathy vote from the viewing public, only this wasn't Project Runway, Heidi Klum and Tim Gunn were nowhere to be found, and I wasn't feeling any sympathy for the man. He was boorish and . . . and . . . and just downright uncivil.

Someone's stomach rumbled. As if the sound triggered a Pavlovian response, Midori reached for a glass and poured herself some lemonade. Jeanette followed, and before long, everyone had a chunky Mason jar filled with sweet tea or lemonade and was munching on a treat from the plate Mama had placed on the coffee table. She might be mad as all get out at Beaulieu, but she wouldn't deny him one of her famous almond icebox cookies. Nana had brought two containers of her goat cheese, along with a package of rice crackers. Then Mama offered to make fried chicken for lunch, but Beaulieu shook his head.

"I'm going to lunch before the outdoor shoot with the models." He downed the rest of his tea, put his empty glass back on the coffee table, and shot a scathing look at Jeanette. "Make sure everything's ready," he said. "After it's done, we're going back to Dallas."

She nodded, her face blank, but her throat pulsed. She could try, but her body betrayed her emotions.

Beaulieu stormed off to the bathroom again, leaving the rest of us feeling muddled and angry. Calling him horrible was an understatement, and I felt enormously sorry for Jeanette. I already had Gracie Flores, but if I'd needed another assistant, I would have hired her just to save her from her horrid boss.

Midori gathered up the Mason jar glasses on the tray and carried them back to the kitchen. Quinton had gathered his camera gear and was at the door, Lindy by his side. "We'll get a bite to eat, then meet you back here. Six models, right?"

"Two for each of us, yes—"

A chilling scream ripped through the air, zapping the rest of the words from my mouth.

My heart shot to my throat and I surged past Jeanette, through the dining room—and smack into Midori, who stood stone-still in the center of the kitchen. She fell into me, knocking my glasses awry, her feet twisting with mine. I caught her wrists, holding her upright as she gripped my upper arms. "What's wrong?" All I could think was that an enormous Texas spider was loose, or that Meemaw was playing practical jokes.

"M-m-m . . ." Midori got stuck on the first letter, and my mind jumped to Meemaw. Except that Midori didn't know Meemaw, and certainly would not attribute any otherworldly goings-on inside Buttons & Bows to my great-grandmother.

"M-m-m . . . ," I mused, and then it hit me. "Michel?"

Behind me, Jeanette gasped.

Midori pointed past me. I turned, following her gaze to the half-open door of the bathroom . . . and to the sprawled body on the floor.

"B-B-Beaulieu," Midori stammered. And then she said what I already knew. "H-h-he's d-d-dead."

Chapter 5

A million thoughts raced through my mind, but I shoved them all away as I barreled past Midori. "No, no, no," I muttered. This couldn't be happening again. He'd been fine a minute ago. He couldn't be dead!

I fell to my knees beside him, pressing my fingers against the flesh of his neck. No pulse. No rise and fall of his chest. I lowered my head, listening for any trace of ragged or faint breathing.

Nothing.

My pounding heart climbed to my throat. I squeezed my eyes shut as if that would make this nightmare go away. But when I opened them again, my head grew fuzzy and my vision blurred. From somewhere behind me, Jeanette and Midori sobbed, but all I could see was Michel flat on the floor in front of me, his nose bloodied, his face drawn and pale.

He was most definitely dead.

It took about two shakes before Hoss McClaine showed up to gather up control of the situation. A dead man in the dressmaking shop wasn't an everyday occurrence in Bliss. Madelyn Brighton, one of my best friends and the official town photographer, showed up, too. Lickety-split, she snapped pictures, wrapped up her photographic cataloging of the scene, and Bliss's finest made a preliminary assessment. Massive coronary. It was unusual given Beaulieu's age, but it was the obvious explanation.

We'd all told the same story. Lindy and Quinton had arrived first, followed by Midori and Beaulieu and then Jeanette.

"His bad attitude might could have made his heart stop tickin'," Mama told her fiancé sheriff, nodding as if that were surely the explanation. I wasn't as convinced that his orneriness had done him in. He was likely cursed with bad genes, poor man.

Beaulieu's body had been taken away and all that was left was a heavy pall hanging over my shop. Well, that and Deputy Gavin McClaine, who stood in front of me with his legs apart, a Bliss Sheriff's Department cap on his head, and a disdainful scowl on his face. True, Beaulieu was dead, and also true, it was a horrible turn of luck that it happened at Buttons & Bows. But there was nothing sinister about it. Nothing that warranted the deputy sheriff hanging around—if you didn't count the fact that this was the fourth dead body I'd been associated with in recent months. My misfortune.

The deputy had been back in Bliss a few months less than I had, and I still had trouble reconciling the shy boy he'd been back in school with the cocky deputy he'd grown up to be. No more ninety-pound weakling. He was lean and lanky and full of attitude. And from the googly eyes Orphie was making at him, she'd noticed, too.

Gavin measured in at about five ten, and while there was no spark between us, he was handsome, khaki deputy uniform and all. Whenever I saw him, he was clean shaven, but I was sure he let his whiskers go scruffy when he was off duty. Another thing I knew from experience that Orphie would like about him.

Normally I could quickly picture a person's ideal outfit to help make his or her dreams come true, but I had been unable to get a vision of him in anything other than his khakis—I'd come to wonder if he ever took a day off.

He adjusted his cream-colored straw cowboy hat, flashed a smile that irritated me to the bone, and cleared his throat, continuing in his heavy Southern drawl. "So he just up and died, is that it?" he said, as if there was more to it than what we'd all already said.

"For pity's sake, Gavin, I told you everything I know. We were all here for the first of two photo shoots. We were getting ready to break for lunch before coming back for the second part of the day. He went to the bathroom, and then he . . . he died."

"Just like that."

"Yes, just like that." Oh, how I wished someone had been with him . . . that we'd had enough time to try to resuscitate him. We could be talking weddings instead of death.

"And you have no idea what happened?"

If only I did. "Maybe he was sick and we didn't know?" I suggested, making a mental note to myself to ask Jeanette if he had an illness. For my own peace of mind. I wanted to get to the bottom of what had happened to Michel Ralph Beaulieu.

"Did you hear anything? Did he cry out in pain? Anything at all?"

"Gavin—"

"Deputy," he said, correcting me.

"Deputy," I said, letting the word slide real slow from my tongue. "I just told you everything I know. He was fit to be tied at having to be here in Bliss, but he didn't seem sick. If I knew anything else, I'd tell you. He. Died."

Gavin dipped his chin and glared at me, and despite the grim situation, I had to smile to myself. The man was too big for his britches and he hated it when I called him by his given name instead of Deputy McClaine. It was a power thing. Being the son of a sheriff his whole life meant Gavin had some big shoes to fill, something he worked mighty hard at doing. "So he did, Harlow. Bad luck for the guy."

"Bad luck for Harlow," Orphie said. "That it happened in her shop, I mean."

Gavin turned toward her, dipping his chin to acknowledge her. "Got that right. But Harlow has a way of attracting death." He winked. "Best watch yourself, little lady."

Little lady? Oh, brother. I ignored his attempt at flirtation with Orphie because something he'd said had taken up residence inside me and I didn't like it. "It was a horrible accident," I said, hoping to God I was right, because no matter how I looked at it, having a man die in my shop was not going to be good for business.

It felt like forever, but finally Gavin McClaine had gotten every bit of information we had to give on the unfortunate death of Michel Ralph Beaulieu. Orphie walked him to the door, where they chatted for another few minutes, him leaning up against the doorjamb, and her with her shoulders curled in and looking at him through her eyelashes. Country courting was sweeter than a thick, creamy bite of pecan pie.

I didn't know if the magazine article was still a go. The models left the second Gavin gave the go-ahead, and Quinton and Lindy Reece had been next to hightail it out of Buttons & Bows, so I couldn't ask them. Plus it didn't feel right to be worrying about it on the heels of Beaulieu's death. As I moved the dress forms to the back of the room next to the portable clothing rack, a hungry stomach growled. I pinpointed it to Jeanette. Her boss had died, but the poor girl was starving. Midori heard it, too, and took Jeanette by the arm. "I am hungry, too. Come on."

"Fried chicken," Mama said from the dining room. "No need to go anywhere. I was fixin' to whip some up."

"Sounds good," Orphie said, closing the door after Gavin finally left.

But Midori shook her head. "No, no. I think we all need a change of scenery."

Jeanette nodded, her face ashen, her lips drawn down on either side of her mouth. I could almost hear every thought going through her head. *What do I do now? Where will I work? Will I be paid? Who'll take care of Beaulieu's appointments and affairs? Why did he have to die?*

This last question was the one that weighed on my mind. I was sure Gavin must have asked it already, but not in front of me—and I wanted to know the answer. "Jeanette, was Beaulieu sick?"

But instead of the answer I'd been hoping for—something along the lines of "Yes, he had a history of heart problems" or "Of course, he's been in poor health for years"—she shook her head emphatically, what little color was left on her cheeks draining altogether. "No. That man was healthy as a horse."

Midori guided Jeanette toward the front door. She still looked like a lost child, wide-eyed and helpless, and I thought Midori might be right. We'd all suffered a loss today, Jeanette most of all. Getting out of Buttons & Bows and going someplace neutral would hopefully help her state of mind.

And then there were four. Mama gathered up the Mason jars, Nana picked up the pitchers, and they headed to the kitchen and Orphie moved around the front room straightening pillows, all of them avoiding the white elephant in the room.

But I couldn't avoid it in my head. Death had knocked on the door of my world since I'd been back in Bliss, but now it had made its way inside.

Chapter 6

I'd known Orphie's visit to Bliss would be filled with wedding craziness. What I hadn't figured on was death darkening my door. We'd escaped the somber veil hovering over 2112 Mockingbird Lane by walking to Villa Farina for coffee and pastries. Now we sat across from each other, the stolen book from Maximilian on the table between us.

"So I guess Bliss isn't so blissful," she said, her expression grim. "Kind of puts things in perspective."

Death had a way of doing that. "It does. Things aren't as bad as we think they are. Let's mail the book back to Maximilian's studio," I said, nodding toward it.

She chewed on her lower lip, finally nodding. "But what if—"

"If they trace it back here, we'll deal with it. Orphie, it's the right thing to do."

She hesitated another few seconds, finally running her fingers across the bumpy cover of the book. "Maybe."

Relief flowed through me. At least she was thinking

about it. One crisis almost resolved. The other—
Beaulieu's death—however, still weighed on my mind. "I
still can't believe he's dead," I said, turning the conversation.

"I guess his time was up."

I'd been trying to convince myself of that for the last
hour, but something didn't add up. "I don't think it's that
simple," I said.

She cradled her white ceramic cup in her hands, steam
wafting off the surface of the cappuccino. "What do you
mean?"

"Remember when you were packing up your bag to
take it back upstairs?" I said.

She nodded. "With those designers around, I was worried about this," she said, dropping one hand to lay it on
the book between us. "What if one of them saw it?"

"They wouldn't have recognized it," I said, but even
as the words left my mouth, I wasn't so sure I was right.
Maximilian's logo was front and center on the book.
Most people in the fashion world probably *would* recognize it.

An idea sparked. "Orphie, you haven't told anyone
else about the book, have you?"

"What do you mean?"

"I mean, did you tell anyone else that you have this
book?" I asked again, not really able to rephrase the
question a different way. I wanted to know if I was the
first person she'd come to with her problem. If I wasn't . . .
well, I didn't know what that might mean, but I still had
to know.

She waggled her head as she said no, a sure sign she
was lying.

I pressed. "Orphie . . . ?"

"I haven't told anyone." She sounded more sure this time, but I still wasn't convinced. Before I could dig deeper, she smiled and clasped my hand. "Tell me about your man."

I laughed. "My man . . . that might be overstating it." Will Flores and I had been victims of the otherworldly matchmaking of Meemaw. She'd laid the groundwork before I came back to Texas, trading my sewing services to teach Will's daughter, Gracie, in return for handyman work around the little yellow farmhouse. "But it's good." I couldn't elaborate to say that he was still adjusting to the realization that Gracie was a Cassidy, too, on her mother's side, and that she, too, had a charm.

Orphie grinned at me, nodding as if she had a secret. "Yeah, I can see it's good from your smile."

I felt a blush heat my cheeks, but before I could change the subject, a hand came down on my shoulder. At the same moment, Orphie tilted her head back, gazing up behind me. "Hey, darlin'," a baritone voice rumbled.

"Speak of the devil," I said, turning to look up at the best-looking man this side of the Brazos River. Will Flores. My heart skittered for just a moment at his smile. Meemaw's matchmaking had hit a home run. Things were definitely good. He was a six-foot-one-inch modern-day rugged cowboy. Goatee, black suede cowboy hat, T-shirt that hung perfectly on his broad shoulders, jeans and Ropers. A tall drink of water, and the longer I knew him, the thirstier I got.

He leaned down and brushed my lips with a light kiss. From across the table, I heard Orphie draw in a breath. "Is this—?"

"Will Flores, meet Orphie Cates." She closed her mouth again and I added, "Orphie, this is Will."

Will took her hand in his, flashing a smile that lit up the dark complexion of his face. "Roommates in New York, right?"

"Right," she said, catching my eye and giving a quick wink. Her approval.

He grabbed a cup of coffee from Gina at the counter, and then turned back to us. "The rumor mills are churning," he said. "A designer died in your shop?"

"Technically, he died in the bathroom off the kitchen," I said. "In my house, not the *shop*." I added air quotes as I said shop, as if the semantics of where I worked versus where I lived made Beaulieu's death better or worse. It didn't. He'd died in my little farmhouse and that was horrible no matter how I looked at it.

I filled Will in on the details of the morning.

"Maybe he drank a lot of coffee," Will said when I commented about Beaulieu rushing to the bathroom.

"But an overactive bladder doesn't cause death."

"Deputy McClaine seemed to think it was a heart attack or something like that," Orphie said. "And I get the impression he has a pretty good handle on things."

There it was again. The flirtation. I guess it went both ways. Sparks between the deputy and my old friend. I sure hadn't seen that one coming.

He pulled up a chair and we chatted for a while, revisiting life in Manhattan. "I had to get away," Orphie was telling Will. Which brought Orphie's problem back front and center.

"Small-town life is a little simpler," I said, pushing my

worry away and not mentioning the murders I'd gotten wrapped up in since I'd been home.

"She had a few things waiting for her here," Will interjected. The implication was clear. *He'd* been here waiting for me.

"People are more real in small towns," Orphie said, as if it were a God-given fact.

"I don't know about that. We have plenty of secrets."

She angled her chin down, threading her thick black hair behind her ears. "Do tell."

I dropped my voice to a whisper, leaning forward so only she and Will could hear. "Murder."

Her brow furrowed and she rolled one hand in the air, prompting me to continue.

I filled her in on the darker side of life in Bliss in the time since I'd been back.

"Harlow's quite the amateur detective," Will said, a little edge slipping into his voice. He thought I needed to steer clear of murder, and I agreed, but I couldn't help it if dead bodies wound up in my vicinity. I had to help the people I cared about. I was a doer, not a watcher.

"At least Beaulieu's death wasn't murder," Orphie said, and just like that, my breath hitched. I glanced down, then around, a coil of nerves settling in my chest.

"Cassidy?" Will had leaned back, folding his arms over his chest. He looked at me as if he could read every last thought spiraling through my mind. "Don't tell me . . ."

I smiled sheepishly. "I've been thinking about it, and some things aren't adding up."

"Like he used the bathroom," Orphie said with a sarcastic laugh. "That's a sure sign of murder."

"I think it is," I said.

I might not be a detective, but I'd had some luck helping to solve the recent crimes in Bliss. Will knew this and paid heed to my instincts. "What's not adding up?" he asked.

How could I put it without sounding as if I was reaching? I racked my brain, finally giving up. Maybe I was reaching, but I ran through my thoughts anyway. "His stomach was upset. He was breathing hard. And he was extra ornery."

"That was probably his normal level of orneriness," Orphie said, but I shook my head.

"No, Jeanette told me he's not usually as bad as all that. Something had set him off."

Will nodded, as if he understood. "Maybe he was hungry. When I need to eat, I'm as grumpy as all get out."

"Or maybe he just didn't feel well," I suggested.

Orphie started, her eyes widening as if she'd remembered something. "Didn't he say he felt sick?"

I nodded. He had. I'd chalked up the comment to how he felt about being stuck in Bliss for the photo shoot, but maybe he'd really been sick.

Orphie stared. "Wait a second, Harlow. You don't think—"

I shrugged helplessly. "I don't know what I think. I just know something doesn't feel right."

"Cassidy, you have a wedding to put on," Will said, not looking convinced that my theories had any merit. "Don't be getting involved in this guy's death."

He was right. And practical. And I knew he wanted me safe and sound and not mixed up in another murder.

The nerves stayed firmly coiled in my chest, but I

tamped down my worry while we chatted. After a few minutes, Orphie checked her watch. "I'll go for a walk," she said.

"I can go with you," I said.

"No, no. I'll give you two lovebirds some time together. I'll meet you back at the house, Harlow."

Will put his elbows on the table and leaned closer to me, winking. He liked Orphie's plan. With good reason. He and I hadn't had much time alone lately. He'd been traveling for his job as city architect, and I'd been wrapped up in my collection and Mama's wedding. "Can you find your way back?" I asked her.

She waved away the question. "Of course. I'll probably be there before you."

I laughed. That almost sounded like a challenge. "I don't think so."

She smirked. "Uh, Manhattan, remember? I can walk a ten-minute mile . . . in stilettos."

Slight exaggeration, but probably not by much. I liked to stroll, but Orphie kept a rapid pace, and even did half marathons, something I'd never even thought about doing.

We agreed, both of us uncertain if the models would show, if the photo shoot would go on, or what else might happen that afternoon. "See you in a little while," I said as she put Maximilian's book in her oversized bag.

"Yep, in a little while." She threw up her hand in a quick wave, her high heels clicking against the bakery's floor as she walked out, leaving Will and me alone, the pall of death still hovering over us.

Chapter 7

Will left to go back to work and I walked home, waving to my friend Josie through the window of Seed-n-Bead, the bead shop she owned as I passed. The shop was a-buzz with customers, so I kept walking, lost in thought. The fact that Orphie had taken Maximilian's book still bothered me. Was she a kleptomaniac? Had she discovered some secret about our former boss? Or maybe she was a woman scorned. Oh no. Surely she hadn't had an affair with him?

I strode down the sidewalk of Mockingbird Lane, heading for my house. I passed under the arbor that was the focal point of my front yard. The wisteria was leafing, fuzzy pods forming and sprouting from the branches, swaying as I walked under it and along the flagstone path. Midori was at the front door, one hand on the doorknob. Jeanette stood beside her. Midori muttered something to Jeanette as they turned to wait for me.

"Did you get some lunch?" I asked, mounting the porch steps.

"Oh yes, at the cute little bed-and-breakfast off the square. It's where we're staying, too. We had scones and tea and these amazing little sweet potato fries."

I knew just the place she was talking about. Hattie and Raylene had bought the old house and spruced it up. Now Seven Gables was the nicest bed-and-breakfast slash teahouse in Bliss. "And that homemade poppy seed jelly?" I said. "It's delicious, isn't it? It's Raylene's specialty."

We made idle chitchat, stalling before stepping inside and into the pall of death that still hovered in the house. When we couldn't wait any longer, I opened the door, stepping in, Midori and Jeanette close on my heels. We all seemed to move slowly, knowing that going back inside would bring Beaulieu and his death right back to the forefront of our minds. As if it had gone anywhere but there.

Everything was in order, but I couldn't shake the sinister feeling of knowing that a man had died right here.

There was no sign of Lindy or Quinton, but Orphie showed up a few minutes later. "Got what I needed," she said, patting the shopping bag she held under her arm.

Good girl. After Midori and Jeanette went back to Seven Gables, we could package up the stolen book and drop it at the post office. Signed, sealed, and delivered.

"No sign of the models?" I asked. If the shoot was off and the article was nixed, there was no reason for any of them to come.

"They came this morning," Midori said. "Too many people for this little shop, so we left them at the bed-and-breakfast."

So they were here whether they wanted to be or not.

Midori scurried around, packing up her garments to keep them safe and sound. "No photo shoot today," she'd told me. "I ran into Ms. Reece at the bed-and-breakfast. She said she has a call into her editor for further instructions."

We all nodded, not surprised. How could they run an article about three up-and-coming designers when one was now dead?

Jeanette roamed around aimlessly, lost without barked orders from her boss. "You can pack up Beaulieu's garments, too," I suggested. I picked up his messenger bag.

"He never lets anyone hold this," she said, taking it from me.

"I understand." I didn't like anyone handling my sketchbooks or sewing kit. They were as personal to me as Madelyn's camera and her Epiphanie camera bag.

Orphie and I sat at the dining table making felt beads for the wedding party while Midori and Jeanette moved around like zombies. "Ask them to leave," Orphie whispered after a solid thirty minutes passed.

I tilted my head and frowned. Mama had raised me better than that. No good Southern woman would kick out her guests, especially ones who'd just suffered a shocking loss.

Orphie read my expression and shrugged. "Southern hospitality, yes, but you're also a martyr," she said. "Suffering in silence."

She had a point, but I couldn't change my upbringing any more than a zebra could change its stripes. Instead of answering her, I pushed the wool rovings, bits of unprocessed combed and carded wool from New Zealand sheep, toward her. I had them in every color of the rainbow. We gathered them in small chunks, saturated the tufts with warm soapy water, and rolled them into tight balls between the palms of our hands. We made different sizes, laying them out on the dining table as they'd be strung on a strand of yarn. "This is all there is to it?" Orphie asked as she finished another round.

"Once they're dry, we attach decorative beads to them, then use a thick needle to string them onto the necklace." I put down the tuft of raw wool I'd been ready to dip, went to the old secretary desk just outside my workroom, returning a second later with a finished necklace. "They'll all look like this," I said.

Jeanette came to the table and sank down. She fingered the marble-sized wool beads I'd laid out. "These are so cool," she said, lifting the necklace and holding it around her neck. Her fingers trembled, the only sign that she was upset about what had gone on today.

"Jeanette? Are you okay?"

She fumbled with the handmade clasp on the necklace, her lower lip beginning to quiver, her eyes tearing. "I . . . I can't believe he's really d-dead."

I couldn't, either, but there it was.

Before I could say anything else, the clinking of glass against glass drew my gaze upward. My chandelier was a handmade Southern contraption made of a dozen old, clear-glass milk bottles. Each one was capped with a galvanized top and perched in a circular galvanized frame. Lightbulbs clustered in the center; the glass of the bottles, embossed with the words "farm-fresh milk," diffused the light. Meemaw had her tricks . . . and this was one of them. Sure to get my gander every time, but I couldn't very well call her out in front of the women in the shop. So I ignored the clinking of glass. Ignored the hairs rising on the back of my neck. The old glass bottles were irreplaceable. If Meemaw broke them, so help me . . .

"Meemaw!" I said under my breath.

"Beaulieu's probably haunting this place," Orphie said, eyeing the swinging chandelier.

Jeanette gasped, her pallor more ashen than it had been a moment ago. "Do you think so?" she asked softly.

I flashed a scolding glance at Orphie. "It's not haunted," I said. But inside, I thought that if Beaulieu was hanging around from the afterworld, he'd be in good company.

We finished all the beads, laying them on a folded bath towel to dry, and Jeanette and Midori finally left. I put the extra wool away, rinsed the bowl of soapy water, and took a few minutes to straighten the kitchen. Mama had left out the pitcher of lemonade, glasses from the morning littered the butcher-block counter, and finger-prints smudged the butter yellow front of the replica vintage refrigerator.

When I returned to the front room, Orphie was chew-ing on her thumbnail, Maximilian's book lying on the table in front of her.

"Are you ready to mail it back?" I asked her, hoping she'd come to her senses.

She shook her head. "I want to show you something first," she said, sliding the book toward me, the embossed "M" with a gold circle around it like an eye on a magic tome.

I laid my own hand on the cover, half expecting a jolt of energy to zap me.

Her guilty expression vanished, but she cast her eyes down toward the book, skittering them to one side, then the other. As if the fashion police were going to make a sudden appearance right here in Buttons & Bows and arrest her for theft. "Take a look," she said.

I lifted open the smooth black cover and braced myself for whatever big reveal I'd find, but the first page held simple pencil sketches of a costumey bustier. It looked like something Lady Gaga might wear, but not the average woman. Still, there was nothing earth-shattering. Nothing that filled me with concern.

I turned the pages and reveled in Maximilian's creative mind. The book wasn't all that different from my own sketchbooks. I recognized a lot of the designs. As Orphie had said, this particular book had to be a few years old. Anything worth producing had been done, and now Maximilian, like every designer, was probably pushing his boundaries and figuring out how to stay fresh and relevant with new designs.

I kept turning the pages, looking at sketch after sketch of rough drawings. Angular figures. Color palettes and fabric patterns. Descriptions of garments and words scrawled across the sheets. Bold. Edgy. Color blocking.

"Do you know how easy it is to steal someone's designs?"

My gaze snapped up to meet hers. "But why would anyone want to do that? That's what I don't understand, Orphie. Don't you want to create your own collections? Show what you can do?" Orphie's aesthetic was unique and utterly her own, so why had she stolen from Maximilian? She might not have his experience—or his bankroll—but she had her own point of view, and that was harder to come by than anything else.

"I'm not—"

I leaned closer to her, my hands gripping the edges of the book. "Orphie Marie Cates, what are you talking about? You're not what?"

She pushed her hair behind her ears. "I admit, when I took the book, I didn't know what I was thinking, but then I saw—"

"Saw what?"

"Look," she said, nodding to the book again.

"I'm looking. They're his sketches. So?"

She didn't blink. Didn't drop her gaze. "Look," she repeated.

"Orphie, blast it, what—"

"Harlow, just look."

I pulled it closer. I still didn't see what she was worked up over, but that didn't stop the anxiety from pooling inside me. "Can't you just tell me?"

Her nostrils flared slightly as she drew in a breath. She spun the book around, flipped through the pages, and then turned it around to face me, again, tapping it with her index finger. "Right there."

I took a good look. More of Maximilian's designs, some sketched in pencil, others in ink, all rough, yet detailed enough to show his point of view and design elements. "Okay . . . ," I said, still not seeing anything alarming. I pushed my glasses up, squinting in case that helped. I looked at the most familiar design. Just like Diane Von Furstenberg's signature wrap dress, this one-shoulder bodice with horizontal darts at the bustline was classic Maximilian.

I looked at Orphie, hating to even ask the question that tickled around the edge of my thoughts. "Is this . . . this isn't . . . you didn't . . ."

"No, *I* didn't," she said, a sad note in her voice. Because we both knew that just because she hadn't used this particular design by Maximilian, she might have used others. She'd taken the book, after all.

"So what—" I stopped short again, but this time it was because I could picture the design in my mind, crafted in a brightly colored piece of chiffon and attached to a black skirt. A wide silk waistband created a visual break between the two pieces and created an hourglass silhouette. "It's Beaulieu, isn't it?" My voice was hardly louder than a whisper. "I saw it in his garment bag. But how . . . ?"

She tapped her finger to her nose, as if we were playing charades and I'd just made a correct guess. "People say he's derivative, but it's more than that. He stole his ideas, Harlow. Remember when we worked for Maximilian and Beaulieu would come around?"

"They were friends," I said.

"Were they? Or was Beaulieu just after what he could get?"

I stared at her. "So you think Beaulieu stole Maximilian's designs, too?" The moment that last word left my mouth, I cringed and bit my lower lip. Too. That one little word lumped Orphie together with Beaulieu as an unethical designer, if not a full-on thief. Which, even if Orphie was, I hated saying the very idea of.

"It's true," she said, giving my hand a squeeze and looking as if she could read my mind. "I did it. I'm no better than he was."

"Yes, you are. You're returning it."

"I know. I will." She nodded, but didn't seem to want to talk about what she'd done. I didn't blame her. It was easier to focus on Beaulieu.

I jumped into the discussion with both feet. "If he altered the designs enough that it wasn't blatant, no one would be able to accuse him of stealing the ideas." She nodded, exhaling heavily. Her relief was obvious, so I kept going. "What if he'd ingratiated himself with Maximilian to get design ideas, and Maximilian figured it out?"

"I've seen some of Beaulieu's stuff," she said. "They're too close to be coincidence."

"Okay, but why wouldn't Maximilian call him on it?"

"And what, risk losing public favor when he has no proof?"

"Or," I said, "maybe he *did* call him on it. Maybe that's why Beaulieu stopped coming around."

I glanced toward the kitchen to where Beaulieu had been found on the floor, dead. That niggling feeling that something just wasn't right about him dying so suddenly returned full force. But that didn't make sense. If anyone were to kill Beaulieu over stealing designs, it would be Maximilian, and he wasn't here.

Not every death was murder, I told myself. Still, the thought stayed with me.

The house phone rang. I pushed away from the table and snapped the handset of the old yellow phone from its wall cradle. It had been there ever since I could remember. "If it ain't broke, why fix it?" Meemaw always said when I'd ask her why she didn't get rid of the old thing and replace it with a new, modern wireless unit.

Now I couldn't bring myself to get rid of the original phone, either. The once tightly coiled cord was now stretched. I wound it absently around my fingers as I answered.

"Sugar, you're not going to believe what I just heard."

Whenever Mama had a secret, her voice was full of the dickens, and I could tell she had a doozy.

"What's that, Mama?" I stretched the phone cord a little farther so I could wave to Orphie. A cloud of sadness seemed to hover around her. It had been a rough day. A rough week. Maybe a rough year.

"Hoss isn't so sure that man just up and died like we were thinkin.'"

I dropped the phone cord and slipped back into the kitchen, that niggling feeling I'd been battling with breaking free and surging through me freely. "Why not?"

There was a rustle and then Hoss's baritone voice hit my eardrums this time. The sheriff had a slow Southern drawl and a lazy way about him, but I knew from experience that he was as sharp as a nail stuck in an unsuspecting tire, and clever, to boot. "I talked to the man's doc back in Dallas. He was fit as a fiddle. No heart trouble. No genetic illnesses. No nothing that could explain his sudden death," he said.

Michel Ralph Beaulieu might not have had a heart condition, but he was sure giving me one. "And?"

The sheriff didn't say anything right off. Trying to get him to spit out the information was like ripping out a seam sewn in very tight stitches. Painstakingly and frustratingly slow.

I pulled the phone cord taut again as I walked farther into the kitchen. Finally I stopped when the cord pulled against the wall. If I went too much farther, I'd rip the unit clear off the wall.

"Gavin and I got to wondering about the timing," he finally said.

"What do you mean?"

"Shame to die just as you're about to get a big magazine break."

Well, that was true enough, but a faulty ticker didn't care about media opportunities. "He *was* talking about how he was going to steal the show with the magazine article."

A heavy pause came over the line. "Was he, now?"

I gulped, realizing too late how that statement could be interpreted. "Yes. We had a little bit of a . . . discussion about it."

"More like an argument."

I'd turned my back to the dining room, but I spun around at Orphie's voice, pulled the phone away from my ear, and held my finger to my lips telling her to shush.

Too late. Hoss had heard. "Argument, huh?"

"He's—was—a little hotheaded, is all. It didn't mean anything."

"Tell me about it anyway."

I folded one arm over my chest, one foot tapping, indignant at being questioned by my mother's fiancé. So what if he happened to be the sheriff and a man happened to die in my shop?

"Cat got your tongue?" he asked when I didn't respond.

"I guess."

"What'd y'all argue about?" he repeated.

"He felt as if he was a better designer than I was. He

was putting down Bliss. A little square town just isn't—er, wasn't—enough for him."

"It ain't enough for a lot of folks."

That was true enough. I'd thought it wasn't enough for me . . . until I came back home. Now it filled me to the brim.

"What are you saying, Sheriff?" I asked, needing him to say it in plain English.

"I'm sayin', Harlow, that you might well have had a murder take place in your shop. I ain't so sure that man died of natural causes."

Oh Lord. My instincts had been right on the money. "Are you sure?"

"We won't be sure until the doc finishes the autopsy. But in the meantime, we're runnin' with this. Don't touch anything. We'll be back to process the shop. In fact, Harlow, go on out on the porch, why don't you?"

He'd asked all nice and pleasantlike, but the truth was, it had been an order. He didn't want me to mess anything up, just in case he was right and we were dealing with something sinister.

"*Harlow*," he scolded. "You have a habit of pokin' your nose into things, and you'd do well to stay out of this one. Let us look into it. Got it?"

"Sure thing, Sheriff," I said, the discomforting feeling of a daze washing over me. Murder. Right here in Buttons & Bows. Not only was Michel Ralph Beaulieu dead, but my fashion design business might be dead right alongside him.

Chapter 8

"How are they going to do an article on three Dallas fashion designers when one of them is dead?" Nana put in words the question I'd been asking myself since the day before. Deputy Gavin McClaine had come back and inspected my shop from top to bottom. If he found anything, he hadn't revealed it. But what he *had* said was that no one—not Lindy Reece or Quinton the photographer, not Jeanette, not Midori, not the models, not Orphie, and not any of the Cassidy women—was to step foot outside Bliss's town limits.

We were all possible suspects in the murder of a top local fashion designer Michel Ralph Beaulieu. The *Dallas Morning News* and the *Fort Worth Star-Telegram* had both picked up the story. Reporters had swooped into town to conduct impromptu interviews and to report on the suspicious death of one of Dallas's own right in front of 2112 Mockingbird Lane. This was not the kind of notoriety I wanted for my shop, but this was the kind I kept garnering.

"I don't know," I answered truthfully. Everyone who'd been at Buttons & Bows the morning before was being questioned, and even people who hadn't been at my shop—like the models who'd been dropped off at Seven Gables before the rest had descended on my shop—were under the microscope.

"The good thing is that the *D Magazine* people can't leave," she said. She scurried around rinsing out glasses, tucking herbs back into the spice drawer, shoving cereal boxes back into the cupboard, and balling up a used piece of plastic wrap. A murder in her granddaughter's house and her daughter marrying the sheriff meant she was all a-flutter inside. Nervous energy that she was channeling in my kitchen.

Orphie took out the broom, starting at the far end of the kitchen. I followed her with the dustpan. "Maybe if they stay around long enough, they'll help figure out what happened," I muttered to myself. "If he was really murdered."

"Right. And maybe," Nana said as Orphie knocked the bristles of the broom against the floor, "they'll find something else to write about here in Bliss that'll dull the blow of the death."

Ever the optimist. "I'm not holding my breath about that." I had the sinking suspicion that the editor would offer the journalist a kill fee on the article and the whole thing would be a no go. After all, they'd have to figure out how to spin it without Beaulieu involved, and the fact was, he was a big name in Dallas fashion. The article, without him, would feel lacking somehow, like a mouth with a tooth suddenly gone.

Despite my skepticism, I had to go forward as if it was

still a go, but I also had other things to work on, namely Mama and Hoss's wedding. My father, Tristan Walker, had been true to his last name, walking out on Mama, my brother, Red, and me, when we were just young'uns. He'd found out about the Cassidy charm and that, as they say, is all she wrote. He left without a backward glance, and eventually they'd divorced. It had been more than thirty years since she'd been married, and she'd even taken her time telling me she was sweet on Hoss McClaine. But now that it was out in the open and she had herself a ring, there was no stopping her. They were getting hitched, and nothing—not even murder—was going to stop the wedding from happening.

I left Nana and Orphie to finish cleaning up the kitchen while I went into my workroom. There was no question in my mind now that something sinister was going on in Bliss, and once again, it had come into my life, uninvited.

The bells on the front door jingled and the door swung open. "I'm here!" Gracie called. "And I have treats for Earl Grey!"

My sweet little teacup pig had been neglected since all the hoopla the day before, but Gracie would turn that around in no time. She loved Earl Grey as much as I did—maybe even more—and other than the fact that the piglet lived here with me, he was just as much hers and her dad's as he was mine.

"He's out on the porch in the pen." Will had made Earl an enclosure. It was the best of both worlds: It had ample room for a miniature piglet to run around and be free, all the while keeping him safe.

Gracie was a typical teenager, minus the attitude. She

had her moments, but for the most part, she was a great girl who loved school, her dad, and sewing. She threw her arms around me and gave me a big squeeze. "My dad told me what happened," she said, letting go. "I can't believe it. He was one of the designers? And now he's dead?"

"Not just dead. It looks like he may have been murdered," I said, cringing as the words left my lips.

She gasped, her lips forming a pronounced O. "Murder?" she whispered. "Are you sure?"

"The sheriff feels pretty certain."

"Oh no." She turned and paced, whirling around to face me again after she'd processed for a few seconds. "Are they going to close your shop? Are you okay? Did you see anything? Do they know who did it—"

"Whoa, Gracie! Slow down."

She took a deep breath and regrouped. "Sorry, I just . . . it's, like, crazy that this is happening."

I'd been saying the very same thing to myself over and over and over. Why was this happening, and why had it happened here in Buttons & Bows? I ticked off my fingers as I answered the slew of questions she'd thrown at me. "The sheriff took some things as evidence, but they're not closing the shop. I'm fine. And no, I didn't see anything, and as far as I know, no, they don't know who did it."

She darted a gaze around the shop, settling for a second on Nana and Orphie in the kitchen, before dropping her voice and speaking in a shaky whisper. "They don't think it was you, do they?"

I gaped at her, sure that if a fly happened by, it would wing its way right into my mouth and I'd swallow it.

Leave it to a teenager to cut to the chase. No hemming and hawing. No beating around the bush. Just right out with the questions gnawing at her gut. "Of course not, Gracie."

She shrugged, a sheepish look coming over her. "Thank God. I was worried the sheriff might think you had something to do with it since he died here. In your house," she added, in case I hadn't felt the full power of her statement.

A shiver crept up my spine. I was speechless for a moment, because, truthfully, she was right and I'd felt the weight of that truth when I'd spoken to Hoss McClaine on the phone. He hadn't said it, but now that Gracie had, I realized that I probably *was* suspect number one simply because of the unfortunate location of the dead body. "I'm sure they'll find whoever did it, and everything will be fine," I said.

She gulped and bit her lower lip. "I'm going to find Earl Grey," she said, and then she turned and was gone, beating a quick path to the kitchen. A few seconds later, I heard the Dutch door squeak open and then slam shut. I could hear the low rumble of Orphie's and Nana's voices, but I tuned them out as I flipped open my sketchbook. Inside was an eclectic jumble of drawings and swatches and commentary about the designs I'd dreamed up. At the end were a few pages of notes I'd taken about the other untimely deaths that had occurred in Bliss recently.

Gracie had planted a seed, and now I couldn't shake it from my mind. Michel Ralph Beaulieu had died right here in my house. I'd already told the sheriff that Beaulieu had disparaged my town, my shop, and my designs. People had killed for less, I'm sure. How long would it take before the sheriff—or his overzealous deputy of a son—turned his attention my way, in earnest? I was sure they'd figure out the truth sooner or later, but why not help them with it?

I racked my brain, trying to remember all the details of that morning. It came to me in bits and pieces rather than replaying as in a movie. The whole group swooping into the shop. The underlying competition between Beaulieu, Midori, and me. The article. Snapshots flashed through my head. My steamer. The dress forms. Mama's wedding dress. Lemonade. Maximilian's design book. They were like pieces from different puzzles, and no matter how I turned them over in my mind, they weren't going to fit together in any semblance of order.

I went through the possible suspects one by one. Lindy Reece and her notebook. Quinton and his camera. Both worked for *D Magazine* and wouldn't be likely to have a grudge against Beaulieu—none that was obvious, anyway. Jeanette and Midori. Both of them could have sketchy motives. Jeanette had taken the brunt of Beaulieu's daily wrath, while Midori, I knew, had struggled to find her footing in the U.S. fashion world. Her connections to Japan were still strong and Beaulieu hadn't had any qualms about pooh-poohing her design aesthetic, but she'd found success nonetheless.

Was any of that enough of a motive for murder, though? I didn't think so.

I moved on to the Dallas and New York models who'd come as part of the designers' entourage. They hadn't actually been in the shop yet, but could one of them have snuck over from Seven Gables and . . . And what? Beaulieu hadn't been hit over the head. He hadn't been startled to death. Could he have been poisoned? That was a possibility. So maybe one of the models had slipped some arsenic, or something, to him somehow.

Was the fact that they hadn't physically been at the shop when he died calculated? From my experience, models could be as cutthroat as the mothers of child beauty pageant contestants. Okay, maybe not quite that bad, but pretty brutal. And they weren't empty-headed. One of them could definitely be a murderer, just as any one of the other possible suspects could have done it.

Still, I couldn't fathom a reason why a model would do in a designer, especially before a photo shoot that could gain said model just as much exposure as said designer.

Which left a small group of people—those closest to me. Orphie's showing up the night before made her a possible suspect. Nana and Mama—

My brain hitched, backtracking. Loretta Mae! She was a ghost right here in this house. Which meant she might well have seen something. Something important. Something incriminating.

Holy smokes, Meemaw could have witnessed a murder. The only problem with this was that Meemaw and I couldn't communicate very effectively. But it was worth a try. I whispered her name into the empty room.

Nothing but eerie silence.

I tried again. "Meemaw?"

Still nothing.

I gave it one last try. "Loretta Mae Cassidy, where in the devil are you?"

Third time was the charm. The latch to the window in the workroom lifted with a creak and the window itself flew open, the sheers billowing from the breeze. In the distance, I could spot Nana's goats munching on the green Texas grass, but inside, the room took on an eerie chill. Normally Meemaw brought comforting warmth with her, but not right now. The pipes in the ceiling above moaned, the garments hanging from the slats of the privacy screen, including a teal tiki dress of Loretta Mae's that I'd found in the attic and had hung up for inspiration, swayed, and the shelves against the west-facing wall rocked, the jars of buttons and trims clanking together.

The air rippled and the faintest hint of a form flickered. I held my breath, watching, waiting, hoping and praying that something would happen, like flipping a switch, and Loretta Mae would come into full focus. But she never quite took shape. This was the way things had been going. My great-grandmother haunted the house, but she couldn't quite muster a corporeal form, she couldn't speak, and communication was frustrating, on a good day. But she was still Meemaw, and having her near made me feel as if I were always wrapped up in a toasty wool jacket with a jewel-toned silk lining.

Even with the unnatural chill in the air, Meemaw was here. "No time to mess around, Meemaw," I said, cutting to the chase. "Michel Ralph Beaulieu was murdered, although I don't know how, and I'm afraid . . ." I trailed off, not needing to put into words just what I was afraid of. Meemaw would know. Her charm had been getting whatever she wanted, whether it was some fabric she'd seen online or me and Will Flores to meet and start dating—which we had. There's no way she wanted me investigated for murder, so I felt pretty sure I'd be fine there, but . . . "It has to be someone who was here in the house or one of the models," I said. "Doesn't it?" I rattled off the names of everyone who'd been here that morning including Mama and Nana, although I knew they were off the hook, too. First, they were innocent. And second, Meemaw wouldn't want them investigated, either.

The air undulated, a whoosh surrounded me, and the dress form with Mama's wedding dress spun around.

I had no idea what that meant.

"Meemaw," I said, needing answers. "Did you see anything? Do you have any ideas?"

If she did, I could tell the sheriff. Mama had told him about her charm. She hadn't mentioned the fact that all the Cassidy women came back as ghosts, but I felt pretty confident he'd believe me. There'd be no evidence, but it could lead him in the right direction. I held my breath, waiting.

The dress form spun around again. I stared. "Does that mean you saw something, or you didn't see anything?"

It whirled a third time, and then fell still. The dense area of rippling air had vanished, and I didn't know if Loretta Mae was still here or not.

"Meemaw?"

Of course she didn't answer, but the pipes groaned and it sounded like a drawn-out vowel. *Nooo. Nooo. Nooo.*

My shoulders slumped and I perched, deflated, on the stool I kept at my cutting table. So Meemaw hadn't seen anything. Which meant we were back to square one.

Chapter 9

My old farmhouse was quaint and had character, both inside and out. From the kitchen, with its vintage-stamped butter yellow retro appliances and red-and-white-checkerboard curtain under the farm sink, to the long row of possum wood trees lining the driveway and shading the house, not a thing about the place was typical or cookie cutter. Usually I found a sense of comfort in being at home in the farmhouse, but today everything seemed a little off. Not even Gracie standing in front of the red Dutch door, cradling Earl Grey in her arms, looked normal. First off, Earl Grey was a tiny teacup pig, not a little kitten. Next, Gracie's outfit was all wrong for her. She leaned toward vintage clothing, always wearing something that had years of history embedded into its seams, but not today. She wore a pair of Levis and a store-bought sleeveless blouse, so nondescript that it said nothing at all about her. And clothing, in my opinion, should tell a tale about the wearer. It should set a mood, give perspective, create an image.

But it was Gracie's expression that made me stop short—and the tingling of my temple where my normally coppery-tinged auburn hair sprouted a blond streak.

"What's wrong?"

She stared past me and into the front room of Buttons & Bows. "They're too tall."

"What's too ta—?" I turned, the rest of the sentence falling unspoken from my lips. Ah, not what, who. The models. They'd shown up, whooshing in as if they were entitled to my Southern hospitality. "We're stuck in this town for a while," one of them had said, "so we came here."

"Height. It's an unspoken prerequisite. Most of the models I fitted at Maximilian were five ten."

She stroked Earl Grey, a slight frown on her face. "Guess that's out as a future career."

"Did you have dreams of becoming a model?" She was a beauty with her clear olive skin, her streaked mahogany hair, and her sixteen-year-old innocence, and she'd planned on modeling my designs for the photo shoot. Her dad was just over six feet, but however tall her mother was kept her eye-to-eye with me. It wasn't unheard of for a model to be five seven, but it wasn't the norm. And truthfully, I had higher aspirations for her. The life of a model wasn't as glamorous as people thought.

"No. Just marking things off the list. No modeling. Check."

I'd let the models mill around the workroom and now they were trying on the designer outfits, completely absorbed in their task. I'd caught a few snippets of their conversation. The one named Esmeralda kept her voice low, but loud enough to hear. "Beaulieu promised I'd be the top model for his line. I had to fly into New York from London and then to Dallas." She looked around the shop. "Then the drive here with the rest of them. What was he thinking?"

A second New York model who went only by Barbi nodded as she piled her hair atop her head. "I hear you. At least we get a chance to look at Midori's clothes up close. She normally doesn't let anyone near them. Better hurry before those Dallas girls come back."

Those Dallas girls. There was a natural rivalry between the models. The New York models disappeared into the workroom and I turned back to Gracie.

"I could be a vet," she said, tickling Earl Grey behind the ears.

"Yes, you could."

She hadn't been around much lately, what with the wedding and the article looming and taking up so much of my time, so I jumped at the chance to get a pulse on how she was doing. Discovering you were a descendant of Butch Cassidy and Etta Place via an affair from a long time ago couldn't be easy. Discovering that you had a magical charm?

Tough for anyone, let alone a teenager.

"Gracie," I said, treading carefully. "We haven't had a chance to talk lately about your . . . about the . . ."

She put Earl Grey down, who promptly scampered off into the laundry room off the kitchen, and lifted her gaze to mine. "About the whole magic charm thing?"

She hadn't belted the words out, but I glanced over my shoulder anyway. The models were still in the workroom. "Something's wrong with these. The hem's uneven," one of them was saying.

"Beaulieu's so much better," the other one replied. "He shouldn't have died."

I agreed. He should not have died. Everyone seemed to agree with that, yet someone had most likely killed him.

The models lowered their voices as they continued looking at Beaulieu's garments. They were so young, in their midteens, if they were a day, so probably completely oblivious of what Gracie and I were talking about. But to be sure, I edged closer and lowered my voice. "Is it getting any easier?"

Gracie's charm was still developing. She'd discovered hers much earlier than I'd discovered mine—which had been just a few months ago. But I'd grown up hearing about the Cassidy legacy. She hadn't.

"Not really." The pallor of her face changed, just barely. It was as if a sheet of gauze had covered her, muting the light in her skin.

The truth hit me between the eyes. "You see images now all the time, don't you?"

Her lower lip quivered, and she nodded. "All the time," she whispered in a shaky voice.

I waved my hand up and down in front of her, as if I were getting ready to utter a spell. "Which is why you're wearing jeans and that top?"

Her chin dipped down again. "I—I can't touch anything old. If I do, I just g-get these flashes of people."

"You can't control it at all?"

This time she shook her head. "If I'm tired, it's, like, worse, you know?"

"Worse how?" I wanted to understand, but I needed more detail than what she was giving me. I'd seen her touch a vintage dressing gown at the old Denison Mansion, had seen her react to whatever she'd seen. She'd known who that dress belonged to just from one touch to the fabric. That had been my first clue that she was charmed.

She drew a circle on the floor with her toe. Nerves. I recognized the signs. Working with nervous brides, new models, plump women wanting to look their best in the outfits I designed for them all brought out similar gestures. "It's like I see clips from a movie, but they're all choppy and broken. Like the old black-and-white ones you see on TV sometimes? You know what I mean?"

"Exactly." The Cassidy charm wasn't refined. Mama's weeds often grew bigger than her flowers, and they responded to her emotions, doubling in size when she was happy or excited, withering when she was angry or sad. Nana's ability to communicate with her goats had helped the locals, once or twice. Will had come to her when he'd had trouble with one of his, for example, but on a daily basis, Nana and her goats didn't help anyone, and her herd got her into heaps of trouble. Goats, after all, will be goats.

And then there was me. When I made a garment for someone, what they wanted—whatever they'd hoped for—came true. It was as if I had a magic wand and was able to wave it around above a person's head, saying, "Bibbidi-bobbidi-boo!" and then, voilà! I cast a spell. Only it wasn't always so easy. If someone wanted something unethical or sinister, I couldn't stop that dream from coming true. I didn't have a charm for that.

But I had an idea about how to help her adjust to her charm. Since she couldn't wear her treasured vintage clothes at the moment, I'd make her something retro, stitching my charm into the seams. Whatever Gracie wanted, once she wore the outfit, would happen, and I'd lay money down that what she wanted was to be able to manage her charm.

We talked for a little while longer and I reassured her that she'd adjust and things would get better. "I hope so," she said, but she didn't sound convinced. "What am I working on today?"

Gracie had become my apprentice. Sewing, tailoring, and design came naturally to her, and she came several days a week after school to hone her craft.

"I'm making a fitted jacket for Mrs. James," I said, heading with her to the workroom. "I'd like you to work on the darts. After that, we'll be adding a houndstooth lining."

"They're awfully quiet," Gracie said as we approached the workroom.

The French doors were closed—not how I'd left them. "They certainly are." They'd asked to look at the dresses they'd been brought out here to model. "We'll never get to wear his clothes again," Barbi had said, her lower lip pushed out in a pout.

I hadn't seen the harm in that, but now, as I yanked open the French doors, they jumped in unison, hands pressed to their chests in surprise.

Gracie and I stared at them in their half-dressed state,

but that wasn't the alarming part. No, what had me tongue-tied was the fact that they were trying on Midori's designs.

An invisible force pushed me forward. It was enough to help me find my voice again. "What in tarnation are you doing?" I demanded.

Esmeralda said, "W-we saw them just hanging there—"

"Hanging there in the garment bags, you mean?" I challenged.

"We just thought we could try them, like, real quick." The dress Barbi had on hung lopsided on her frame, the hem on one side dragging on the hardwood floor.

"You cannot just come in here and act like you own the place," I said tightly. "Take them off."

Barbi got the picture. She began stripping off the color-blocked dress. "I'm so sorry, Ms. Cassidy. I didn't mean . . . I won't do it again."

Esmeralda blew an adolescent raspberry from between her lips. "This stuff's too old for us, anyway. Zoe must have one leg longer than the other. Stupid dress," she muttered.

Barbi scoffed. "Yeah, the fit sucks. She's way overrated."

Enough was enough. "Girls," I said, channeling my authoritative voice, "you have five minutes to get my workroom cleaned up and get those clothes back in their garment bags."

"Chill out, Harlow—"

My blood had been simmering just under the surface of my skin, but now it revved up to boiling. "Esmeralda, don't tell me to chill out when you are messing with expensive clothes that don't belong to you." I looked her up and down. "Even if it *does* hang oddly."

They stared at me. "We're just—"

"Uh-uh." I wagged my finger at them just the way Meemaw used to do to Red and me when got into trouble. "Take. Them. Off."

"Let's just go," Barbi said under her breath to Esmeralda.

Esmeralda's pointed jaw pulsed and her lips drew into a thin line. She hesitated, looking as if she was ready to refuse, but then she waved one hand in the air and lifted her chin defiantly. "Fine. You're way too serious."

Sympathy for rail-thin übertall women who complained about things not fitting? I shook my head. No one was ever satisfied. One of my missions with fashion design was to help women see themselves as beautiful, no matter their shape or size. I designed for the everyday woman, not some unrealistic idealized version. Another reason why Bliss was where I belonged.

I wasn't sure if I was a keen observer of human nature, but the Dallas models hadn't come to play dress-up with Beaulieu's clothes, and my esteem for them went up a notch. It took Esmeralda and Barbi almost fifteen minutes to put things to right in my workroom. They finally left, still mumbling under their breath. "His stuff blows the rest away," one of them said. "Totally. They fit, for starters."

Gracie set to work on the darts and I took a few minutes to think about what I'd make for her to help her find some peace. Later I'd study my favorite sewing blog, Gertie's New Blog for Better Sewing. It was one of my go-to spots on the Web. Gertie's personal passion for all things vintage was perfectly aligned with Gracie's, so I knew I'd find inspiration there.

But before I could do that, I had a long list of other tasks to work on, starting with the beading on my mother's dress.

Chapter 10

Loretta Mae had been a big proponent of the family meeting. Whenever there was anything to discuss, the Cassidy clan would get together in the gathering room of the yellow farmhouse—which was now the front room of Buttons & Bows—and discuss whatever needed to be discussed.

Spending an hour working on embellishments for my mother's dress didn't do anything to take my mind off Beaulieu's death, and I had a hankering to call a meeting to talk it all through. Who would have wanted him dead, and why?

But it wasn't up to me to call a meeting, so Lindy Reece's call came at just the right time. She wanted to get the models and designers together for an update about the article she'd planned to write. Perfect. An hour later, I dropped Gracie off at home and rumbled to the Historic District of Bliss in Buttercup. When I got to Seven Gables, Midori, Jeanette, the New York models, Barbi and Esmeralda, and the Dallas models, Zoe and

Madison, were milling around the parlor of the bed-and-breakfast. "Looks like there's no article," Esmeralda said as I walked in.

That wasn't a huge surprise, and while I'd hoped it would still be a go, I'd prepared myself for the whole thing being called off. "Is that what Lindy said?"

Jeanette interjected, "Not yet, but why else would she call us all here? It makes sense, right? With Beaulieu dead and all, I mean."

Midori's eyes were black-rimmed and bloodshot, and I wondered if she'd slept at all. For all we knew, whoever had killed Beaulieu could be targeting designers in general. My instincts told me that wasn't the case, but maybe I was wrong. "If he was really murdered, one of us could be next," she said, echoing the very thoughts I'd just had.

"I'm not going to sit around here and wait to be killed," Esmeralda said. "I'm leaving. They can't seriously keep us here, can they?"

"Actually, I think the sheriff can," I said. "If someone killed him, it stands to reason it could be one of us, and he wouldn't want the suspects scattering in the wind."

Madison, the blue-eyed, fresh-faced model from Dallas, shook her head, her hair-sprayed blond hair staying firmly in place. "I thought he had a heart attack."

"The sheriff said there was no history of heart disease, or any other illness. So far, there's no cause of death at all."

She looked at me, puzzled. "So do they think it's murder, or do they just not know?"

Oh boy. I'd already said more than Hoss probably would want me to. I shrugged helplessly. "I think they just want to be sure about what killed him," I said as noncommittally as possible.

"This is stupid. I want to go home," Esmeralda said, pouting. "I miss my mom."

Those last four little words shook me to the core and were a reality check. Esmeralda and Barbi were teenagers. With their heavy makeup and staying here on their own, I'd forgotten how young they really were. The heavy makeup Esmeralda wore was a mask, I realized, and I wondered who she was when she took it all off and was alone. Did she go back to being a normal teenager, missing her mom and her regular life?

The Dallas models were a few years older, not typical, but not unheard of, either. Zoe spoke for the first time, sweeping her honey-hued hair behind her shoulders and looking like the savvy older sister next door. "The man is dead," she said. "We should help if we can. If that means we're stuck here for a few days, that's the way it goes."

"The sheriff will get to the bottom of things." Or maybe I'd get there first.

"I need to get back to my studio," Midori said. "I have projects and deadlines."

"No assistant?" Jeanette asked, her raised eyebrow making it clear she'd take the job—if there was one.

Midori scoffed. "No one touches my designs but me."

"Really?" Buttons & Bows was a small business, but even I had Gracie. I couldn't do it all myself, and Meemaw had taught me the beauty of many hands working together. We were stronger together, and looking around the room punctuated that very idea. Someone here had to know something.

"Midori, you can use my atelier," I offered. A sewist without a machine and a space to work was like an addict without a fix. I could only imagine how she had to feel, especially if she did it all herself.

Before she could reply, Lindy Reece and Quinton walked in. Lindy instantly commanded the room, her voice loud and confident. "Thank you all for meeting us here," she began, gesturing toward the table. Hattie and Raylene had it decked out with doilies and silver-plated forks, spoons, and knives. The tearoom itself was done up with floral wallpaper, complete with a border running around the top of the wall at the ceiling in lieu of crown molding to give the room an old-fashioned look. Lace curtains and doilies dotting the furniture added to the feeling that we'd all stepped out of twenty-first-century Texas.

As if on cue, Raylene bustled in wearing an outfit I'd made for her. Sweet girl—I knew she'd liked it, but it was thoughtful of her to wear it when she knew I'd be visiting. She stopped at one end of the group, cleared her throat, and addressed us all.

"I'd like to welcome y'all to Seven Gables, so named for the seven peaks in the roofline. What with all the hoopla yesterday over at Buttons and Bows, none of you had a chance to see the grounds. I'm happy to give a tour later for anyone who wants it."

If there was an upside to Beaulieu's murder, which was a stretch even to my optimistic way of thinking—it was that Seven Gables had no vacancy for the first time since it opened. All the people clustered around the tables were staying at the bed-and-breakfast.

A few people nodded, another couple of them mur-

muring an unenthusiastic "Sure." The out-of-towners were not here to partake of Bliss's history, that much was clear.

Raylene picked up on the mood in the room and carried on. "We have a good variety of tea. Go on and help yourself to a cup and saucer." She pointed to a heavy metal-and-oak baker's rack against the far wall. It fit into the old Victorian setting perfectly with its antique bronze finish and turn-of-the-century style. Dainty teacups and saucers in different shapes and styles sat on two of the shelves, while large clear glass canisters held an array of loose-leaf tea.

Nobody moved. It was as if they'd never been to high tea before, or if they had, they'd only experienced it at places like the Ritz-Carlton or the Hyatt. This was tea, Southern-style. "Looks amazing, Raylene," I said, leading the charge. I bypassed the rack of tulle and flowered hats and boas Raylene and Hattie had set up for little girl tea parties, stood in front of the rack, and chose a delicate cup and saucer. I told her which tea I wanted and went back to my seat. One by one, the others followed suit, picking their cup and their flavor.

"I'd like to talk about the fate of the article," Lindy continued as we all settled back at our places.

"Oops," Esmeralda said. "Fate, as in finished. We're stuck here, we're not even going to get to be in the magazine, and we have to sit here around all this food."

Barbi frowned, immediately pressing her finger to the space between her eyebrows as if the pressure could stave off a future wrinkle. "The tea looks okay."

Esmeralda, even with her plastic made-up skin, looked more like a Tawny or a Tiffany. There wasn't anything exotic about her other than her name. She shook her head at Barbi, who fit her name perfectly, right down to her disproportionately tiny feet. "Not the tea. Being *stuck* here." She wagged her finger between them. "It's not like either of us had anything to do with this. *We* didn't kill anyone. *We* were just in the wrong place at the wrong time, but will that hillbilly sheriff and his deputy dog listen? I can't wait to leave."

The disdainful look she gave the room Raylene and Hattie had spent days on end decorating made my gut clench. "I mean, seriously, I didn't want Michel dead! He helped us create our portfolios. He worked with that photographer until he got it all right. I didn't want him dead." She looked at Barbi. "Did you?"

Barbi shook her head. "Not me, no way."

All of us moved our attention from Esmeralda to Barbi and back.

Lindy caught my gaze and raised her eyebrows. I got the feeling she didn't know if she should let them continue ranting, or if she should rein them in.

I voted for reining them in. "Someone killed him," I said. "Maybe someone here knows something."

"We didn't want him dead," Esmeralda said. "He made his *samples* for us." She whipped her head Midori's way. "And everything he designed hung perfectly. No weird hemlines or heavy stuff. None of those weird frogs," she said, referring to the closures Midori often favored on her Asian-inspired pieces. "And no kimono wraparound things. Michel was hip."

Midori's jaw went slack for a split second, and then she stood up, tossing the gown she'd been doing handwork on to the back of the Victorian couch. She looked

ready to spit fire at the teenage models. "How do
you—"

I jumped up. "Everyone just needs to take a deep
breath and simmer down," I said, wanting to throttle Esmeralda myself. She'd crossed a line when she and Barbi
had been in my workroom, and now she was destroying
the line altogether with her attacks. Midori's designs
blended cultures and styles. They could be worn by every
woman, not just rail-thin seventeen-year-old twigs who
had to have a minimum height requirement of five ten.
"Beaulieu's death is horrible," I said, trying to simmer
down myself, "but getting ugly with each other isn't going
to bring him back, and it's not going to change the fact
that you have to stay here awhile longer. The article—"

A guttural noise from Lindy cut me off. "My editor's
thinking of killing the article," she said.

There it was. Nana'd asked me if they'd go with the
story given that one of the designers was now dead. The
answer was no.

Midori flattened both of her hands on the table, her
porcelain skin blushing an angry red. "That is not fair. It's
not our fault Beaulieu died! I've worked too hard for
this." She flapped one hand in the air, vaguely waving at
me. "*We've* worked too hard for this. I am very sorry this
happened to him," she continued, her gentle Japanese accent coloring her words slightly, "but I do not think I—
we—should be punished because of it. Make the article
about the two of us. Women designers taking on the DFW
Metroplex fashion world." She rolled her hand, directing
her attention to Lindy. "You're the journalist, surely you
can figure out how to keep the story alive. Don't you
write for other papers and magazines?"

Lindy scribbled in a spiral notebook. "I do, and believe me, I'm trying. I like that idea, too," she said. "It's a good angle. Michel said he had some other leads for me, but now those are gone."

It hadn't occurred to me until now that Midori, the models, and I weren't the only ones losing out from Beaulieu's death. Lindy and Quinton lost the opportunity, too.

"That could work," Lindy muttered. "You have to have something unique to be noticed."

"Same with modeling," Esmeralda said.

"You could do a tribute to Beaulieu," Zoe suggested. Bless her heart, she was a true Southern woman, trying her best to be conciliatory. Problem was, while Beaulieu's work was good, I didn't think it would fly as a special feature.

Lindy shook her head. "I can do a mention, but D isn't in the habit of doing in-memoriams. It's about what's hot and exciting in the city *now*."

Midori hadn't simmered down. She stared at Lindy as if she could send laser beams right through her.

Jeanette sat motionless, looking from one person to the next, her lip quivering. "Beaulieu's dead and you're all talking about the article. That's not . . . not . . . it's just not respectful of the dead."

Jeanette's voice trembled, her emotions just on the surface. "She's right," Midori said. "You're right," she said to Jeanette, patting her hand.

"You're right, of course," Lindy said, "but the rest of the world doesn't stop because one designer died, as heartless as that sounds. If I can get an article out of this, I'm going to try."

In unison, the models' spines seemed to crackle and they lifted their chins in attention. "So we'll still get to model? Will there still be a photo shoot?" Esmeralda asked, looking at Quinton. "We flew out here for Michel, but if he's dead, will we still be part of the shoot?"

"I'll photograph whoever she tells me to," he said, notching his thumb toward Lindy.

Madison, one of the Dallas beauties, spoke up. "We're Midori's models. She makes her samples for *us*, so *you're* not getting in them."

Esmeralda faced Madison, her lips tight and her left eye twitching slightly. "Too late."

Madison placed her hands on the table, palms down. "What do you mean, too late?"

Esmeralda held her gaze. "I mean, we already tried them on."

"What?" This time Midori jumped up, her eyes blazing.

Esmeralda was fearless, and no petite designer was going to faze her. "She let us in," the girl said, pointing to me.

"What!" Now I jumped up, swinging around to face Esmeralda. "I gave you permission to look at Beaulieu's garments, not to look at, and certainly not to try on, Midori's designs."

She shrugged, clearly unconcerned with little details like that. "We're stuck here now, and we want to be paid and we want to be in the magazine." If she'd stood up and jammed her hands on her hips, she would have come across as a petulant five-year-old. Not what she'd been going for, I'm sure.

Midori leaned over the table, her voice laced with venom. "Those are my designs. You had no right."

"They're crappy, anyway," Esmeralda said.

"They didn't even fit," Barbi said. She gestured to a heavy silk dress lying haphazardly over the gold velvet sofa in the adjacent parlor. "All that uneven weight and that one back at the shop with the beading. They're too heavy."

Midori seethed. Any second, steam would start pouring from her nostrils. "I don't tell you how to walk the runway. How dare you tell me how to design clothing?"

Barbi stared her down, clearly not realizing—or not caring—that criticizing a designer's work did not earn brownie points. She got up and in two seconds was across the room, her hands on the silk dress.

Madison picked up the attack for Midori, careening toward Barbi, plowing into her arms so she couldn't take hold of the dress. "You are only here because of Beaulieu, and he's dead. His clothes aren't going to be showcased—"

Esmeralda flung her arm out, pointing at Lindy. "Didn't you hear her? They might kill the story and none of the clothes will get to be showcased, but if they don't kill the story, we want a chance to do what we were brought here to do."

Zoe, the other Dallas model, leaned back in her chair. "It doesn't matter what we want. They're going to make the decision," she said, lifting her chin toward me and then toward Midori. She and Madison leaned their heads together and she added in a harsh whisper, "But Midori made her samples based on us wearing them, so they shouldn't even bother."

Oh boy, this could get ugly. Being caught in the middle of a throw-down between the beautiful people wasn't high on my list of things to do. I couldn't make *D Maga-zine* run the article, and I couldn't tell Midori what to do. Loretta Mae had always been full of homegrown wisdom, and one of her oft-repeated snippets came back to me now: The true test of a person's character comes down to how she deals with a trying situation. I felt I was being tested right now. "If they go with the article, I'll need models, too. Between Midori and me, I'm sure all y'all will get a chance."

The back-and-forth continued until Raylene came back into the dining room carrying tiered trays of tea sandwiches, mini scones, fruit, crème fraîche, and a lightly sweet, soft pink poppy seed dressing. Hattie followed with individual teapots filled with steeping tea.

The models picked at the fruit, while Midori, Jeanette, and Lindy placed a sandwich and scone and spoonfuls of the condiments on their plates. Quinton, who I realized never said much of anything, piled his plate high.

I was somewhere in between, with a few of the dainty sandwich triangles, two of the mini scones, a pile of fruit, and healthy dollops of the cream and dressing.

"Enjoy!" Raylene said once everyone had been served their tea, but her voice was muted, her excitement forced. I caught her eye and she notched her head toward the kitchen.

"I'll be back in a flash," I said to the group. I might as well not have spoken for the response—or lack of response—I got, which was nothing more than a bunch of blank stares.

There was no abundance of Southern congeniality here. The kitchen felt a mile away, and my feet felt like lead as I trudged across the hardwood floor, but I finally got there. Stepping into the freshly painted mint green room was like drawing in a desperately needed breath. I dodged a precarious stack of boxes, circling the center island until I stood next to Raylene and Hattie. The resemblance between them was strong. They both had the same rosy cheeks, and their hair was Miranda Lambert blond. They looked sweet as apple pie, but while Raylene really was quiet and lovely, Hattie was a spitfire if there ever was one. I'd seen both of them riled up. Raylene's emotions tended to get the better of her and she shut down while Hattie wound up like a coiled snake, ready to strike at the first opportunity.

"Bunch of fun-loving people out there," Hattie said, uncharacteristically calm. Almost intentionally so.

I smiled. "Yep, a real barrel of monkeys."

Hattie finished spreading a dill-infused mayonnaise on miniature pieces of pumpernickel bread, laid thin slices of cucumbers atop them, and then capped them with another square of the dark bread.

"Everything's beautiful," I said. "Y'all have done an amazing job with Seven Gables."

The compliment fell on deaf ears. They had something else on their minds.

"Harlow," Raylene said as she wiped her hands on her apron. Her expression grew slack, and for the second time in as many days, my heart dropped.

"What is it, Raylene? What's going on?"

Hattie handed me one of the miniature pumpernickel cucumber sandwiches. Everything, right down to the small floral napkin she set it on, was coordinated. She hemmed and hawed, starting to speak and then stopping, starting, and stopping, but the cat held firm to her tongue. Which was so unlike Hattie. I'd known her since childhood and the girl never held back.

"For pity's sake, Hattie, what is it?" I finally demanded.

She leaned back against the white-tiled counter and folded her arms, that defiant Hattie expression planted firmly on her face. "What's the story with Gavin McClaine?" she asked.

Raylene was at the swinging door, heading back to the dining room with her loaded, tiered tray. She stopped with her shoulder against the newly refinished oak. "He was in here yesterday poking around, asking questions about your mama and the sheriff—"

"What kinds of questions?" A red flag went up in my head. Gavin had that effect on me. For whatever reason, he didn't approve of his dad's relationship with my mother. As if the McClaines were too good for the Cassidys. We were the Hatfields and McCoys to Gavin's mind.

Hattie and Raylene locked gazes for a second before Raylene answered, "He wanted to know how many guests, the general plan for the reception, asked to see all the accommodations, seems worried that we can't handle the guests if the . . . the . . . murder . . . er, if the other guests are still here."

"Did he say how long he and his dad were going to request that they stay?" I asked, tilting my head toward the dining room. After all, either one of them could release the group from Dallas and New York. They didn't have any evidence to hold anyone.

They both shook their heads. "No, but I got the impression they weren't going to be set free any time soon,"

Hattie said, "and I also got the feeling it wasn't necessarily because of that man dying."

My jaw tightened, right along with my fists. If Gavin McClaine was using Beaulieu's murder to throw a wrench into the wedding plans, he had another think coming. All the more reason I wanted this resolved, even if I had to get involved to make sure that happened. Nothing was going to stop this wedding from happening, least of all a hotshot deputy with a wild hair in his craw.

Chapter 11

The sheriff's department, which used to be the old Baptist church, was part of Bliss's historic registry, a plaque affixed to the outside entrance announcing the building's importance in the town, since circa 1898. It was spittin' distance from Buttons & Bows and was now home to the city offices. But being as old as it was, the devotion from years and years of prayer had seeped into every board, every brick, and every crack. It still looked like a church. Its faded brick siding and peaked roofline would never be changed, and entering the building made me feel more like praying than confronting my soon-to-be stepbrother, aka the deputy sheriff.

I walked into the vestibule, past the old sanctuary to the left with the pews still pushed up against one wall and the solemnness hovering in the air. I stifled my urge to hold out my arms in reverence, instead plowing down the hallways toward reception, searching for Deputy McClaine. I sucked in a calming breath, and walked up to the cutout window. "Hey, Dixie," I said, throwing up my hand in a friendly wave. Meemaw always said you can catch more grain moths with apple cider vinegar, which was a spin on the catching flies with honey metaphor. It was another thing I never understood when I was a little girl, but now that I was grown and in my thirties, I got it. What's sweet to one person may not tickle someone else's taste buds. The trick was always getting to the nitty-gritty and finding what people responded to. It was true in fashion, in cooking, and in everything else, too.

I racked my brain for what I knew about Dixie. She'd been a few years ahead of me in school, had been the head cheerleader from Bliss High School, and had married Jake Stannis, her high school sweetheart, who'd been the star quarterback of the Bliss Bobcats. I knew she and Jake had three kids. She worked here to make ends meet while Jake coached football at the high school. I'd heard the catty women around town say that her receptionist job was so she'd have spending money for her spray-on tan and hair bleach, but I imagined she was good at her job.

"Hey yourself, Harlow," she said, giving me a good once-over. I couldn't tell if she was impressed by my outfit—a prairie dress, belted low on my hips, paired with my favorite red Frye boots—or if she was holding back a mocking smile.

Either way, I had to find some common ground with her. I smiled real big. "Did I hear that your daughter was in the play at the middle school?"

The hard lines on her face softened and she smiled. If the way into a man's heart was through his stomach, the way into a woman's was through her kids. "She sure was.

Four days of auditions. She had the starring role," she said.

"Wow, congratulations. If she's anything like you, I bet she was great," I said, completely sincere. From what I remembered, Dixie had starred in several of Bliss High School's plays.

We chatted about her kids for a few minutes, my blood pressure finally getting back to normal. "I've been meaning to come by your shop," she said after I'd been fully updated on Jake Junior, Heather, and Tiffany. She scrolled through pictures on her smart phone, bragging on her kids in true mother style. Dixie still had a cheerleader's personality, but she'd also grown up and seemed like a great mother. "Fashion's Night Out is coming in the fall. We don't have a mall nearby that's going to participate, but the town council wants Bliss to be part of it. Kind of a block party, all about fashion."

I knew about Fashion's Night Out. It was an annual event from Manhattan to Milan to L.A., and everywhere in between. The Galleria in Dallas always took part, I knew the suburban city of Southlake drew a big crowd, and the shops at Highland Village joined in, but I'd never imagined Bliss being in the mix. "Sounds like fun!" I said, a trifle too enthusiastically. I was calm, but still distracted by my desire to chew out Gavin McClaine. I'd waited a few hours to simmer down before coming to talk to him, but time hadn't helped in this instance. I was still worked up. Taking on a new project like Fashion's Night Out would have to wait until after my mother's wedding, and after the weight of Beaulieu's murder was lifted off the town.

"Great! I'll come by real soon," she said with a toothy smile. "Now, Harlow, what can I do you for?"

"Is Deputy McClaine around?"

"He's right back in his office," she said, pointing to the hallway behind her.

I hesitated. "Can I . . . ?"

"Sure thing." She pressed a button underneath her desktop, and a buzzing came from the door, followed by a click.

I'd been to the department before, but I usually entered through the city offices side of the old church. Being buzzed through was a new experience. "Do you know where to go?" she asked once I'd passed through to the back.

"Sure do. Thanks a bunch, Dixie. Come on by anytime so we can talk." I waved and headed down the hallway and into the maze of offices. Will had an office at the opposite end of the building with the other city employees. This side was the law enforcement side. I really wanted to take a hard left and go see Will, but I stayed my course, heading for Gavin's office instead.

His door was cracked open slightly and his Southern drawl carried into the hallway. I paused long enough to listen to the snippets of conversation, suddenly recognizing the other voice. What was she doing here?

I'd been taught not to eavesdrop, so I lifted my hand to knock, but the sound of my name stopped me. My hand froze midair and all my good Southern breeding went out the window.

"I plan to win that Pulitzer one day," Lindy said. "I've done some research, and I won't stop until I have what I need."

"And?"

"And yes, she has a name in the industry."

There was a weighty pause. Gavin's voice changed slightly, almost turning forlorn, as he said, "Does she, now?"

"At least she's starting to. She left Manhattan and her job at Maximilian, but she's still just starting out."

My breath caught in my throat. *Why* were they talking about me? My thoughts hitched. I couldn't possibly be a real suspect in Beaulieu's murder, could I? Gavin and Hoss McClaine knew me better than that.

"That can't be why she's here," Gavin said.

Lindy met Gavin's refusal to believe head-on. "It certainly could be."

I could supply her with the truth. What Loretta Mae wanted, Loretta Mae got. And she'd wanted me back home in Bliss, so here I was. I dropped my hand back to my side. Why in the world did they even care? I debated on what to do—tiptoe out of here and leave them to their discussion, or barge in and demand to know why they were talking about me.

I went with option number two. I was my mother's daughter and I didn't back down from anything. I was the great-great-great-granddaughter of Butch Cassidy, which gave me extra gumption. I wouldn't turn my back on the likes of Gavin McClaine when I had a beef with him about interfering with my mother's and Hoss's wedding, and certainly not when he was asking around about me and why I was even back in Bliss.

My hand fisted and I rapped my knuckles against the door, pushing it open at the same time. "I'm taking her at face value. She came to help her friend with her mama's wedding and with that photo shoot," Gavin was saying. "Nothing more."

I poked my head in and saw Gavin reclined in his

chair, his heavy black boots on the corner of the desk, his fingers linked behind his neck. Lindy turned in her chair from where she sat at the far side of the desk. But before either of them could say another word, the realization of their last sentence hit me. They hadn't been talking about me.

Oh Lord. They'd been talking about Orphie Cates. And Gavin was trying to believe she had nothing to do with Beaulieu's death.

"Sorry. Wrong office," I said, the words spilling from my mouth before I had time to think. The fact that the deputy was questioning why Orphie was in town, and given that Beaulieu had been murdered just after she arrived, was probably a big ol' red flag. Until the murder was solved, I was pretty sure Gavin would be focusing all his brainpower on that, which meant he'd have Hoss's ear, which meant the sheriff would be spending his time involved in a murder investigation instead of enjoying his upcoming nuptials with my mother.

Which also meant that Gavin could wedge his foot between my mother and his father, if he was so inclined.

"Harlow Jane," Gavin said, "were your ears a-burnin'?" Gavin met my gaze, his dark eyes boring into me as if he knew perfectly well that I'd been standing outside the door, listening.

"Why would they be? Were you talking about me?"

Lindy tucked her notebook in her satchel, but her spine was straight, her shoulders back. She was on high alert and while she might not be taking notes, not a single detail of the conversation we were having would slip past her.

"Sure was," Gavin said. He dropped his legs down, the soles of his boots hitting the hard pile of the industrial carpet with a dull thud. "You have a lot on your plate, what with the wedding and the magazine article—"

"*If* that's still even happening."

He ignored my interruption and continued. "And the murder at your shop, of course."

My heart ratcheted to a thunderous rhythm, but I made my voice remain steady. "I work better under pressure."

"Then a murder under your roof shouldn't slow you down in the least."

My fingers twitched and I forced my feet to stay rooted to the spot. "I'm sure you'll figure out what happened."

"Working on that very thing. Top of the priority list." He pointed at Lindy. "We were just discussing it, in fact."

Orphie's face appeared in my head, front and center, her infectious smile tainted by the murder that had happened in Buttons & Bows. "Oh?"

"I've been talking with all the people who were at your shop that morning. Wanna go through the list with me?"

How could I refuse? "Sure thing, *Deputy*."

Gavin's eyes narrowed. He usually had to remind me to address him as deputy, and calling him Gavin was so much more fun because it got under his skin, but bless his heart, he just kept going. "Great."

I went through the list in my mind, ticking off one person after the next. "Lindy," I began, looking at her and offering a quick smile. "And Quinton. Beaulieu, of course, his assistant—"

"Jeanette?" Gavin had flipped open a file folder and

alternated between looking down at his notes and looking at me.

"Yes." I went on. "Midori. Her models—"

"Zoe and Madison?"

"Right. And Beaulieu's models, Barbi and Esmeralda."

"Esmeralda," he murmured, shaking his head. "Who names their kid Esmeralda?"

Who named their kid Hoss or Bubba or Betty Sue? Texans, that's who, and I imagined Esmeralda was a family name since the girl didn't look as though she came from some exotic place far away from the South.

"Your mother, too, right?" Lindy asked.

As if she didn't know with absolute certainty that Tessa Cassidy had been there. "Yes, my mother, my grandmother, and a friend who's visiting—"

"Orphie Cates," Gavin said, his lips lifting just slightly on one side. He looked up at me, an innocent, Barney Fife look on his face, as if I couldn't tell he was smitten with her. If someone who looked like Timothy Olyphant could summon up Barney Fife, that is.

"Yes, Orphie Cates. My *friend*."

Gavin met me gaze again. "And you, of course." He chuckled, but the sound sent a chill down my spine. He had a truckload of Southern charm he could employ when he wanted to, just like his daddy, but underneath it all, he was shrewd and wanted nothing more than to get the job done.

"And me."

He flipped a page in his file, scanning it before looking back up at me. "Let's go through them all, one by one, shall we?"

I got my feet to move forward and sat in the hard, ladder-back chair next to Lindy. Wanting to hightail it out of there might be at the top of my list of things to do, but making sure nobody I knew and loved ended up in some horrible state penitentiary was higher on my to-do list. "Sure."

He looked at Lindy. "I'll talk to you later, darlin'," he said.

Some people liked a Southern man's endearments, but from the tense look on Lindy's face, she wasn't one of them. She stood, slinging her satchel over her shoulder, and with a quick, almost nonexistent wave, she was out the door.

Gavin dipped his head and held his palm out to me. "I want your perspective on the suspects, Harlow."

I nearly fell out of my chair. "Since when do you want to hear what *I* have to say? Haven't you already interviewed everyone?"

He sat perfectly still for a good ten seconds. "I have," he finally said, "but I'm interested in what you observed."

I wasn't quite speechless, but I was stunned. *"Okay."*

"Let's start with Beaulieu, shall we? What do you know about him?"

I perched on the edge of the chair. No amount of effort could stop my heart from hammering in my chest. "I know of him and his designs," I said, not really sure what Gavin wanted to hear. "I met him last week when we did the first photo shoot in Dallas. He was just as surly then as he was here. Almost."

He took out a fresh sheet of paper and started jotting down notes. "What's his reputation in the fashion world?"

"He's a good stylist," I started. Orphie's description of him came back to me. "I guess he's, er, was, a bit derivative."

Gavin stared at me, his head shifting forward on his neck as if he were a turtle darting its head out of its shell. "Derivative how?"

Beaulieu wasn't on trial and I felt guilty at speaking ill of the dead, but then again, understanding the victim of a crime could help Gavin figure out what really happened. "He sort of"—I made air quotes—"*borrowed* from other designers."

"Did he borrow from you?"

"No!" I understood the question, but the idea was absurd. A sliver of doubt about Gavin's motives worked under my skin. Maybe I'd fallen prey to his Southern charm. A little barrier went up, just in case.

"What about from Midori?"

Oh boy. If Beaulieu routinely used my designs, or Midori's, adopting our aesthetic and point of view, and one of us happened to be at the right place at the right time when Beaulieu was murdered, we'd be the first suspect. But I shook my head. "From what I gathered, they didn't like each other, but no, his aesthetic was more influenced by other big-name designers, like Jean Paul Gaultier. If you put their collections side by side, they'd be pretty similar."

"But this Jean Paul Gaultine character—"

"Gaultier," I corrected.

"I stand corrected. This Gaultier character wasn't at your shop, or in Bliss."

I sat back on the hard chair. "No." And the odds of him sneaking into Bliss to kill Beaulieu over some stolen designs were zero. Which brought the focus back onto me and Midori.

"Anything else you know about him?" With Gavin's heavy Southern drawl, the French elegance of the dead man's name was lost, another thing Beaulieu would have been cringing at. The first being his murder, of course.

I shook my head. "Not really, no." He had no connection to anyone who'd been in my shop that I was aware of. "He brought in his own models from New York," I offered.

"I ran into them at Seven Gables," he said, the corner of his mouth lifting in a smile.

A sudden thought occurred to me and I framed a question that could help with my own personal investigation. "Hattie and Raylene mentioned you were there. Something about the wedding?"

He waved his hand dismissively. "Harlow, I ain't gonna lie to you. You Cassidys? I think y'all are nuttier than a tornado chaser, but my pop is happy, and if your mama makes him that way, I'm not gonna poke the fire."

I was speechless for a second, finally managing a hoarse "Really?"

"Sure. I'm not gonna break up two people in love. I'm not heartless."

"So why were you grilling Hattie and Raylene?"

He chuckled again, but this time it wasn't directed at me, and no chill wound its way up my spine. "Grillin's the wrong word, Harlow Jane. That Raylene makes a mean pecan tart," he said. "I'd do just about anything for a truckload of those."

I peered at him, my protection mode kicking in. "So you're not interested in the models?"

"As suspects? Of course. Other than that? Hell, no. What kind of man do you think I am?"

Maybe a better one than I'd given him credit for. "And Orphie . . . ?"

"I ain't talkin' about my personal life with you. Unless you wanna start sharin' about you and Flores?" He winked because he knew good and well that I wasn't about to tell him a thing about my relationship with Will, which meant whatever he might or might not feel about Orphie was going to stay his business. My only fear was that he was making nice with her only to ferret out more information, but deep down I didn't believe that.

He grinned, looking like a cat who'd swallowed a canary. "Tell me about Midori." He paused. "Isn't that a drink?"

I'd have to deal with whether or not to open Orphie's eyes about Gavin later. For now, I stayed zeroed in on the murder. "Midori sour," I said, nodding.

"Does she have a last name? Or maybe that *is* her last name?"

I sat back, trying to relax a little bit. He was doing his job, nothing more, nothing less. If you didn't count the fun he wanted to have along the way. "I don't know, actually. All I know is that she's from Japan, she goes back pretty often, the other models here are from Dallas and she uses them regularly, and she's known for being very . . ." I hesitated, thinking about how to phrase it. "Persnickety," I finally settled on, "when it comes to her designs, who's showing them, and who buys them." And who makes them. She was a bit of a control freak, I realized.

"So she's high-strung. Great." He gestured with his hand so I'd go on.

"Jeanette works for—" I stopped and regrouped. "Worked for," I corrected, "Beaulieu. She was his assistant."

"And you just met her."

I nodded. "Yes. She's staying at Seven Gables, too. Seems pretty lost right now. On top of her boss dying, she's lost her job. I sort of got the feeling she'd love it if Midori hired her, but Midori doesn't use an assistant."

"Anything else about Jeanette"—he glanced down at his notes, then back up— "Braden?"

"I like her," I said, and I did. She was what we Southerners called a sweet gal. "I hope she can find a job with a better boss than Beaulieu has been. Someone who doesn't chew her out and—" I stopped when the conversation, if you could call it that, between Jeanette and Beaulieu came back to me.

"Spill it, Harlow."

"Spill what, Gavin?"

He pointed his finger at me. "You're a dang open book. I can see it in your eyes. You're thinking something, but you're not sure you should tell me. Look here, darlin', your allegiance should be to the sheriff's department, not to some girl you just met, who you don't know, and who might could have killed that man."

I was brimming with turmoil. On the one hand, he was right. I needed to let the sheriff's department do its job. Let Gavin do his job. But I liked Jeanette and maybe my wayward thoughts meant nothing at all.

"Harlow . . . ," he said, his voice heavy with warning.

"Okay," I said, making up my mind. I was a fashion designer, not a detective, and I didn't have any business getting involved. "Beaulieu was pretty rough on Jeanette. He humiliated her, right there in front of all of us."

Gavin nodded, encouraging me to go on.

"He chewed her out for wrinkling a garment and he told her to press it. She was pretty upset about it."

He jotted down some notes. "Interesting. Good. Now, tell me what you know about the models."

"I don't know anything about them," I said, and then added, "Except that they're like oil and water."

"The Dallas girls don't get along with the Yankees?"

"Exactly."

"A little friendly competition between them?"

"Competition, yes. Friendly? No. We all had tea a little while ago at Seven Gables. Let's just say the Dallas girls aren't too happy to have Beaulieu's girls here, and Beaulieu's girls think they're better models than the Dallas girls. Not much love lost between them."

"I got that from them, too," he said, "but do you know if there was love lost between any of them and Beaulieu?"

I shrugged. "I have no idea."

"We can't forget the *D Magazine* people. Quinton Holstrom and Lindy Reece."

I hadn't really given them serious consideration. They'd been sent to do a job, but weren't connected to Beaulieu. At least not that I knew of. But I nodded anyway. They had been present, after all. But with Beaulieu dead, their story was out the window. Neither one of them had a motive that I could see.

He hesitated, writing something on his piece of paper before raising his gaze to me again. He hesitated and his lips curved downward as if he didn't want to ask his next question. But finally he did. "And that brings us to your friend Orphie. Do you keep in touch with her?"

Instantly the coils in my stomach tightened. "Orphie didn't have anything to with this."

He nodded, and I knew he agreed with me. "But it was mighty bad luck for her to show up just before a murder."

"All the more reason to think she wouldn't be involved. Why would she conspicuously show up only to kill someone?" I shot back. "That makes no sense."

"That's the thing about murder, Harlow. It never does make much sense, now, does it?"

He had a point and my shoulders sank. "No, I guess it doesn't."

I didn't have anything more to offer, and he had the good sense not to hurl accusations at my mother and grandmother for being present, so I stood to go. Back to Buttons & Bows. Back to the wedding plans. And back to talk to Orphie about Maximilian's book, because the more I thought about it, the more I thought the deputy had a point. The timing of Orphie's arrival in Bliss could be seen as oddly coincidental, and I didn't want Gavin McClaine digging around and finding a way to connect her to Beaulieu.

Chapter 12

I arrived back at Buttons & Bows to find both Midori and Jeanette sitting on the white rocking chairs on my front porch. They were rocking in unison, but as I parked my truck and came through the side gate from the driveway, they fell out of sync with each other. Midori rocked forward as Jeanette rolled back. I'd get dizzy if I watched them for too long.

They were each dressed just as they'd been earlier. Midori wore a sleeveless red silk blouse that hung loosely over a fitted black skirt. Jeanette still looked harried—but who wouldn't after their boss had been murdered? She had on jeans and a hand-done silk-screened T-shirt, the design on the cotton colorful and abstract.

My boots crunched against the granite footpath, the sounds of my footsteps finally quieting as I turned onto the flagstones that led to the house. "We had to get out of Seven Gables," Jeanette said as I mounted the porch steps.

So they'd escaped to the dressmaking shop. I'd offered Midori the workspace, so it made sense. I'd have done the same thing.

I blinked and just like that, my charm kicked in, as if a switch had been flipped, illuminating a pitch-black room. Images of them came to me in different outfits. Midori's was a raglan-sleeved blouse in black and white, and tailored, tapered slacks. Jeanette, true to her more casual style, but also in black and white, had black jeans and a white sleeveless blouse embellished with silver strands of shimmery cording. In my mind, the draped cording flowed artfully as she moved, looking fluid and sleek.

I blinked again and they were back in their original outfits, my vision gone. It was just as well. With the wedding, I had no time to begin planning outfits for the two of them.

"How are you feeling?" I asked, but given the fact that they were at my shop instead of in their rooms at the inn, I had a pretty good idea.

"Those girls," Midori said, shaking her head. "They fight and bicker and I cannot stand it another minute."

I didn't think I'd be able to bear it, either. I nodded, gesturing toward the door. "I bet. Come on in."

They stopped rocking, nodding at the same time, like mirror images of each other. They might not have known each other before they'd come to Bliss, but murder had a way of bringing people together.

They followed me inside. Midori glanced around, her gaze continually drawn to the kitchen where Beaulieu had died. Jeanette set about tidying the throw pillows in the seating area. Nervous energy. I could put that to good use.

"Did you know my mother's getting married soon?" I said, but I stopped, a red flag shooting up in my mind. Something was off inside the shop. Had Meemaw been nosing around? I looked around but didn't see anything out of place, but the feeling stayed with me.

"To the sheriff, right? Gossip in a small town," Jeanette said with a faint smile. "The Seven Gables sisters were talking about it. They're having the reception?"

I nodded. We'd tossed around a passel of ideas for the reception, finally deciding on the bed-and-breakfast. Their outside space was landscaped and lush and would make the perfect backdrop for the party. "I'm finishing my mama's dress. Then I have to make mine still, and I'm designing a special outfit for a . . . for my . . ." I stumbled on how to describe Gracie. The daughter of the man I was dating. A friend. My half cousin once removed—or something like that.

"For my assistant," I finally settled on. "You'll meet her later."

Midori's attention zeroed in on me, her brown eyes widening, the slight curve of a smile touching the corners of her lips. "Let me design your dress for the wedding."

Me, in a Midori design? "Oh no, I couldn't ask you to do that."

"You didn't ask me, and you didn't ask for this . . . situation. We've all descended on your life—"

"Beaulieu dying wasn't your fault," I said.

"But we're stuck here, and if I can help . . ." She twisted her hands together, and I understood. The corner of Midori's sketchbook peeked out of the oversized bag she hauled around. A designer could have a million sketches, but to take one and bring it to life, to choose fabric, cut the pattern pieces, stitch the seams, and breathe life into it, all for one specific person, well, that was what brought out my Cassidy charm, and for Midori, I got the feeling it brought her a sense of peace and purpose.

"Tell me about the wedding," she said, pulling her sketchbook out and opening it to a clean page.

Maybe this was where my hesitation came from. Midori's designs were stylized, full of angles. Her aesthetic was completely different from mine. I had no doubt I'd like what she created, but would it fit in with the overall style of the wedding? I wasn't so sure.

She sat on the settee and looked expectantly at me as Jeanette sat opposite her on the love seat. She held a mechanical pencil poised over the paper, a thin piece of graphite poking out from the tip.

Everyone brainstormed design ideas differently. I had no idea how Midori worked, so I just launched into the background. "The bride is Tessa Cassidy. The groom is Hoss McClaine."

She nodded. "And your mother was here yesterday?" She was the one making tea and lemonade?"

"Right," I said. "She and my grandmother."

Midori looked past me in thought. "Are they very, how do you say it, lovey-dovey?"

I laughed. "Hoss McClaine is a curmudgeonly man who's a lot of gruff and a little bite."

She stared at me, blank-faced, so I tried again. "They're plenty lovey-dovey," I said. "Hoss is a good ol' boy who loves my mother." They were the perfect match. Tessa could give as good as she got, and Hoss could take it. He didn't put up with any shenanigans from her, but they'd found a way to balance each other's personality.

"You must get to see them all the time. How nice."

The slight melancholy tinge to her voice gave me pause. "Do you have family here?"

"No, no, all in Japan," she said. The tip of her pencil danced along the surface of the paper, the faint outline of a shape taking form. "I go back each season."

I smiled to myself. Just like a designer to think in terms of seasons rather than months.

"I'm sure that's got to be really hard. My great-grandmother passed," I said, "but she used to say that she'd always live in my heart. It's true. I feel her with me." I was instantly surrounded by a warm cocoon of air. Meemaw was present and accounted for. "Sometimes quite literally," I added. A little inside joke between Meemaw and me.

"My mother died a few years ago." Jeanette's lips quivered, but she managed a smile and flattened her palm against her chest. "I do feel her with me."

We sat in silence for a moment, holding on to the memories of our families. Finally Midori cleared her throat, blinking away the glaze that had surfaced in her eyes.

"Is the wedding inside or outside?"

The question was a good segue back to our shared passion. "Outside, in the bluebonnet field at the church off the square. Unless we get a summer storm, in which case we'll go inside."

"There's nothing like a good summer thunderstorm," Jeanette said, her voice steady and even again. "My daddy sits outside with a cigar, a jigger of scotch, and a book, and if there's thunder and lightning, he forgets all about the book and watches the show."

In my mind's eye, I could see Will sitting out on his back porch with a set of blueprints or a war novel, breathing in the summer air. Must be a guy thing. Me, I'd always rather be in my atelier, sewing or designing or crafting. "I'm making felt beads for the bridesmaids and the flower girl," I said, getting back to the wedding. "And Mama had a pretty good idea of what she wanted for her dress."

I went into the workroom, lifting the dress form with Mama's dream gown on it. The fitted bodice had a lacy top, and the lightweight taffeta sprang from the waistline, ending in an angled hem that was shorter in the front than in the back. "She'll be wearing these underneath," I said, holding up one of the bedazzled boots.

"Interesting," Midori said.

It was only one word, but it set me on the defensive. "Tessa Cassidy is stubborn as a mule, and when she sets her mind on something, there's no changing it. This fits her to a tee."

She waved one hand apologetically. "Sorry. I did not mean anything. I think it's quaint. A real country wedding."

"I don't know if it's everyone's idea of country, but it's certainly my mother's."

"And you need something to complement the wedding gown, but a little more . . . you?"

"Exactly. No small order."

"And you're a bridesmaid?"

"Maid of honor," I corrected. Mama had plenty of friends, but having a secret like a magical charm tended to bring you closest to the people who knew about it, and further from those who didn't. We were mother and daughter, but we were also best friends.

She lifted the tip of her pencil from her notebook. "And she didn't pick out a dress for you? That's very trusting of her."

"That's my mother. She wouldn't dare try to tell me what to wear, just like I wouldn't tell her what flowers to grow in her garden. She'll grow what she wants to grow, and I'll make what I want to make."

Midori narrowed her eyes slightly, nodding. "I see. She sounds like an interesting woman."

"All the Cassidy women are," I said brightly.

"So, will you let me design a dress for you?" she asked.

"Midori, I appreciate—"

I stopped when she held her finger to her lips. "I want to," she said, setting her sketchbook on the table and standing. "I can't sit around and do nothing while I'm here in Bliss. I'll go crazy."

"You can read," I suggested. "I have stacks of books upstairs."

She looked at the floor for a beat. "Reading in English? No. I need to sew."

Her voice had grown thin and desperate, and I understood.

Usually I was the one creating for other people. To have the tables turned was exciting. "I'd be honored," I said.

She nodded, just once and very formally, but I could see the faint smile appear again. "Good." She perched back on the edge of the settee, picked up her sketchbook again, and went back to her drawing. In the matter of a minute, she was lost in her imagination, her pencil flying across the page.

I noticed the design book lying open on the coffee table and drew in a breath. A minute ago, it had been closed, the red cover with the blogger who'd written it on the front cover. Earlier it had been in the workroom, and before that, I'd found it in the kitchen. Meemaw. She'd been moving the thing from one room to another. She had a message to give me.

I peered at the page, a vintage design for a sweetheart sundress staring back at me. I inhaled sharply, but this time it was because of a revelation. This was the perfect outfit for Gracie! It had a simple bodice, and it could be worn strapless, but for Gracie, I wanted straps. A halter was an option, too. It might not need boning if it had straps, but to hold it in place, the bodice would need some sort of structure.

"She's an old soul," Jeanette said, picking up the book.

"She sure is." From what I knew of Gertie, she was a contemporary woman enthralled by the history of design and clothing. A girl who could have walked off the set of *Mad Men*, and a girl after my own heart.

Jeanette stayed with me as I took Mama's gown and the dress form back to the workroom. She shot a quick glance over her shoulder. "Can I ask you something?" she said quietly.

"Sure." I situated the dress form next to Meemaw's old Singer and the privacy screen, keeping it safe and out of the way, but near enough that I could look at it, contemplate the design, and see what else needed to be done to it. There was something . . . I just couldn't put my finger on it.

She fidgeted, shifting from one foot to the other in her sensible navy flats. Another reason Beaulieu probably hadn't liked her. She didn't dress with the keen sense of fashion one would expect a designer to have. She dressed for ease and practicality, from her plain slacks to her thin cardigan sweater set. I was all for feeling comfortable, but I liked my outfits to express my fashion sensibilities as well.

"What is it, Jeanette?" I asked.

"It's just . . . why did you . . ."

Poor girl couldn't get the words out. "Why did I what?"

"Why did you leave Manhattan? I mean, you worked for Maximilian, right?"

Coming back to Bliss had been one of the most difficult decisions I'd ever made. Meemaw had passed, I'd found out that she'd given me the little yellow farmhouse and made me a homeowner, and truthfully, I had missed small-town life. But leaving the fashion world of New York felt more like giving up a dream than coming home. "It wasn't easy," I said, trying to figure out how to put my decision into words. "Working for Maximilian was great experience, but I wasn't creating my own designs or following what was in my heart. I was part of the team that made his designs a reality."

"But wasn't that exciting? Working for a real designer, I can't even imagine that!"

"You worked for Beaulieu," I said. "It's the same thing."

"But it's not. Beaulieu . . . his stuff wasn't . . . he didn't . . ."

She looked over her shoulder again, looking into the front room, and I did, too. Midori had just started riffling through the rack of ready-made clothing at the far end of the shop, and I suddenly realized what had been bothering me when we'd first entered. The outfits on the rack were all out of order, mixed up, one or two of the pieces falling off the hangers. I bit my lower lip, processing. It was as if someone had been riffling through them.

Not knowing why the clothes were askew bothered me, but I pushed the concern aside. It could have been Meemaw, after all. Midori straightened the garments on the hangers as she looked. At least she'd get a better sense of my aesthetic by looking at what I'd made. I hoped. Showing up at my mother's wedding in a traditional Midori outfit meant I'd probably steal the show, and that couldn't happen. A wedding day belonged to the bride, and the bride alone. The rest of us had to complement her, not steal the attention. I had to trust that Midori understood this and could produce an understated design for me to wear.

I put my hand on Jeanette's shoulder, encouraging her to speak. "He didn't what?"

"He wasn't like Maximilian. *He's* one of a kind."

"What do you mean?" I asked, although I had a feeling I knew where she was going.

"He wasn't very creative," she said.

"No?"

"No. I almost laughed when I heard him talking about integrity and originality. I think he'd really convinced himself that he was better than he was."

My smile was halfhearted. Orphie had been on the verge of becoming nothing more than a copycat. At least she'd had the good sense to quit before she'd jumped across that line with both feet. "It's easy to get sucked into the glamorous life of high fashion. Sometimes that integrity line blurs," I said. "All the celebrities coming out at Fashion Week with their toy dogs and sunglasses. It's a different world."

She stared off over my shoulder as if she were imagining such a scene. She was Dorothy stepping out of her house in Oz and seeing everything in Technicolor. "I want to be part of it."

"Then you should," I said. Me? I preferred the slower pace of the small town, and I loved my shop, but everyone needed to choose their own path. "It's hard work, and it's really competitive, but if you want it bad enough, you can do anything." The words hung in the air like a cloud of mist. Someone had wanted Beaulieu dead enough to kill him. Jeanette had been right here. She had disdain for her boss because of his lack of integrity; she'd made that much clear. But was that enough of a motive to kill him? After all, if she wanted to go to New York so badly, Beaulieu would have been her best opportunity. She would have wanted him alive. She couldn't just step into his now empty shoes and take over.

"What will you do now?" I asked.

She wandered around the workroom, looking at everything with wonder in her eyes. "Midori said she may have some opportunities for me. She has regular buyers here in the U.S., but she said she's been thinking about expanding. Or I could start my own collection and see if I can get backing."

"That's definitely the hard part. It's not easy to find investors."

She laughed. "Not for Beaulieu, but then again, blackmail works if you do it right."

My brain skidded to a stop. "What?"

She sucked her lower lip in, her eyes going wide. "Nothing. Never mind."

"Jeanette, was Beaulieu blackmailing someone?"

For the third time, she peeked through the open French doors between the workroom and the shop area of Buttons & Bows. Midori had moved from the ready-to-wear rack to the coffee table, sitting on her haunches and flipping through my magazine stash, perusing my lookbook, and going back to her sketchbook.

Jeanette dropped her voice to a faint whisper. "I heard him on the phone a few times. I could be wrong, but it sounded an awful lot like keeping a secret in exchange for money."

Oh boy. "Did Beaulieu have the secret or the money?"

"From what I could tell, he knew something about someone, and the only way he was going to keep quiet was if he got some money."

"Jeanette," I said, "did you tell the sheriff about this?"

She recoiled, her chin dropping, her eyes bugging. "No! I don't want to get involved, Harlow. I should never have mentioned it." She grabbed my arm, her gaze boring into mine. "What if I'm right and . . . and that's who killed him? They could come after me! You can't say anything."

"Say anything about what?" Midori stood in the threshold between the two rooms, looking up from her sketchbook just long enough to ask the question. Lindy stood just behind her, notebook in hand. I looked past her to the front. It was open. The bells that normally jingled to announce a visitor were on the floor and kicked into the corner. Lindy had appeared the way a ghost might, throwing us a little off balance as ghosts were known to do. At least in my house.

Jeanette's eyes flew open wide, but she swallowed and her voice remained steady. "Harlow was just telling me how she feels about sewing and design," she said, thinking far more quickly than I'd been able to.

Anxiety emanated from Jeanette like heat off a Texas highway, and a thought struck me. Jeanette and Midori had had lunch the day Beaulieu died. What if Midori had been the one being blackmailed by Beaulieu, had made some allusion to it, and Jeanette had figured it out? And what if Midori had somehow killed the man to stop the blackmail?

"I'd love to hear your thoughts," Lindy said, closing the door and coming farther into the shop. Something in her voice gave me pause. Was she talking about my thoughts on sewing and design, the thoughts racing around in my head, or Jeanette's plea that whoever had killed Beaulieu could come after her?

"Are you going ahead with the article, then?"

"Come hell or high water, as they say."

Which didn't precisely answer my question.

Midori tucked her sketchbook under her arm and clapped her hands. "So your editor said to go ahead?"

"Mmm, not quite, but just about," Lindy said. The slight shake of her head made me think the not quite was the more accurate part of the answer. She seemed to sense my doubt, because she offered more. "Look, newspapers and magazines are going under all the time. I need to write great stories. Win a Pulitzer. Something, you know? I'm going to write a damn good story and I'll find someone to buy it. And then maybe I'll rework it from another angle and sell it again."

She was nothing if not tenacious. She fit right in with the Cassidy women. "Okay," I said, pushing my glasses back into place. If she was willing to put in the time to write the articles, we could answer her questions. "Ask away."

We sat down in my cozy seating area, Jeanette and Midori on the couch, Lindy on the love seat, and me on the settee. "You said you were talking about how you feel about sewing and design," Lindy started. "Can you elaborate on that?"

I thought for a minute, trying to put what I felt into words. "Women are nurturers," I said. "That I'm a woman means I want to help people, encourage them, fulfill longings they have—sometimes needs they don't even understand themselves." My charm came in very handy in those circumstances. "But I'm also an artist, which means I see beauty and sensuality all around, and I want to find a way to represent that beauty through my designs. It's always challenging to figure out how to give a woman what she wants while balancing that with something that's luxurious, practical, and sensual. But that's exactly what I try to do with every single design, no matter who I'm making it for."

Lindy's hand flew across the page as she transcribed what I'd said. Designing for real women of different shapes and sizes was a balancing act. But truthfully, I preferred real curves to a shapeless skeletal figure, another reason I loved being home in Bliss.

We talked design for a few more minutes before Lindy turned to Midori and asked her the same question. "I needed to make something of myself," she replied. "My family, they do not understand. They do not see what I see with color and pattern and shape. But they support me, and here I am. I donate my runway clothes."

Lindy's eyes lit up and I could tell she saw a new angle to her story. "So everyday women can buy your designs?"

"Yes, exactly. I have a buyer and customers who wait. That, above all else, gives me joy. That my dresses carry with them something for everyone."

Lindy nodded, hurriedly taking down notes on what Midori had said. "That's fantastic." As they kept talking, a concentrated gust of air gathered behind me and, like two hands on my back, pushed me off the settee. "Oomph!"

Jeanette jumped up, putting her arms out to block me, but I caught myself just in time, regaining my footing and stopping just before plowing into her. Jeanette stared at me as if I'd lost my mind. Which to her I probably had since it had to have looked as though I'd launched myself across the room. "Are you okay?"

I shook off my frustration with the ghostly antics of my great-grandmother. "I'm so sorry! I'm fine." I pulled her aside, away from Lindy and Midori and their puzzled looks. "Sorry!" I said to them with a quick wave.

"Are you sure you're okay?" Jeanette asked.

I batted away her concern. "Yes, yes, fine. I was wondering, though . . ." I hesitated, not sure how to broach the subject tactfully, but the pause gave Loretta Mae another chance to gather up her energy and push me again. I whipped around, ready to scold her as if she were a precocious five-year-old. "Meemaw!" I said under my breath with a hiss. "Cool it."

This time, Jeanette stared at me. "Who's Meemaw?"

I laughed off Jeanette's question. "Oh, no one. Just my great-grandmother. All this talk about my sewing philosophy made me think of her. She taught me to sew."

Jeanette gaped, looking for all the world as though she didn't believe a word I'd just said, but I was sure that the alternative—that a ghost had shoved me—wasn't even on her mind, so she finally shrugged, letting it go. I seized the bit of privacy we had while Lindy monopolized Midori. "Jeanette, I really think you should talk to the sheriff."

She backed away. "I can't, Harlow."

"If you really think Beaulieu was blackmailing someone, you have to."

She didn't budge, and I didn't think there was any way she'd tell her suspicions to Gavin or Hoss. I could do it, but before I did, I wanted some proof. If someone was running scared, he or she might resort to murder . . . again. If Jeanette was right, someone had been blackmailed by Beaulieu, and quite possibly, one of them had resorted to murder to stop it.

Chapter 13

I'd decided that Buttons & Bows was the Bliss equivalent to Grand Central Station. No sooner had Jeanette and Midori left to head back to Seven Gables than Mrs. Zinnia James burst into the shop, standing tall, chin up, paper-thin skin pulled taut over the angular bones of her face, and dressed like Nancy Reagan in a smart suit, hose, and pumps.

Mrs. James was a senator's wife, but more than that, she was the matron of Bliss. She had her hand in everything, from sitting on committees to running charitable events to organizing some of Bliss's oldest traditional events. And she'd elected herself my personal patron, taking me under her wing.

"Harlow Cassidy," she said, her cadence slow and her accent thick. "What in tarnation is going on around here?"

Every time I saw Mrs. James, I envisioned her in a new outfit, each one more individualistic and arty than what she normally wore. This time, it was a maxi dress.

The fabric looked to be a shimmering gold cloque lamé like one you might find in Paris, the fibers of the cotton blistered to produce bumps and folds and then woven together with another fabric. Or it could have been a guimpe, the ribbons wrapped around a fibrous yarn. Either way, it was bold and was sort of an upscale version of the typical Texas bling.

Before I could answer, Orphie waltzed in looking more relaxed than I'd seen her since she'd arrived. "Mrs. James, meet Orphie Cates. We roomed together in Manhattan. Orphie, this is Mrs. James."

Orphie smiled warmly, extending her arm. Mrs. James, on the other hand, narrowed her eyes and gave Orphie a discerning look as she clasped her hand around Orphie's in a firm grip. "You look like you're in love," she said.

Blunt might have been Mrs. James's middle name.

Orphie's smile wavered. "No, not yet, but it could happen."

I gawked. "You don't mean with Gavin?" I said, cringing at the horrified edge in my voice.

Mrs. James was silent for a beat before letting loose an amused chortle. "Gavin McClaine?"

Orphie's smile was completely wiped from her face. She looked from me to Mrs. James, and then jammed her hands on her hips. She thrust her chin up defiantly. "Yes, *Deputy* Gavin McClaine. And what, pray tell, is wrong with that?"

Oh boy. She looked so serious and ready to defend Gavin at all costs. "Darlin'," I said, "Gavin mentioned something to me earlier today."

"You saw him?"

I nodded. "At the sheriff's station. I went to give him a piece of my mind—"

She huffed. "A piece of your mind about what?"

"I thought he might could have been trying to interfere with the wedding."

She gasped, staring at me as if I were crazy. "He wouldn't do that!"

"You don't know him, Orphie."

"He's not the same guy he was when you were kids, Harlow. People grow up."

I stared at her as if *she* were the one who'd gone off the deep end. "You just met him."

"Sometimes you just know," Mrs. James said matter-of-factly.

Orphie nodded. "That's right. Sometimes you do. Thank you, Mrs. James."

They shared a look that defied logic. After all, they'd just met, too, yet here they were, forming an alliance about love at first sight.

"We went to that bakery on the square and shared a cannoli," Orphie said, and her eyes got all dreamy again.

I didn't want to burst her bubble, but I had to dig a little. "Did he ask you why you came to Bliss?"

She met my gaze head-on. "Yes, he did. He told me he thought my timing was coincidental. Me arriving just before Beaulieu was murdered didn't look too good for me. But," she said, "I told him about the book—"

"You did!" I gaped, absolutely stunned that she'd fess up to Gavin about that.

"I did, and you know what?" There was that blissful expression again. "He didn't care."

Okay, that didn't make sense. "He's a deputy. How can he not care about a stolen book?"

Mrs. James had been listening quietly, but now she interjected. "A stolen book? Harlow, dear, am I missing something? People lie every day. Every ten minutes, for heaven's sake. Love is blind, as they say. If there's an attraction between two people, a previous indiscretion surrounding a stolen book isn't going to be a deal breaker."

I breathed in and out, unclenching my fists. It was Orphie's life, not mine, and maybe Orphie was right. Maybe Gavin really had changed and I was still seeing him as the cantankerous teenager he'd been fifteen years ago. "All I'm saying is that he was asking about you and why you were here."

"Well, he knows why, and we're going out again tonight." She hesitated, just barely, but enough that I noticed, before squeezing my hand. "Don't worry about me, Harlow. I'll be just fine."

I knew she would, and I also knew in my heart that Orphie had nothing to do with Beaulieu dying. But she was keeping something from me. I just had to figure out what it was.

Chapter 14

Midori, Jeanette, Orphie, and I spent the next two days buckled down in my workroom, sewing. We each had our projects. Midori was working on my maid of honor dress. I still hadn't seen the entire thing, but I liked the fabric she'd chosen. It was a sunny orange, my mother's favorite color, and looked fresh and happy—the opposite of the mood in my shop at the moment.

Orphie was trying to recapture her sewing confidence after her confession of copying Maximilian's designs, Jeanette was trying to elevate her game by working on a Peter Pan–collared blouse, and I focused on the sweetheart dress for Gracie. I'd chosen a bright teal-embroidered cotton voile, cutting the neckline and straps out of a contrasting white cotton pique.

"Has she seen it yet?" Orphie asked as I cut another rectangle two and a half times Gracie's front waist measurement, doing the same for the back, out of a plain weave habutai for the lining.

"No, it's a surprise." I wasn't sure if Gracie's charm ex-

tended to fabrics, or if she saw visions only from clothing
that had been worn by someone else. This would be a test.

She looked up from the center cutting table, studying
my progress. "Scalloped edge. Very tricky."

"So no hem?" Jeanette asked. "Is that why you picked
the voile?"

I grinned. "Maybe."

I'd gathered the waistline of the skirt and lining on
the sides only in an effort to make the dress a little less
full, had attached it to the bodice, matching the side
seams, and had inserted the zipper. The last step was slip-
stitching the bodice lining around the zipper. Gracie
would have to try it on before I could adjust the straps'
lengths, making sure to get them in the right place.

"Are you adding crinoline?" Orphie asked.

"I don't think so," I said. I'd thought about it, looking
back to Gertie's picture in the book. Tulle was another
option, but while I knew Gracie loved vintage, I didn't
think she'd want the poufy look.

The front door opened and shut so quickly, the bells,
which I'd rehung after the last time they'd ended up on
the floor, hardly had time to chime. At the same time, the
Dutch door in the kitchen slammed shut and a second
later Mama's boots clacked against the hardwood floor.
"That's it," she announced, peeling off her jacket as she
came into the workroom. Nana padded in behind her.
"The weddin' is off."

I stared at her, stunned into silence.

Mama slid her jacket half off, her cropped hair standing on end, and her glare wicked enough to turn me and
everyone else who happened across her path to stone.
"Did y'all hear me? The weddin' is off."

The air in the room stilled; all the sewing stopped. The wedding was in just two days, and up until this moment, I'd never seen Mama happier. I stood and jabbed my fists on my hips. "Mama, for Pete's sake, what are you talking about?"

She stood stock-still. "It wasn't meant to be, is all."

I thought it had been eerily silent a minute ago, but now it was like the quiet before the storm, clouds funneling in the sky above, a tornado formation imminent. Mama wasn't a crier. She was a stomper. After my father walked out on her, she hadn't hollered or wept. There'd been nary a tear in sight that hadn't belonged to me or Red.

Mama had just clomped around the yard, the flowers and plants around her withering. Even seeing Meemaw again, albeit in the form of a very wispy ghost, hadn't brought tears to her eyes.

She was strong, yes, but her quiet stony mood right now was like nothing I'd ever seen. "Not meant to be? What in the world are you talking about?" I demanded. "You and Hoss are meant for each other."

She whipped around, her newly cut and styled dark hair falling in loose curls around her face, the Cassidy blond streak in her hair more distinct because of whatever she was feeling. It was like a touchstone for her, as it was for each of us. My own scalp tingled from seeing my mother in emotional turmoil. She opened her mouth, sounds coming from her throat but not quite forming words. One by one, she looked at each woman in the workroom, and then her mouth closed.

She crooked her finger at me and shot a glance at Nana. "Come over here," she said to us.

We obliged, Nana scurrying back to the kitchen to slip

on her Crocs and me stepping into my cowboy boots. Twenty seconds later, we stood by the arbor in the front yard, the purple wisteria flowers, which had been in full bloom, turning brown along the edges before my eyes. "Mama, what's going on?"

"What's going on is that Gavin . . . the *deputy* . . . is hell-bent on you taking the fall for that man's murder."

One of the wisteria flowers had turned completely brown. The wind picked up and the dried petals were pulled from the stalk, moving through the air until they disappeared. "What?" That couldn't be right. He'd just asked for my thoughts on the suspects. "Why would he want me to take the fall?" I demanded. My mind whirled. "I just talked to him two days ago. He didn't launch a single accusation at me. He's dating Orphie—oh no."

"Oh no, what?" Nana asked, her arms folded over her chest.

"Maybe he really is a conniver and he's just using honey to try to trap a fly."

Nana shook her head. "I always knew that boy was no good. Wearing a badge and a uniform don't change that." She glared at Mama as if she'd birthed Gavin and his troublemaking ways were her fault. "What makes him think Harlow had anything to do with what happened?"

"And what does that have to do with you and Hoss and the wedding?" I asked, trying to stay calm. Gavin was a pill, but he wasn't stupid. I knew he was just trying to solve a murder, and I definitely didn't like him pointing his finger my way. But I also knew that he wouldn't be able to pin Beaulieu's murder on me because I didn't kill the man. No, he was up to something. And then I realized exactly what. He'd said he wasn't going to interfere with love, but that's just what he was doing. Investigating me had gotten under my mother's skin so much that she was contemplating how to go ahead and get married. Maybe that had been Gavin's plan all along.

Fire smoldered behind Mama's eyes. I could almost see her blood boiling. She'd blow any second if we couldn't calm her down. "I cannot marry a man who's trying to put my child behind bars," she said slowly.

And there it was. Gavin's success. I dropped my hands from my hips to my sides. "Is he . . ." The words tried to slip back down my throat, but I forced them out. "Does Hoss think I killed Beaulieu?"

Mama's head waggled like a bobble-head. "He said Gavin knows how to do his job, and that you"—she pointed her finger at me—"have a darn good motive."

"I don't have a motive!" I backed up a step, stumbling on an uneven piece of flagstone. "I didn't even know him!"

The anger on Mama's face was worse than a torrent of tears would have been. A sad Tessa Cassidy could be consoled and made to feel better, but a scorned Tessa Cassidy? I now understood why Mama was fired up and she was right. There likely wouldn't be a wedding in two days, because she wouldn't marry a man who thought ill of her kin.

"Oh," she bit off, "but you do. According to the *deputy*, you were being upstaged by Beaulieu in the magazine article, and everyone around town is talking about how he steals other designers' concepts and makes them his own, and how surely he's doing that to you, too."

I gaped. Who in the world would have started *that* rumor? "It's not true. He hasn't stolen anything of mine." My disheveled ready-to-wear rack came back to the front of my mind. Could Beaulieu have riffled through it before he died and I just hadn't noticed? I felt as if my mind was playing tricks on me.

"Tell *that* to Gavin." She slid her jacket back on and faced Nana and me. "I can't do it. No," she corrected, "I won't do it." She hitched up her blue jeans as she shook her head.

"Mama, they're just doing their job. They've got to consider everything," I said, but still, I was unnerved.

She frowned.

"And I didn't have anything to do with Beaulieu dying, so there's nothing to worry about.

"And," I finished, "you love Hoss McClaine."

Her stony expression faltered for a split second, but she bucked up, hardening the lines of her face again, blocking out the emotions that I knew were tucked away inside her. "I love you more, darlin'. Loretta Lynn mighta wanted to stand by her man, but I want a man who'll stand by me and mine. Period."

I started to argue but stopped. I wanted a man who'd stand by me, too. I thought that Will might be that man. I wanted nothing less for Mama, and while I was pretty sure Hoss McClaine was the cowboy for her, she had to know it in her heart.

Which left me no choice. I'd go have a sit-down with Hoss and his deputy son, proclaim my innocence, see what Gavin was really up to, and figure out what else I could do to help them find the truth. I'd already been thinking about the murder, wondering how it could have happened in my shop, and why. But now? Now I needed to save Mama's wedding—and her heart—and if that meant inserting myself into another murder investigation with both feet, then that's what I'd do.

Chapter 15

Nana and I both tried to get Mama to come back inside, but she threw her hand up, said, "Bah!" and stormed down the street.

"She'll come to her senses," Nana said when I turned to her. "We should just give her some time to cool off."

"Will she?" And if she did, would it be soon enough? I only had two days to set things right between Mama and Hoss, which meant I had two days to figure out who had killed Michel Beaulieu.

A minute later, I had slipped back inside Buttons & Bows, taking a moment to watch the women before they realized I was back. Jeanette, Orphie, and Midori looked as though they hadn't moved from their tasks. Orphie had moved on to stitching together the pieces of the sweetheart dress. Midori had her back to me, orange fabric pooling over her lap. And Jeanette cursed at the rounded collar on the Peter Pan blouse.

The pressure of just forty-eight hours to save a wedding sent my thoughts circling. Who was the likeliest suspect? Midori. Gavin McClaine's reason for suspecting me of murder held for the Japanese-American designer, too. Beaulieu had had a big presence. While I hadn't been threatened by him, Midori might have been.

My gaze drifted to Jeanette. Public—and repeated—humiliation could be a strong motive for murder. Rage whipped through people over being cut off on the road, so Jeanette's losing control after Beaulieu's outburst wasn't all that implausible. And then there was the iron.

Finally I looked at Orphie. We were old friends, and I couldn't fathom the idea that she might have had anything to do with murder. That was beyond anything she was capable of. No, it couldn't be Orphie. I went back to Midori and Jeanette, but couldn't quite see either of them in the role of murderess, either.

Which still left six other suspects. Quinton and Lindy Reece, and the four models. I couldn't formulate even a simplistic motive for the photographer or the journalist, but the models? I could actually see one of them killing Beaulieu. Lack of food could make a girl cranky.

The three women chatted together as I continued to think about the models. Barbi and Esmeralda from New York wouldn't have had reason to kill the designer who'd favored them to model his clothing. Of course for all I knew their relationships with Beaulieu could have been more complicated than I was aware of. Still, I dismissed them for now and let my thoughts trail to Zoe and Madison. They still had clothes to wear on the runway since they were Midori's go-to girls. And, as far as I knew, they didn't know Beaulieu.

"Earth to Harlow." The voice sounded softly in my ear.

"There she goes again, woolgathering."

I blinked and yelped, immediately lurching backward when a blurred face loomed in front of mine. "Lord almighty, Orphie, don't do that!"

Her face lit up with a big smile. "Sorry. I didn't mean to startle you, but jeez, you were somewhere far, far away. Are you okay? Is the wedding really off?"

"I don't know," I said.

Jeanette and Midori left their projects and came to stand at the French doors of the workroom. "Oh no," Midori said with a sad shake of her head. "But I thought you said they were lovey-dovey."

"They are. Or they were. There's more," I said. The idea that any of these three women could have killed Beaulieu was absurd, but mixing silk with denim was absurd, too, and that happened. But it didn't happen often, and I figured it couldn't hurt to simply be straightforward. "Apparently the deputy suspects *me*, and the sheriff hasn't ruled that possibility out."

Orphie's face drained of color and she stumbled back. "That can't be right."

"And your mother can't marry a man who could think you'd be capable of murder?" Jeanette said, her lower lip quivering. "More tragedy from one man's death."

Orphie regained her balance. She spun around, searching the room for something, finally landing on her purse. She grabbed it, took me by the arm, and steered toward the front door. "You did not kill an enemy designer." She scoffed. "He said he'd never even met you, so what's the motive, huh? No. No way. Let's go, Harlow. I'm serious, we need to have a talk with that *deputy* and set the record straight."

I pulled back. "No. Gavin's going to think and do what he wants. I'm not going to beg him to cross me off the suspect list. What I *need* to do is figure out what really *did* happen so Mama and Hoss can get married, as planned."

Orphie hesitated, but Jeanette surged forward. "I'll help you, Harlow."

Midori waved her hands. "Wait. Ladies, you are not detectives. Won't you get in trouble for interfering? Is it not an official investigation, or something like that?"

"I'm not going to interfere," I said, "but I'm not going to sit around and let my mother's relationship with the sheriff fall apart and I'm also not going to just do nothing while the deputy suspects I killed a man."

Jeanette threw out possibilities, rattling them off as if she'd been making lists in her head, just as I had. "What about the models? Maybe the Dallas girls were so upset about not getting to wear his clothes that one of them did it? Or maybe it was the other girls. I mean, they're tough. They're from New York. Maybe ... Oh! Maybe Beaulieu was going to give the Dallas models a chance, the New Yorkers got mad, and"—she drew her finger across her neck—"did him in."

"Maybe." They were the same thoughts I'd already had, and they were as good a guess as anything else.

"What about Quinton or Lindy?" I asked.

Jeanette tapped her finger against her lip, thinking. After a hefty pause, she finally answered. "I don't know about Quinton. I don't think he runs in the same circles as Beaulieu. At least I've never seen him around. But Lindy's written articles for the *Dallas Morning News*. I know she's interviewed Beaulieu once or twice before."

That fact jettisoned to the front of my mind. "Really? So she knew him?"

Jeanette lifted her shoulder slightly. It wasn't quite a shrug, but wasn't *not* a shrug, either. "She's definitely met him before."

I wondered if Lindy had shared that with the deputy, and I made a note to myself to find out.

Orphie was quiet. She put down her purse and went back to the sweetheart dress.

"I think the wedding will go forth," Midori said optimistically. And to prove it, she picked up my maid of honor dress to keep working on it. Jeanette and I kept throwing out ideas. Finally Orphie threw down Gracie's dress and blurted, "How are we supposed to prove you didn't kill Beaulieu and figure out who actually did?"

Her questions were so basic, and so direct, and yet I didn't have answers. "I don't know yet," I said. "But I'm working on it."

I picked up my sketchbook and flipped it open to a blank page. I could get lost in my drawings, thinking and processing through any dilemma. It was mental therapy for me.

Start with the basics. The idea circled in my head, over and over again.

"Really?" Orphie demanded. "You're going to draw?" She threw down the dress, marched over to me, and grabbed the sketchbook from my hands. "You don't have time to sit there and sketch, Harlow. We can't hole up here and sew!"

"It helps me think," I said, taking the book back from her.

She huffed, but didn't try to fight me for it. Instead she perched on the edge of a stool and watched.

I started sketching and before long I had the most basic design for a sheath dress. Nothing fancy. Nothing complicated.

Meemaw used to say, *Got a dilemma? Make dilemmonade*. She was right, but everything felt wrong at the moment. Sour. I was hoping that with a little creativity, I could figure it out and make everything sweet again.

"We can't go off willy-nilly, trying to solve a crime without having a clue about what we're doing," I said when she didn't budge.

But patience wasn't one of Orphie's strengths. "We have to figure out something, Harlow, and quick. We can't just sit here and do nothing."

I sighed and nodded because she was right. *Start with the basics.* And suddenly I knew the first thing we could do to try to figure out the truth. Just the two of us.

Chapter 16

"I need some fresh air," Orphie said.

Good girl. I'd caught her gaze and flicked mine toward the door, giving a slight notch of my head, hoping she'd get the message that we needed a powwow.

Without another word to us, she headed outside.

"Poor thing," Jeanette said after the front door had opened and closed.

Orphie deserved an A-plus in acting. She'd been pitch-perfect. I waited a few minutes, the second hand on the clock moving excruciatingly slow. Finally, after I thought enough time had passed, I put down my sketchbook. "I better go check on her. Jeanette, would you mind?" I picked up Gracie's unfinished dress and handed it to her, not waiting for her to reply. If I didn't give her a choice, she couldn't refuse.

"Oh, sure, er, no, I'd be happy to." She took it from my outstretched arm, but she couldn't hide the disappointment on her face. I got the feeling she wanted to check on Orphie, too. Either that or she couldn't stand the idea of being left out.

"I'm going to make her walk around the square," I said, and before either Midori or Jeanette could argue, I escaped outside, leaving them with their projects.

Orphie wasn't on the porch. I walked to either end, looking to the side yards for her. She was nowhere to be found. "Orphie?" I called, and then I waited, listening.

I hurried down the porch steps, across the flagstone path, and through the arbor and gate to the sidewalk beyond. "Orphie!"

Once again, I cocked my head and listened. "Where'd you go?" I muttered under my breath. I whipped around to head back into my yard, calling her. "Orphi—oomph!"

Orphie had come up behind me and I'd plowed right into her, knocking my nose against her shoulder. She rubbed her shoulder. "Ow."

I touched my fingers to my nose. "Yeah, ow."

"Okay, what was that about?" she said, notching her head toward the house.

"If we're going to investigate, we've got to get moving."

"We're really going to investigate?" she asked, her mouth forming a surprised O.

"Of course. Mama and Hoss are getting married, if it's the last thing I do."

She looked unsure, but after a few seconds she nodded. "Okay. Where do we start?"

"At Seven Gables."

"The models?"

"No, Hattie," I said.

One eyebrow rose in skepticism. "And who is Hattie?"

"She and her sister own the inn. It's where Mama and Hoss are having their reception, but," I added, a conspiratorial tone seeping into my voice, "it's also where Beaulieu was staying."

"And you want to look in his room?"

I nodded, and a slow smile slid onto her face. "Diabolical, Harlow Jane Cassidy. Let's go."

I laughed as she dug her keys from her pocket. Ever prepared. It was one of the things I loved most about Orphie. "Now who's diabolical?"

With a quick look behind us, we raced back through the arbor and gate, hopped into the sedan Orphie had road-tripped from Missouri in, and sped away from Mockingbird Lane.

Bliss isn't a big town. We arrived at Seven Gables in about six minutes. I didn't want to see Quinton, Lindy, or any of the models who were staying here. We had to get in and get out without them catching sight of us.

"Will Hattie and Raylene let you see the room?" Orphie asked as we crept through the cottage garden, making our way to the back entrance of the house.

"I helped them out pretty recently, so I think so." At least I hoped so.

We mounted the brick steps leading to the kitchen door. I peeked through the window, making sure none of the guests were in the kitchen before I knocked. All clear. I quietly rapped my knuckles on the door and we stood back and waited.

It was utterly silent.

Orphie peered through the window. "Maybe they're not here."

"One of them is always here," I said. They wouldn't

leave the inn unattended. I knocked again, a little louder this time, but still there was no answer.

"Should we go in?" Orphie asked.

I hesitated, but only for a minute. I didn't think Hattie and Raylene would mind us coming in. They were counting on the reception, so they'd want me to find a way to make sure the wedding was a go.

I turned the doorknob, slowly opened the door open, and entered the kitchen.

Orphie tiptoed in behind me.

"Hattie?" I called quietly. "Raylene?"

It was utterly quiet.

"You're friends, right?" Orphie whispered, stepping around the boxes and the center island and stopping at the door to the dining room. "You sure they're not going to get mad at us and call the police?"

"I hope not," I said. More than anything, I was pretty sure Deputy Gavin McClaine wouldn't like us sticking our noses into his investigation. But that's precisely why we'd come, so we had to be very careful.

"Hattie? Raylene?" I called to them one more time before pulling Orphie by the arm, dragging her away from the swinging door between the dining room and kitchen. "There's a back staircase," I said. "Let's just take a quick gander."

We crossed to the opposite end of the kitchen and hurried up the stairs, keeping our footsteps quiet. I had no idea which room had been Beaulieu's. In a crime drama television show, there'd be yellow crime scene tape still strung across the threshold of the room. That was too easy, and this was a small town. I was pretty sure crime tape wasn't something the sheriff's department stocked up on.

I was right. Nary a clue in sight as to which room the designer had stayed in while in Bliss. Only one door was cracked open. Voices drifted into the hallway. I crept forward, motioning for Orphie to follow me. I felt like the Pink Panther, creeping down the hallway, pausing to listen, moving forward a few more steps, pausing again . . .

We stopped at the first door, leaning close and listening. The low sound of the television came from inside. Hattie and Raylene had named each room after a famous Texan. They ranged from the fashion world, ironically, to politics. Texans had infiltrated every major industry, and we were proud of each and every one of them. The Tom Ford Room. Former creative director of Gucci. Apropos for this particular group of guests. But with the sounds from inside, this one couldn't be Beaulieu's room. I crooked my finger and we tiptoed across the hallway and listened at the next door, the Dwight D. Eisenhower Room.

We could hear the steady rumbling sound of snoring. My first thought was that this had to be Quinton's room, but women snored, too, so it wasn't necessarily the photographer. Whoever's it was, it wasn't Beaulieu's room, so we moved on, stopping at the next door. Complete silence. Orphie and I looked at each other, both of us nodding. This one was a possibility.

The door of the room across the hall was cracked open, the voices louder. The Farrah Fawcett Suite. Women's voices. Southern drawls. "Zoe and Madison," I whispered to Orphie. "The Dallas models," I added, thinking that they'd ended up in the right room. Farrah had been Texas's own favorite gal, and always would be. We stood completely still, barely daring to breathe, trying to make out what they were talking about.

Snippets of sentences drifted out to us. "...some nerve...," one of them said. The other murmured something we couldn't hear, and then the first, Zoe, I thought, said, "They think working with him—those photos are like fashion porn—"

"Shhh." Madison this time. They fell silent, but I heard a slight rustling and the light padding of feet slapping against the hardwood floor. Orphie clawed my arm. I froze. There was nowhere to run. Nowhere to hide. If they whipped open the door and looked into the hallway, we'd be caught eavesdropping, no ifs, ands, or buts.

I squeezed my eyes shut and held my breath, waiting for the indignant outburst. Instead there was a faint click and the voices started again, too muffled now to understand.

I opened my eyes, clutching at my chest as I drew in a ragged breath. "That was close," I whispered.

Orphie nodded, her face pale. "Too close," she said under her breath.

We tiptoed past the door and listened at each of the other three rooms. Another TV played, cartoons, if I wasn't mistaken, and the others were silent. No way to tell if someone was inside sleeping or if the rooms were vacant.

Orphie's gaze traveled over each of the rooms, one by one. "How are we supposed to know which one was Beaulieu's?"

I racked my brain for an answer. The best option was waiting until Raylene and Hattie showed up to ask. I motioned for Orphie to follow me and I hurried to the front staircase. I paused at the top, listening for sounds from below. Nothing. Hugging the wall, we scurried halfway down, stopping again to listen. This time, I heard Raylene's distinct twang, followed by Hattie's equally twangy response.

The registration desk was our destination. "Let's go," I said, my voice still a whisper as if someone from upstairs might hear us.

Orphie's voice floated softly from behind me. "Right behind you."

We skirted down the steps, staying close to the edge to avoid the creaking stairs in the old house, then tiptoed across the entryway to the L-shaped counter. Raylene had her back to us, chatting with Hattie, who sounded as if she was in the kitchen.

"Raylene," I said.

She yelped, spinning around and clutching her chest. "Harlow! Lord a'mighty, you startled me."

"Sorry." I smiled sheepishly. I'd gone to school with Raylene and her sister, Hattie, and we'd become fast friends recently. I'd even become honorary godmother to Raylene's son, Boone. "How's the little guy?" I asked.

"Home with Grandma," she said, an automatic grin sliding onto her face, "and precious as ever."

I introduced her to Orphie, but before I could say what we'd come for, Raylene launched into an overview of the wedding reception plans, detailing the menu. "We're makin' braised barbecue chicken wings, coleslaw, fried okra, potato salad, baked beans . . ." She went on, rattling off every last dish she and Hattie were planning to make. "Your mama is goin' to love it," she said.

"She certainly will."

Orphie tilted her head, looking puzzled. "But didn't your mother say—"

I flashed her a hush-up look. I planned on saving the wedding, not giving in to Mama's foolishness about canceling. Which meant Raylene needed to go forward, as planned. "You may never get Hoss to go home, what with all that good food," I said to her.

She smiled, looking mighty pleased. I wanted Seven Gables to be a hot spot in Bliss. Hopefully this would be the first of many wedding receptions Raylene and Hattie would plan.

"What brings you here?" Raylene asked after another few minutes of chitchat.

Automatically, my gaze lifted to the old-fashioned cubbies behind the counter. The unit looked like a turn-of-the-century apothecary, with notes and keys sticking out from each slot. Hattie and Raylene had wanted to create the entire old-fashioned experience at Seven Gables, and they'd succeeded.

I cleared my throat, suddenly a little less confident that she'd just open up Beaulieu's room and let us search.

"Harlow? Are you feelin' poorly?"

"No, no. I'm just fine." I tended to slip further into my Southern drawl when I was around folks who dropped their "g"s and had a strong twang. And also when I was nervous. "I'm just pokin' around . . . er, that is to say, I'm investigatin' what happened to the designer who died in my house."

Her eyes widened. "You are? I'm not surprised, you know. Did you know she helped solve another murder not so long ago?" she said to Orphie.

Orphie shook her head, looking at me as if I were a mystery to her. "Did she?"

"It was nothing," I said, waving away Raylene's praise.

"It was not nothin'. She fell off a roof and discovered a dead man. And now she's happened across another one. She'll solve it," Raylene said. "Just as sure as I'm standin' here, she'll get to the truth."

"That's why we're here," Orphie said.

"Yeah?"

No point in dillydallying now, so I charged ahead. "We'd like to take a look at Beaulieu's room. Do you think we might could do that?" I hurried on, quieting my voice and offering an explanation. "See, we think he might have been blackmailing someone, and I thought maybe we'd find some evidence of it."

Raylene hesitated, chewing on her lower lip. "I don't know, Harlow. What if I'm not supposed to? Gavin didn't say not to, but . . ."

"Did he tell you no one could go in?"

Slowly, she shook her head. "No, he didn't say anythin' like that." She hesitated again, but finally pulled her lip from her mouth and straightened up. "I guess it'll be okay.

"He's in the Cynthia Ann Parker Room."

The famous Texans Raylene and Hattie had chosen to name their rooms after included the tenacious Cynthia Ann who'd been kidnapped and raised by Comanche Indians early in the 1800s. She'd endured her childhood and had grown up to become the mother of the last Comanche chief. Some might think naming the room after Cynthia Ann was an odd choice, but I saw the little girl, and the woman she'd become, as a survivor. Beaulieu hadn't been so lucky.

Raylene slid the key from a cubby and handed it over. "Thank you," I said. "We'll be back in no time."

Orphie and I hightailed it back up the stairs, stopping in front of the room marked with a Cynthia Ann Parker placard. The coast was still clear. Before I could change my mind about what we were doing, I plunged the key into the lock and we slipped inside.

I collapsed against one wall while Orphie pressed her back against the opposite wall, listening for Lindy or Quinton or any of the models. Breaking and entering, even though we had Raylene's permission, wasn't something I did every day. "This is crazy," I whispered.

"Maybe," Orphie said, "but we're on a mission to save your reputation and your mother's wedding."

Just the right thing to say. "Right." I pushed off the wall and surveyed the room. Floral wallpaper gave it a period look, but the style was slightly contemporary, so it didn't feel too froufrou.

A queen-sized four-poster bed, a tower dresser, one nightstand, and a small table and chair were the only pieces of furniture in the room. Beaulieu's suitcase wasn't in sight. We'd left in such a hurry, we hadn't thought to bring gloves, and its being summer meant Orphie and I were both wearing short sleeves. "Just look," I said. "We shouldn't disturb anything."

"Right."

"Use your hem," I told her. Even though I knew Gavin and his team had already been here and done their thing, one could never be too careful. "Let's don't touch anything."

"Got it." She started with the dresser drawers, hiking her sundress up and using the fabric to pull open each one. While she did that, I headed for the satchel lying flat on the writing table. It was lying flat, was made from heavy navy wool with a thick red stripe down the center, and, as luck would have it, the top zipper was undone. I was wearing jeans and a light linen short-sleeve jacket over a beaded tank top. No hem to pick up and use like a glove. I grabbed a tissue from the box on the nightstand, using it to lift the top open enough to peer inside.

Behind me, I heard the dresser drawers sliding open and closed. "Anything?" I whispered over my shoulder. If there was anything to find, the deputy would have discovered it already, but I didn't let that stop me from continuing the search.

"Not yet." She left the dresser, heading to the closet.

I grabbed a second tissue and riffled through the bag, pulling a sketchbook halfway out, followed by a printed catalogue of Beaulieu's fall collection, and a few loose papers. I quickly flipped through them, but nothing struck me as important. My nerves coiled and twisted as I held on to the sketchbook. It could hold a clue as to what Beaulieu was up to. Or it could simply hold his sketches. Did I dare take it all the way out and look through it?

We'd come this far. One little peek might ease my mind, or it might point me in the right direction. I wouldn't know unless I looked.

Out it came. At the same time, a dresser drawer closed and Orphie came up beside me. "Nothing. He unpacked a few things, but just clothes, scarves, socks. He brought only an overnight bag—it's in the closet. It doesn't look like he planned on staying for very long."

"And nothing that could give us a clue about who might have wanted him dead?"

She shook her head. "Not that I can see, but I'm no detective. No note from the murderer or anything like that."

"Yeah, that would be a little convenient. Maybe this will give us something," I said.

She swallowed in an audible, loud gulp when she saw what I was referring to. "Do you think we should?"

"If there's a clue, it's not going to be out in the open, is it?"

Her gaze stayed glued to the book and I could see her mind whirling. She'd stolen one designer's sketchbook. Looking through another was another step down a slippery slope, and from the suddenly green patina of her skin, she didn't relish revisiting her crime.

I didn't blame her, and I didn't want to force her. "I'll look," I said. "Did you check the bathroom?"

She nodded. "Nothing. He probably just dropped his stuff off and headed to your shop."

Of course she was right. He and the others had come to Buttons & Bows first thing that morning, so he wouldn't have had time for anything else. Not to mention that what little I knew of Beaulieu told me he wouldn't have wanted to spend his time holed up in an old-fashioned inn.

Orphie didn't budge, so I opened the book, careful to only touch the corners and only with the tissue wrapped around my fingers. The book itself was a low-budget version of Maximilian's. It had a coated cardboard cover, nicer than what you'd find at an office store, but certainly not custom-made. No embossed monogram on the cover. The pages inside were off-white and slightly textured. The grain added additional depth to the sketches.

One by one, I turned the pages. I recognized many of the drawings from Beaulieu's most recent collection. Some pages had two drawings: a smaller sketch in the top left corner, and a larger sketch, with some key elements modified, but overall quite similar to the smaller drawings. "Was he copying these?" I mused aloud, tapping on the two similar drawings of a tailored jacket.

"It sure looks like it."

I kept turning the pages, stopping once or twice when I noticed words or phrases jotted down. They seemed to be notes about fabric and color or pattern choices, though, nothing that gave a hint about who might have killed him.

"I don't think this is going to help," Orphie said as I turned to the next page.

"Maybe not." I started to agree with her, but stopped. The next page held a small design in the corner, a modified sketch in the center. Close-up drawings of French seams, an attached lining on a jacket, and a wide hem were also highlighted on the page.

But the thing that struck me the most was the color-blocking and slightly asymmetrical design. It was a signature style. And it sent shivers dancing over my skin.

Oh boy.

"Midori," we both said at the same time.

Chapter 17

"Those look like some of Midori's designs from last season," Orphie whispered.

I agreed. Beaulieu's renditions were modified enough that, while there was a definite resemblance, saying he'd stolen a design would be difficult to prove.

But that's just what it looked like That was definitely what it looked like from where I was standing.

I tucked the book back into the satchel, not really sure what to do with the ideas forming in my head. I had too many questions, first and foremost: Did Midori know that Beaulieu had been using her designs as inspiration?

"It's not like I can just ask her," I told Orphie after we returned the key to Raylene and headed back to Buttons & Bows.

"No, that would mean telling her that we snuck into his room, and that could get back to Gavin, and—"

"And we definitely don't want that," I said, although I

suspected we had different reasons for wanting to keep our activities quiet.

When Orphie suggested she drop me off and she'd run to the market, I was all for it. "Nachos make everything better," she said.

She had a point. A block of Velveeta and a can of Rotel made the perfect *queso*. It was a Texas delicacy, and I wouldn't turn it down.

A little time alone would give me time to think about the implications of finding Beaulieu's drawings and what they might mean.

Instead of taking me all the way home, she dropped me at the corner of Mockingbird Lane off the square. "I'll walk from here," I said when I saw Madelyn Brighton leaning into a shrub, snapping a picture of something with her camera.

"You know," I said as she pulled up to the corner, "Gavin wants to solve this case. He's an 'act now, ask forgiveness later' kind of guy."

"Don't worry about me, Harlow," she said.

But I did. I wanted her to protect her heart and not fall for Gavin too fast. "Just be careful, okay?"

She squeezed my hand. "I will."

I watched her drive off, wondering if we had the same definition of careful.

I didn't have time to contemplate what trouble Orphie might be getting herself into with Gavin because Madelyn turned and saw me. She instantly straightened up, rushed over, thrust her camera toward me, and said, "Look at this. Just take a look."

A close-up of a spiderweb, its strands delicately strung

between the branches of a bush, lit up the digital screen. "It's a work of art," she continued. "Each bit is dependent on the one next to it. Without each strand, the web would lose its beauty."

Her description was an awful lot like the pieces of a pattern. One missing or wrongly cut piece would change the entire look of a garment.

We fell into step together, walking in comfortable silence around the square. I looked over at her, struck, not for the first time, at how beautiful Madelyn's skin was. It was the color of fine milk chocolate and had the dewy, unblemished look people paid thousands of dollars to get through moisturizers and skin treatments. "It's genetics," she had a habit of saying, her British accent emphasizing the "t" in the word. No matter what, she sounded highbrow and elegant, and I always sounded Southern casual. We were quite a pair.

We walked side by side, a big floppy pink hat covering her black hair and shading her face—another reason why her skin stayed so lovely—and me brushing my curls out of my face as the breeze kicked up.

Madelyn was a good sounding board. I filled her in on what Orphie and I had discovered in Beaulieu's room and waited for her to give me some much-needed perspective. "So Midori has a motive?" she asked.

"She might." I wasn't actually sure if seeing the sketch qualified as a motive. "I don't know if Beaulieu ever made the jacket, and if he did make it—or something else—does she even know? I've never seen anything by him that looks like it might have been inspired by her work. If she didn't know, it wouldn't be a motive, but if she did . . ."

Madelyn stopped in front of a plate-glass window and swung around to face me. "If she did, love, she'd have a very solid motive."

"Yes, she would, wouldn't she?"

Madelyn started walking again. "How do we find out if she knew?"

Exactly what I'd been wondering. "I could ask her."

"I don't know how well that'll go over given that she'd probably get defensive."

She was right, of course. Which meant I had to think of another way.

We turned the corner and walked past Two Scoops, the old-fashioned ice cream parlor with the red-and-white awnings and the quaint white wrought-iron chairs and table, past the florist, turning again as we reached the next corner.

My ringing cell phone interrupted us. I ducked under the overhang of one of the historic buildings to answer. Hattie's voice burst into my ear. "Harlow, what the devil is goin' on?"

My heart dropped to the pit of my stomach. "I'm so sorry, Hattie. It's all my fault. I talked Raylene into letting me look around Beaulieu's room—"

"What? Oh Lord, I don't give two shakes about that. I'm talking about your mama's weddin'. We already bought all the food. Raylene's been workin' her behind off preppin' everythin'. I've got the flowers for the tables bein' delivered in the morning. We might could cancel the flower order," she said, the pitch of her voice getting higher, "but we can't return all this food, and we can't afford to lose that money."

A different vise tightened around my insides. Hattie

wasn't upset I'd snooped around in Beaulieu's room. No, she'd got wind that Mama was canceling her wedding.

Madelyn, looking like a hunting dog catching a scent, waved at me before wandering off toward the center courthouse. I smiled tightly and waved. "Don't worry, Hattie."

Her voice grew shrill. "I can't help but worry. We're goin' to take a big ol' bath on everthin' we bought, and, Harlow, we can't afford that!"

I leaned back against the brick wall, cupped my hand over my eyes, and shook my head. "I'm working on it."

"She just called, Harlow. Said plain as day, 'The weddin's off.'"

Mama was as mule-headed as they came, and for some reason, she was digging in her heels on this, but I knew how much Hoss loved her, and how much she loved Hoss. I remembered that one of Loretta Mae's core beliefs was that love will always win out. That might be the case, but I knew that I had to help love along right now. I could hear Mama's fiery voice in my head making her proclamation, but I wasn't going to have any of it. They were a good pair, the two of them, and they'd be getting hitched in two days if I had to drag them both to the altar myself.

"No, it's not," I said. "Keep Raylene cooking and take those flowers in. There *will* be a bride and groom walking the aisle Saturday, and we *will* be descending upon Seven Gables directly afterward. You have my word."

Chapter 18

The way I saw it, I really had two problems. One was figuring out the truth behind what happened to Beaulieu, and the other was convincing my mother that true love didn't come around all that often and she should not be a damn fool and let it go.

I was pretty sure that solving the murder would be a whole lot easier than talking sense to Mama. I'd never be able to do it alone, which meant I needed backup. Reinforcements. Madelyn was off taking pictures of who knew what? I sent her a quick text telling her I was heading home, and ten minutes later I was back at Buttons & Bows.

Once on the porch, I instantly felt Meemaw's presence, but something was off. Instead of the typical cocoon of warm air, a burst of coolness encircled me, chilling me to the bone. Maybe her equilibrium was thrown off by the death of Beaulieu in what I still often thought of as her house. Or maybe she was upset by the state of Mama's wedding. Either way, I figured we could commiserate. "Meemaw?"

The leaves and flower petals in the garden rustled in response, the movement of the air increasing, but she didn't suddenly decide to materialize and she gave no sign she was actually here. Our communication skills were sketchy, at best. She'd written me messages in the steamed mirror in my bathroom, and she was particularly fond of using words and passages in books, flipping back and forth between the pages to get her meaning across. But could she hear my thoughts? I'd tried to send her silent messages, but so far, that hadn't worked. Still, my experiments on telepathy weren't definitive and I hadn't given up the idea.

But right now I wanted to be more direct.

"Meemaw," I called again, keeping my voice low enough so I wouldn't catch Jeanette's and Midori's attention inside, but loud enough that Meemaw could hear me if she was around.

A low hiss came from the spigot, followed by the sputtering of water as air forced the liquid through the hose and out the end. I leaned closer, hoping she'd give me more than that little sign she was present. Nothing. The water turned to a trickle and the spigot did a half-degree turn, as if an invisible hand was on it cranking it to the right.

"Loretta Mae," I said, trying one last time, and with her given name to show her I was serious and needed her.

The shrubs next to the porch shook, the leaves dancing with the movement. The slow breeze that had been spiraling around me dissipated and then, before my eyes, it gathered like storm clouds, concentrating in the rustling bush. A low gasp escaped from my lips and I leaned over the railing, watching as the milky white mist grew more opaque.

"Come on, Meemaw," I said, my breath catching in my throat. She'd come close to manifesting in front of me a few times, but each instance, it was as if she'd run out of energy and hadn't been able to appear.

My words seemed to fall like stones, breaking apart the focused energy of the moment. The mist became loose and airy, finally disappearing, and the burst of air went from cool to warm to icy, all in a matter of seconds. I reached over the railing, stretching toward the shrub and where I was sure she'd been, but nothing was there. "Don't go, Meemaw," I called, fighting back the tears pooling in my eyes.

The door behind me opened and someone stepped onto the porch. "Harlow! There you are!"

I turned to see Jeanette holding up the sweetheart dress. "Look at this. It's just about done. Have to finish slip-stitching the lining to the zipper and waist, and then your—what is she again? Your niece? Or your cousin?"

"Cousin," I answered, glad I didn't have to explain just exactly how she was related. That was too complicated a story. I threw a lingering look over my shoulder, still hoping I'd see another sign that Meemaw was still here, but all was silent.

Jeanette continued. "Well, she needs to try it on so we can do the straps, and then it's a wrap."

I refocused on her and smiled. It was perfect. Contemporary, yet with a vintage style that Gracie would love. "You're really good," I said, fingering the voile overlayer of the skirt. "Fast, too."

She smiled as she pulled together the sides of her cardigan and blushed. "I'm great if I have a pattern. I'm even great at making patterns if I have a starting place.

But custom designs still take me a long time. The creative eye takes a lot of effort for me."

"It takes a while to gain confidence in your design abilities," I said, "but once you have a few under your belt, you'll start to develop your personal style and it'll all come so much more easily."

"I hope so," she said as she hung Gracie's sweetheart dress on the privacy screen.

Midori had been quiet, hunched over my maid of honor dress. It crossed my mind that I should tell her she didn't need to break her back to get it done because Mama had canceled the wedding, but I couldn't bring myself to utter the words. I was as stubborn as Mama was, and I was committed to saving the Cassidy-McClaine nuptials. "Where's Orphie?" she asked, finally looking up. "I thought you went for a walk."

"She's gone off to the store," I said, sitting down at Meemaw's old Singer. I grabbed two squares from a pile of fabric I kept handy for moments like these, placed a smaller square of cotton batting between them, and stitched an X across it. I tossed it onto the teetering stack of completed squares, picked up another two, and stitched again. It was mindless and quick to slap two pieces of fabric together and before long, I'd have enough to stitch the squares together into rows, and then I'd have enough rows to sew together into a big rectangle. I'd fray the edges and voilà! I'd have a rag quilt.

Restless, I got up and paced, going back into the front room.

If Mama were here, and if she weren't completely preoccupied with her wedding that wasn't going to happen, she'd have insisted that Midori and Jeanette stay for dinner. Or when she saw that I hadn't insisted, she'd have swatted me on the arm for my lack of hospitality. I was failing as a Southern hostess.

Three quick taps came on the front door before it swung open, bells tinkling lightly. Will stepped in. Gracie followed, and, as if he'd heard her coming from a mile away, Earl Grey scampered down the steps and straight to Gracie.

"We're here!" She scooted toward me, her eyes wide. "You really have a surprise for me, Harlow?" she asked before Will had even closed the door.

"Hey," he said, flashing her a "you have better manners than that" look.

She laughed, scratching Earl Grey behind the ears. "Sorry. But a surprise from Harlow is, you know, gonna be awesome!"

She looked more rested than she had the day before. Maybe she'd figured out something about her charm. Even if she hadn't, the sweetheart dress would hopefully help. It was hard to know what you had until it was actually on a body, but no matter what, it would be free of history, and it would also kick in my charm and help one of her dreams come true. Will, Gracie, and I were almost our own little family, which pleased me to no end, and I knew not even a murder on the premises could rip us apart.

I took her by the arm and led her to the workroom, swinging my arm wide toward the dress I had designed for her. She skidded to a stop behind me, her arms going a little slack. Earl Grey fidgeted until she finally crouched to let him free. He scampered away, disappearing into the kitchen.

"Is that for me?" Gracie asked, her voice suddenly filled with wonder.

Jeanette beamed, walking up to it and slipping it off the hanger.

"It's for you," I said. "For the wedding. We just need to fit the straps, and it'll be done."

Will caught my eye, his lips tight under his closely shaved goatee. "I heard something about that," he said.

"What's that?" I asked, knowing full well what he'd heard. Bliss was a small town, after all, and if Mama had called Seven Gables, she'd also probably called Babe's Chicken House, where we were supposed to have the rehearsal dinner, the florist, the bakery, and who knows who else? She never did anything halfway.

"Shep, over at Johnny Joe's, he mentioned something about the wedding being off."

Gracie gasped. "Dad, that cannot be true. Ms. Cassidy and the sheriff aren't getting married?"

"Shep Shepherd's wrong," I said. "There *is* going to be a wedding."

I ushered Gracie to the privacy screen to try on the dress, and a minute later she emerged, a vision in vintage. "I love it!" she said, twirling in front of the full-length mirror. I could see the peace on her face. It suited her perfectly, fit her even better, and best of all, it was history free. No distracting visions.

Jeanette marked the positioning of the straps, made a few adjustments, and Gracie disappeared again.

"She has a few pieces of clothing that don't seem to bother her," Will said into my ear, low enough so that only I could hear.

"Now she has one more," I said, squeezing his hand. "It'll get easier for her. I promise."

She stepped out from behind the screen again, this

time dressed in her cutoff jeans and another cheap T-shirt. As she hooked the hanger holding the sweetheart dress back on the screen, she froze and her body lurched. A visible trembled passed over her, like a mini seizure. She fell against the screen and I could see her left hand clutching the fabric of the tiki dress that had once belonged to Meemaw.

Will and I hurried to her. I eased her hand free of the cotton. Poor thing. Her charm, at least for the time being, took her by surprise and threw her way off-kilter. It was like having an allergic reaction to dust—something you couldn't escape.

Midori and Jeanette stared, clearly not sure what to make of what was happening. "Is she okay?" Midori asked.

Will nodded. "She's fine. Just a . . . condition she has. Don't worry."

We led her out of the room, and out of earshot. Her chest rose and fell as she dragged in heavy breaths. "What did you see?" I asked her once she'd calmed down.

She shook her head, but I got the feeling she was trying to shake the images out of her mind as much as she was responding to my question. "It was weird this time. Really jumbled. I mean, it's always jumbled, but this was different." She closed her eyes as if she was pulling up the images she'd just seen. "Color. Red and orange and yellow. Like angry flames. And then piles of white."

She opened her eyes, shaking the tension out of her arms. "It's all gone now."

Will wrapped her up in a hug and a minute later she scooted up the stairs in search of Earl Grey.

Will ripped his Longhorns cap off his head, slapping it against his open palm as he paced the length of the room.

I knew Gracie would adjust, just as all the Cassidy women did, to her charm. "She'll be okay," I reassured him.

He breathed, visibly calming himself. "I know," he said, and then more forcefully, "I know."

"Can we talk?" I asked after a minute.

He nodded. I left my little atelier and followed him to the front porch. The second the door closed, he had me in his arms. "I missed you," he said.

"I miss you, too." We hadn't had a chance to talk since Beaulieu had died. "I've been running around—"

I stopped when his lips met mine. "Mmm-hmm. Doing a little sleuthing."

I sank into him, thinking I could deny it, but he knew me too well. "Maybe a tiny bit."

"Because he didn't die naturally, did he?"

I shook my head, regaining my equilibrium. Being so near Will made me never want to leave his side. True love. Meemaw believed in it, and I did, too. The idea made me think again about Mama and Hoss. They had it. I just had to help them remember. Which brought me back to figuring out what had happened to Beaulieu.

"I think he was blackmailing someone, Will. What if that person just wanted it to end?" I took him through the discovery of the body, the sheriff's department combing my house—once again, Midori's fight with the designer, and his belligerent behavior. I left out sneaking into Beaulieu's room at Seven Gables since I wasn't sure if we'd discovered anything or not. There were a lot of different possibilities, but none of them sounded quite right.

Will nodded, but his expression had turned serious. "I also heard something about you, uh, being *looked* at."

Being looked at. That was a nice Southern euphemism for me being a suspect. I wanted to deny it, but another thought occurred to me. Could it all have been a plan to set me up? Or maybe to set up Midori or Jeanette! Although their motives were weak, they were still the most likely suspects. "Why was he killed that day and in my house?" I said aloud. "Whoever did this riffled through my designs and made sure that it happened after Beaulieu had been with his rival designers, including me. What if that was the plan all along?"

He leaned against the porch railing. "Who would have done that?"

"It could have been any of them. If he had something on one of them . . ." I came back to blackmail as a motive. "They all drove up to Bliss together."

"You know, Harlow, you could let the sheriff do his job. You don't have to be the one to solve the crime."

"No, but I might be able to help and get it done faster, and if I do, Hoss and Mama won't have any issues, I won't be a suspect, and the wedding can go on as planned."

"Hoss and Tessa love each other," he said. He wrapped his arm around me again. "We'll figure this out, darlin', and everything will be okay."

Not *you'll* figure this out, but *we'll* figure this out. Will considered us a *we*. Warmth flowed through me, in part at his commitment to Tessa, Hoss, and true love, but mostly because he saw us as a team.

"Already working on it," I said.

Chapter 19

I'd taken to calling the ancient pickup truck that had come to me along with Meemaw's house Buttercup, in part because of the mellow butter yellow color, and in part because of the curved fenders and cab, both of which reminded me of the delicate petals on the flowers. But not even being cocooned in the cab of the old Ford could shake off the chill that had settled inside me.

"No." My voice sounded hollow. I'd been around murder too much lately, and it was beginning to wear me down. Then again, I'd had a hand in solving each one, so that counted for something. Heck, instead of accusing me, Gavin should be knocking on my door asking for my help.

I saw Orphie's car pull away as I parked on the street in front of Seven Gables, hopping down from the truck and trudging up the walkway. I tried to muster up some enthusiasm for the wedding so I could talk with Hattie and Raylene about the plans, but the door was flung open before I even got to the porch and Raylene's expression made me stop cold. "Is your mama's weddin' on or off? The way I heard it, Miss Tessa isn't even talkin' to the sheriff, she returned his ring, and there ain't gonna be a weddin'."

I felt my eyebrows V. Oh Lord. "She returned the ring?" I said, zeroing in on that little fact. Mama loved that ring. Things were a lot more serious than I'd thought. For the first time, I started to doubt that I could stop the wedding from derailing altogether.

She nodded, her lips drawn into a thin line. Behind her, guests milled around. Esmeralda held a teacup. Midori flipped through a magazine. Jeanette walked into the kitchen, plate in hand. And Lindy descended the staircase, slowing as she saw me.

"What am I supposed to do, Harlow?" Raylene demanded. "The flowers?"

Assuming Mama hadn't canceled the order, of course. "Take delivery. Is everything else on schedule?" I asked.

"Yes, but—"

"No buts. There will be a wedding, Raylene, and we'll all be here just as soon as it's over. Y'all just go forward as planned."

It took another few minutes to reassure her, but finally she was ready to go back to her homemade barbecue sauce, her bacon, cheddar, and cranberry dip, and her petite biscuits. As soon as she did, I turned and bolted back toward Buttercup, jumping into the cab and hightailing it straight to Mama's house. She could avoid me all she wanted, but she couldn't run and she couldn't hide, and it was high time for a major intervention.

Mama lived in an unincorporated area of Bliss. The road to her house led me past the Bliss Country Club and up a winding road and into Hidden Creek, a small country neighborhood where I'd grown up and my mother still lived. The house was an old Craftsman style with stone columns and front steps leading to a flagstone porch. The closer I got to her house, the more abundantly the flowers and flora grew. Her charm in action. Trees. Weeds. Flowers, particularly bluebells and daisies. I pulled onto the long driveway, passing a thicket of knockout roses, parking in an asphalt slip across from the house.

"Mama!" I yelled, slamming the truck door behind me and storming across the grass. I plowed past the flower stems that stretched across the steps and grabbed the door handle, bursting in. "Mama, what in tarnation are you thinking?" I bellowed. "You are not calling off your marriage to Hoss McClaine."

I'd realized that it was more than simply calling off the wedding; it was calling off the whole love affair and the happily ever after. It was the one thing the Cassidy women, excepting my grandmother and my granddaddy Dalton, hadn't managed. Love didn't tend to last for us. I'd wondered if it would last for Will and me, but I was coming around to the idea that he could accept and love me, despite—or maybe because of— my Cassidy quirks.

"Mama?"

No response. Nothing but silence. I passed the dining room, the sitting room, and stopped at what she liked to call the gathering room. I knew she was here. The garage door outside was open and her burnt orange Jeep was parked inside. The front door had been unlocked, and while a lot of people in Bliss didn't regularly lock up, Mama had taken to sliding the dead bolt when she wasn't home. "Too many deaths in Bliss, darlin'," she told me.

"Mama!" The word sounded loud in the empty house, despite the upholstered furniture and carpeting to absorb my voice.

I glanced in the kitchen—nope—called upstairs—nope—and then hung a right and went through the laundry room and out the back. The screen door banged closed behind me. "Mama!" I bellowed again.

I didn't see her anywhere in the yard, so I trudged across the lawn, straight toward the cedar, slope-roofed greenhouse she'd added in her backyard ten years ago. It was a small structure on a cement pad, complete with electricity and rows of benches for her plants. Her charm never waned, so she grew plants year-round, never worrying about what the weather was like outside.

"Mama—!"

She popped her head out from the top of the Dutch door, her curly hair held off her face with a wide headband. Mama was the spitting image of her mama, Coleta, who looked just like Loretta Mae. All the Cassidy women looked alike, from their wavy auburn hair to their trademark blond streak sprouting from their temples. Only right at this moment, Mama was looking a might frazzled. Not her usual put-together self.

"Good Lord, Harlow, is there a tornado coming?"

I jammed my hands on my hips, planting my feet and leveling my gaze at her. "No, there is not a tornado coming."

"Well, then, what in heaven's name are you hollering about?"

"Mama," I said, trying to keep my voice even, "you know perfectly well why I'm here."

She feigned an innocent look, batting her eyes like

Mae West. "I'm sure I don't," she said, as if she were some traditional Southern belle instead of the feisty, fiery Tessa Parker Cassidy.

"I'm sure you do," I said, dishing it right back. "You are not going to call off your wedding, so you can just stop telling people that."

"It's my life," she said as she turned away from the door and disappeared back into the greenhouse.

I marched over to the Dutch door and clamped my hands on the base. "And you're meant to spend your life with Hoss McClaine."

She held a pair of clippers, her hands covered in snug leather garden gloves, and she snipped at the miniature bonsai tree. Just as soon as she cut one sprig off, another appeared in its place. "I can spend my life with whomever I want, darlin', and not you or Hoss or anyone else can tell me what I'm meant to do."

Okay, so maybe that had been the wrong tactic. Mama was superstitious to a fault, tossing salt over her shoulder, avoiding black cats, and never stepping on cracks. But she was also fiercely independent, the result, I was sure, of my father's walking out on us and of her having to raise Red and me on her own. "But I can tell you what I know, Mama, and that's that you love Hoss, and he loves you. You belong together."

I caught a faint glimmer in her eyes before she looked back down at the bonsai and clipped at it some more.

I'd struck a chord. Opening the door, I stepped inside. "I didn't kill Beaulieu, Mama—"

She whipped around, flailing her clippers at me. "Well, of course you didn't! And shame on anyone who could think you did."

I filled in the rest of the sentence that she left hanging there between us. *Like Hoss McClaine.*

"They're just doing their jobs, and the man was found dead at my shop. Of course they're going to look at me," I said, sounding far more practical about it than I felt inside. I didn't want Hoss and Gavin suspecting me any more than Mama did, but I understood it. They had to follow any leads in a tough case.

"Pft," she said, attacking the poor bonsai. The plants all around her seemed to give a collective shudder in response to her.

"I told Raylene that the wedding is on."

She froze, clippers open, and slowly lifted her chin to look at me. "Darlin', I appreciate what you're tryin' to do, but you just call her back up and tell her to cancel everything."

"No, Mama. *I* appreciate what *you're* trying to do, but I'm not going to let you ruin your future over this."

She didn't blink. Didn't hardly move a muscle. "That's the point, isn't it? How can I have a future with a man who could think my daughter could kill a man?"

My eyes teared. Her love for me filled my soul with warmth, but damn it, she was misguided and as stubborn as a damn pack mule. "Mama, you're the one who told me what a good man Hoss is. You told me he accepts you and your charm, and he's fair, loyal, and as honest as the day is long."

"All of which has nothin' to do with him even givin' a whisper of a thought to you or any of my kin bein' capable of murder."

"Maybe not, but you have to trust him, Mama. Just as surely as he accepts you for who you are, you have to

know that he's got to do his job. And that's what he and
Gavin are doing. They're good at it, too. They're not out
to hang me, or anyone else. They just want to figure out
what happened."

She finally set her clippers on her potting table, leaning one hip against the freestanding cedar table as she
peeled off her gloves. Her lower lip quivered, just barely,
and her left eye twitched. Around her, the flowers she
tended so lovingly began to droop, their color fading to
a paler version, their stems and stalks turning brown and
taking on a brittle look.

I felt the confusion emanating from her. The tips of
my fingers tingled and I swallowed the emotion bubbling
up inside me. It wouldn't do for both of us to lose control, and from the looks of the plants all around us, she
was not winning her battle. One of us had to keep it together. "Where is he?"

She looked up at the slanted ceiling, chewing on her
lower lip. "How should I know? We split up."

"No, Mama, you are having a momentary lapse in
judgment, is all. I'm going to find Hoss and we're going
to sort this all out."

She released her lower lip and a second later, one side
of her mouth lifted in a faint smile. "You know somethin'?"

"You mean besides the fact that you're getting married tomorrow to the man who completes you?"

She laughed. A good sign. "Yes, Jerry Mcguire, besides that."

I smiled to myself. She hadn't nixed the wedding
again. A very good sign.

"Mama, how about a deal? If I can figure out which

one of the people with Beaulieu killed him, you get hitched, as planned. Your dress is ready. My dress is almost ready. Raylene and Hattie are ready. Even the weather is cooperating! There's no reason for you not to become Tessa Parker Cassidy McClaine."

Her answer was a hefty shrug of her shoulders. "We'll see," she said, which in my experience meant it could go either way. But I took that as a lifeline, choosing to be optimistic. The planning and preparations would go on.

I left her to her plants and spent the drive back to town thinking about Midori, Jeanette, the Dallas and New York models, and even, to my dismay, Orphie and her secret about Maximilian's book. Could Beaulieu have known about it, and could he have been blackmailing her? I still didn't think Orphie could kill a man, and certainly not Beaulieu, but it got me thinking. How far and wide was his reach? Of everyone who'd come to Bliss with him, who did he have the longest relationship with?

I ran through the list in my head one more time, stopping short on someone I hadn't really given much thought to. Lindy Reece. She'd done an article on Beaulieu before, had been to his atelier, and had her pulse on the fashion industry. Could he have been blackmailing her, and could that have led her to murder?

Or perhaps there was a different reason altogether.

Either way, I had to find out, and I knew just where to start.

Chapter 20

The Jebediah James Library was one of the newer buildings in Bliss. It was nondescript and flat roofed, but still,
it had character. It was named after Senator James, husband to Zinnia James, who was one of my biggest fans.

I hadn't had much spare time to read, so I hadn't
signed up for a library card since I'd come home to Bliss.
No time like the present. My boots thudded lightly
against the tight loops of the carpet inside the building.
The library was completely quiet.

"Afternoon." The librarian, a woman with gunmetal
gray hair cropped close to her head, clasped her hands in
front of her at the circulation desk. "What can I do for
you now?"

Looking at the librarian, I got a vision of her in jeans,
a blinged-out T-shirt, and a lightweight Southwestern
vest. Nothing that I would or could make for her, but it
was her style more than the mousy pants and beige
blouse she currently wore. Somewhere down deep, she
had a sassy side she hadn't tapped into yet. Either that or

she felt compelled to dress a certain way for her job. After all, people had a certain perception of what a librarian looked like, and this woman was definitely living up to that expectation.

But she wasn't a client, so I told her what I was after and within minutes, I was sitting in front of one of the library's computers, scrolling through back issues of the *Dallas Morning News.* Jeanette had said that Lindy Reece had written the article about Beaulieu about a year ago. I typed in Beaulieu's name and narrowed the search to twelve months prior. Turns out there were more than half a dozen articles by Lindy that referenced Beaulieu. They talked about different designers, up-and-coming trends, and at least two were about controversial goings-on in the industry. I skimmed each one, cringing at the dirty underbelly of fashion that she so diligently outlined. Models not being paid, or worse, being abused by photographers. Nothing struck me as relevant to Beaulieu, so I moved on, scanning the other articles by Lindy. Only one was about Beaulieu specifically.

I didn't know what I was looking for, but I was hoping that something would jump out at me.

It didn't. The article detailed Beaulieu's climb to the top, sharing his early propensity for art, growing up in a single-parent household, and his love of all things New York. *Many designers study the craft and aesthetic of the competition. Some, I daresay, even steal ideas, and it's reprehensible, but I don't pay attention to other designers or their work,* he said in the article. *You have to keep your eye on what's coming, of course, but getting hung up on what's happening now stifles the forward progress of your own aesthetic. Designers like Midori and Jean Paul Gault-*

*ier contribute their own new ideas to the fashion world,
but Midori's designs with the color blocking and the wide
hems and heavy lapels—they're great, but can she do anything else? And Gaultier, well, he took me under his wing
and taught me a good deal of what I know. I'll always be
grateful for that. But I have to be true to my own vision.*

Had he intentionally been obtuse, talking about other
designers stealing ideas when he so blatantly was using
Midori's designs for inspiration? I'd seen it in his sketchbook, for heaven's sake. What a lot of bullpucky, as my
granddaddy would say.

Beaulieu came across as totally self-involved and disdainful of almost all other designers. That was nothing
new. I'd gotten that from him after one brief meeting. No
matter how hard Lindy Reece might have tried to mask
that side of him, she couldn't rewrite his direct quotes,
and she couldn't change his stripes. He was who he was,
and the pompousness couldn't be hidden.

I scanned the rest of the article, but didn't come away
with any new ideas, nor did I conjure up a motive for
Lindy, herself. The article wasn't quite window dressing,
but it wasn't hard hitting, either. It fell somewhere in between and while it might not be Pulitzer prize quality, it
wasn't horrible.

I was back to the drawing board, unless . . .

There was a little disconnect between the Lindy
Reece who'd been talking to the deputy in his office and
the Lindy I'd seen at Buttons & Bows, and even at Seven
Gables. Her articles weren't strong investigative reporting, yet she'd told Gavin that she was working toward a
Pulitzer. How was she supposed to achieve that if she
wrote fluff?

I searched Lindy's name one more time to see if I'd missed anything, or to see if a new idea sparked.

She'd written an article the previous year that dealt with imported Japanese fabrics and the influence of Japan on the current fashion. Midori and Jeanette were both quoted, along with another prominent Asian designer. There were articles about anorexia and bulimia and drug use in the modeling community, but the reporting stopped just short of revealing any serious truth about the industry.

Still, I couldn't quash the notion that maybe Lindy wasn't who she was portraying herself to be when she was around all of us. Had she seen a different side to Beaulieu when he was alive? Could he have been blackmailing her?

A wild idea planted itself in my mind. How badly did Lindy want that Pulitzer prize I'd heard her mention? Maybe she'd dug deep and found out something about Beaulieu—his bogarted ideas, for example. And what if he'd tried to pay her off to keep her quiet? He could have turned that into blackmail, and voilà! Lindy Reece suddenly had a motive.

I thanked the librarian and drove off, formulating a one-two punch for the sheriff.

Chapter 21

I stopped myself from barging into the sheriff's office, pausing to knock on the door instead. A few manners could go a long way, and I wanted mine to help me take Mama and Hoss all the way to the altar.

"Yup," a slow, deep voice intoned.

I opened the door to find Hoss McClaine at his desk, pen in hand, looking like a craggy cowboy with his iron hair, sun-scorched skin, and soul patch under his lower lip. "Do you love her?" I demanded, stopping just inside the doorway. That was the first punch from my arsenal.

"Harlow," he said calmly, as if it were perfectly natural for people to barge in on him and ask such a personal question.

"Don't *Harlow* me," I said. "She wants to call off the wedding. Call off the *marriage*," I said, as if he wouldn't understand the ramifications.

He tilted forward in his chair and steepled his fingers. "I'm well aware."

"You're aware?" I strode to the desk, put my hands on

it, and leaned in. "You're *aware*? What are you going to *do* about it?"

"She won't talk to me, Harlow, so there ain't much I *can* do about it at the moment."

"She won't talk to you?" My voice rose. "She won't talk to you? And you're going to leave it at that?" This was not acceptable behavior for a man willing to enter into matrimony with a Cassidy. "Just because Mama doesn't want to talk doesn't mean you can't make her listen."

"She's hot under the collar—"

"Yeah, just a little bit. Because you think her daughter—me—that *I* might have killed Michel Ralph Beaulieu. Which," I added, throwing my hand up, "is completely ridiculous."

He leveled his smoky gray eyes at me. "First of all, I work in facts and evidence, and right now a few things point in your direction."

"I can't believe you'd think—"

"But," he said, cutting me off, "I do not think you actually killed the man."

"That you'd think I could . . . Wait, what? You don't think I did it?"

"Good God, Harlow, of course not. You may be just as hot under the collar as your mama, but a murderess you're not. I'm no fool."

"What about Gavin?" I said. If Hoss really didn't think I had anything to do with Beaulieu's death, then maybe he'd listen to my thoughts on Lindy Reece. "And why don't you just tell Mama what you just told me?"

He gestured to one of the straight-backed chairs facing his desk. "Have a seat, Harlow." His voice was grim.

I perched on the edge of the chair, fidgeting. "You can just spit it out," I said.

"I love your mama, Harlow. You know I do."

I sensed a *but* coming.

"*But*," he said, right on cue, "there was a murder at your shop and I have a job to do. I have no choice but to keep you on the suspect list until I can clear your name."

My leg shook from the coiled nerves inside me. "But you just said you know I didn't kill anyone."

"Like I said, we have to have proof about what happened." He opened up a plastic evidence bag, took out some creased sheets of paper, and slid them across to me. "We found these on his person."

I reached out, my hand hovering over them. "Can I touch them?"

"They've been processed, so yes."

Even with them upside down, I could see they were sketches, but when I turned them to face me, the truth smacked me right in the face. They were sketches of *my* designs. I flipped through them, instantly recognizing Mama's wedding dress—the same one Beaulieu had mocked—a flouncy skirt that had been on my ready-to-wear rack, and a stylized woman's jacket that had been hanging from the privacy screen in my workroom. I looked up at the sheriff, feeling my eyes go wide. "He had these on him?"

"Inner pocket of his vest. One of the deputies noticed that these look very similar to some of the outfits you have at your shop." He watched me closely, gauging my reaction.

"That's because they *are* my designs."

"Why would he have drawings of them?"

"Good question, Sheriff. Beaulieu has a . . ." I hesitated, wondering how to broach the designer's reputation. "Let's just say he borrowed designs from other designers." Including me, apparently.

"Interesting."

"Yeah." I looked more carefully at the sketches. He'd made notes on the page in a quick scribble, more rushed than his notes in the sketchbook I'd seen in his room at Seven Gables.

"There's been a new development."

I refocused on the sheriff, planting my feet firmly on the floor and leaning forward. "What's that?"

"It looks like there was poison in his system. Several people there said that Beaulieu had looked queasy, like he might upchuck."

"Yes, he did."

"Well, it turns out that he did, upchuck, I mean—in the toilet in your bathroom."

I searched my mind, remembering that he had gone to the bathroom after he first arrived. "Oh no," I said under my breath. "What kind of poison?" I asked. Whoever killed Beaulieu had to have left clues.

"It's called sago palm," he said, brushing the pad of one thumb against the thatch of hair under his lower lip. I knew him well enough to know that this meant he was weighing his thoughts. He wasn't one to jump to quick conclusions. He was slow and steady. It could be infuriating, but at the moment, I liked that about him.

I stared at him. "What is that? A palm tree?"

"It can grow mighty tall, yes, but not to tree size. More common in south Texas, but they're pretty hardy and can survive the freezes we get if they're covered."

I cataloged the garden at 2112 Mockingbird Lane, trying to picture any palms I had. Even if I had one, there hadn't been time for someone to dash outside, spot a poisonous plant, do whatever had to be done to make it ingestible, and then get Beaulieu to drink it. My yard was more of an English garden, lush and floral rather than fronds of tropical plants jetting out here and there. "*Okay.*"

"Every part of 'em is poisonous," he said.

"I certainly didn't see him eat any greens. Honestly, he wasn't there for very long. Nana brought out some goat cheese and crackers, but no one ate any. There was tea and lemonade. No palm bushes on the menu."

"The poison most likely came through the seeds. Ground up, they'd be easily digested."

My mind hiccupped as it tried to remember something, but it was just out of reach.

"Sheriff, I don't even know what that palm bush looks like, let alone that it's poisonous," I said.

"I believe that, Harlow. I'm just followin' the clues and the evidence. If you have any ideas, I'm all ears."

The perfect opening to the second part of my one-two punch. I told him about Lindy Reece wanting to write a hard-hitting investigative piece. "If she discovered proof that he stole other designers' ideas, it could have turned ugly between them."

He rubbed his thumb against the thatch of hair under his lip, thinking. "But wouldn't she be the one dead in that scenario?"

And that was the problem. Without knowing if he'd somehow turned the tables on her, my theory could be hard to prove.

"And the wedding?" I said after we'd spent a minute in silence, both pondering the scenario I'd brought up.

"She's as stubborn as all get out," he said, "but I can live with that. Bein' stubborn's better than a poke in the eye, but she's done dug her heels in on this. Truth be told, I think it's an excuse. She don't want to believe I won't up and walk out on her like your daddy did."

I had a feeling that his armchair psychology was right on the money. I stood up and faced him square on. "Look here, Sheriff, we don't need to go to Babe's for any rehearsal dinner. In fact, we don't need anything more than you and Mama professing your love to God. So if I can get her there, will you be at the church?"

His smile lit up his craggy face. "I reckon so, Harlow. Yes, I reckon so."

Chapter 22

After a quick trip to the fabric store for a zipper, a few spools of white thread, and hook and eye closures, I parked in my driveway under the possum wood trees, walked through the side gate and through the yard, and up the front porch steps. No matter how I was feeling inside, coming home to 2112 Mockingbird Lane made my heart beat slow, my breath come easier, and filled me with ease.

I mounted the porch steps, ready to finish the last-minute projects for the wedding. I had to go on as if the wedding was happening. A strange heaviness settled over me as I stepped onto the porch. I was used to Meemaw haunting me, her invisible presence flittering in and out of the various rooms in the house at a whim, but this, once again, was different. I could almost feel my great-grandmother's sadness, as if she were magnifying everything I was experiencing.

I closed my eyes, working to keep my mind still and empty, thinking only of Loretta Mae, wishing she were here and that we could talk. The bushes and plants and flower petals remained motionless, not a rustle or whisper to be heard. The spigot stayed firmly in the off position, no hiss or sputtering or flow of water sounding. Not a creak, and nary a sound came from anywhere around me. "Meemaw?" I finally said aloud, wondering if my voice would have the power to summon her this time.

The sound of cars passing by on Mockingbird Lane and the occasional slamming of a door hit my eardrums, but I got no other signs that Meemaw was near.

"Woolgathering again?" a man's voice said through the dining room window.

I jumped, my heart shooting to my throat for a split second before I recognized the voice. Will Flores.

I spun around to face him, seeing his shape through the dark screen. "I guess so," I said with a smile, coming closer. "What are you doing?"

"Waiting for you."

I frowned. "I hope you don't have bad news. I'm not sure I can take that right now."

He laughed. "Not a bit of it, but I think you can handle whatever's thrown at you. You're a pioneer like that, ready to dig in and do what needs to be done."

I didn't feel that way right now, but it sounded nice. Reassuring. The kind of thing you wanted the man you . . . cared about . . . to say. His face disappeared from the window, reappearing a moment later at the front door. He emerged, pulling me into a hug and dipping his head until his lips nuzzled my neck. "You worried about the wedding?" he asked, his breath warm against my neck.

"That, and the murder."

"First things first," he said after another few seconds of nuzzling. "We can make sure Hoss and your mama get hitched. You worry about getting the sheriff to the church and I'll handle your mother. She won't be able to say no to me, no matter how hard she tries."

I already had Hoss taken care of, so we were halfway there. I smiled. "I bet she won't. I know I can't."

The heaviness of the air on the porch abated slightly and the sturdy white rocking chairs behind us started up, moving back and forth, back and forth. They creaked, and with each forward motion of the curved legs it sounded like someone—namely Meemaw—saying *ah*, and with each backward rock, saying *love. Ah, love. Ah, love. Ah, love*.

Will must have heard it, too. He shot a surprised glance at the chairs, but then his face relaxed. Bless his heart, he'd accepted the Cassidy charms better than I ever could have hoped for. Including the glimpses of Meemaw's presence he saw every now and again.

Meemaw and her matchmaking had made a good pair with the two of us.

"Now, about Beaulieu, what's on your mind?"

I told him the latest about the sheriff's suspicion of poison and the fern. "I searched it on my phone to see what it looks like and I don't have anything like it here on my property."

"If it grows in Texas, anyone could have gotten hold of it," he said. "Access to something like that is a lot different than getting hold of a monitored narcotic or some other drug."

"Easier," I said, "but you'd have to know that it was

poisonous." Another check in Lindy's column. She knew how to do research, was a Texas native, and who knows? Maybe she had the stuff growing in her Dallas yard.

"So, what's your plan now?" he asked. He didn't like that I tended to get wrapped up in mysteries wherever I went, but he didn't fight it, either.

We sat on the rocking chairs, keeping them going with our feet pushing against the wooden slats of the porch. A cocoon of warmth moved around us in a constant stream. If I could see it, I would have described it as a figure eight in a pattern of continual light. "I want to find out if Lindy knew Beaulieu more than she's been letting on," I said, following my hunch. "She's too focused on him, and an article about him dying—murdered, even, for his designs? That could be way more powerful than the article she was going to write about three local designers. What if she plotted the whole thing?"

"You think she'd kill someone to make the story better?"

I shrugged. "Sounds a tiny bit better than killing because your boss is a jerk and humiliates you, or because you don't like the latest designs he wants you to model." Which was the best motive I'd come up with for Barbi and Esmeralda.

"How was the poison administered?" Will asked. "No matter who did it, he had to ingest it somehow, right? If we figure that out, maybe it'll help narrow the suspect list."

There it was again. We. As in part of a team. I reached over and dusted the tips of my fingers over his forearm. I drew in a bolstering breath, peeking through the window behind me to make sure we were alone.

"No one's home," he said, answering my unasked question.

"Orphie?"

"Wasn't here when I arrived. I haven't seen her."

"She's probably with Gavin," I said. "They're, um, seeing each other."

Will stopped rocking, planting his booted feet on the floor. "Is that right? Gavin McClaine and your friend?" A low chuckle started in his throat and moved into a full laugh. "Maybe it'll make him nicer, you think?"

I grinned, his laughter contagious. "We can hope."

"The poison," he prompted.

"Nana brought over some of her goat cheese. We had crackers. Mama made lemonade and tea—almost dumped a pitcher of it on Beaulieu, too. Mama and Nana served all of us. But neither one of them has a motive, of course, and no one else fixed the food or drinks. I don't think any of it was ever left unattended, either. The sheriff took the glasses and pitcher, though, so if that's how he took it in, Hoss'll find out."

"So it could have been any of them," he said. "The models, the photographer, the journalist, the designer. They were all right here."

"Not the models," I said. "They were dropped off at Seven Gables before the rest of them came here."

"Which lets them off the hook."

We sat, just rocking, both of us thinking. It was comfortable silence like nothing I'd ever experienced before. The only sounds were the creaking of the chairs and the cicadas hidden in the trees. The occasional truck rumbled by, but Mockingbird Lane was a quiet street. Almost ominous at the moment given my somber mood.

"Why else would someone have wanted him dead?"

I mused aloud, not really expecting an answer, but Will offered one anyway. "Midori could be jealous of him as a designer."

"I think he was stealing her designs," I said, hoping he didn't ask how I knew that. I hurried on. "He was trying to steal *my* designs. The sheriff found sketches in his pocket of pieces I have in my shop." I snapped my head up. "He hated Bliss. He made that perfectly clear from the second he walked in, but if he wanted my designs, he had to come here."

"Okay, but you didn't kill him. Midori could have, but again, how?"

"And unless she knew he was using her designs, she'd have no motive."

"But maybe she *did* know. Hoss had to consider *you* as the killer for that very reason. If he was stealing her designs, she might have wanted to put a stop to it. Can you ask her?"

Oh yes, that had risen to the top of my list of things to do. Right after I made sure Mama and Hoss got hitched.

My cell phone rang from the depths of my oversized purse. I riffled through the contents until I found it, glancing at the screen. Madelyn.

"Hey," I said, happy to hear her voice.

"You'd best get down to Presby," she said in her British accent.

"To the hospital?" My insides clenched. Mama? Nana? Granddaddy? All the people I loved—with the exception of Will because he was sitting next to me—raced through my head.

"Your friend Orphie."

The nerves in my gut jettisoned to my head, making me feel as if it were stuffed full of cotton. "What happened?"

"I don't have the full story, but from what I gather, she was at the bead shop when she just collapsed. Josie said she turned green, acted like she was nauseated and headed for the restroom, and then she just fell. Josie called 911 and they brought her here."

"How did you—?"

"I'm here to get some statistics for the Bliss Web site I'm working on for the town. I saw the emergency team wheel her in on a gurney."

The vise around my insides tightened. "Is she . . . will she . . ."

"I don't know, love."

I stood without thinking, grabbing my purse from the porch and blindly walking down the steps. "On my way."

Will was by my side the next second, guiding me by the elbow. "What's going on?"

I headed toward my truck as I told him what Madelyn had said, my voice sounding hollow as I heard myself utter the words, "Orphie . . . collapsed . . . hospital . . ."

He took the keys from my hand, opening the passenger door for me. "I'll drive," he said.

"Good idea." I slid in, and seconds later, I was having a déjà vu experience. Not so long ago, we'd driven to Presbyterian, Bliss's only hospital, to stop a killer, Now we were speeding down the road toward praying we'd find Orphie alive and on the mend.

Chapter 23

We stopped at the information desk where an elderly volunteer gave me Orphie's room number and pointed us in the right direction. She'd already been moved from the ICU to a regular room, a very good sign. Will stayed by my side as I half walked, half ran down the wide hallways, rode the elevator up two floors, and finally found her room. The cloying mixture of antiseptic and sickness filled my nostrils, pushing down into my gut until I was nauseated with it.

It hung around me like a nebula lying thickly around a lone planet. "She'll be fine," I muttered, trying to reassure myself.

Will kept silent, his hand on my lower back as we found her room and pushed open the large, pneumatic door. It closed behind us slowly and with a soft *whoosh*.

The curtains around the first bed were drawn. The second bed was empty. No overcrowding at Presby. At least Orphie had her own room.

I found the opening in the curtain and peeked

through. The bed was slightly inclined and she was propped up by several pillows. Her eyes were closed, her breathing steady, her hair spilled gently over the pillow. Even in repose, she had that angelically lovely quality about her. I had a flash in my mind of her in a lightweight clingy knit skirt and a ruched top with a crisscrossed front, both in soft lavender. I took it as another sign that she was going to be fine. At least that's what I told myself. "Orphie?"

Her eyelids fluttered.

"Orphie?" I said again, this time slipping through the curtain and taking her hand. "Can you hear me?"

Her eyelids quivered again, but this time they cracked open. "Harlow."

I perched on the side of the bed and took her hand. "How do you feel?"

She managed a little smile. "Like a million bucks."

I couldn't pussyfoot around, so I just blurted out my question. "What happened, Orphie?"

What there was of her smile faded. "I felt a little sick, but I tried to just keep going. Your friend Josie was showing me how to string felt beads. And then it just hit me. I . . . my stomach . . ."

She stopped, glancing over my shoulder at Will.

"Your stomach was upset?" I asked, letting her off the hook for giving us the down and dirty details.

She nodded. "I thought I could make it back to your house, but . . . but . . . I couldn't. I lost it in the bathroom, and then I . . . I just collapsed."

Behind me, the door whooshed open, followed by the thud of cowboy boots hitting the linoleum floor. I turned to see Deputy Sheriff Gavin McClaine hurry in. He was clean-shaven but still managed to look tousled. He could have stepped right into a TV show about a powerful, good-looking Southern lawman. The women would fall at his feet.

Me? He got my craw and I just wanted to throttle him for showing up here after Orphie had gone through such an ordeal.

Except they were, apparently, seeing each other.

He slowed once he saw us next to the hospital bed, nodding at Will as he sidled past him. He came up beside me, moving so he was next to the bed and leaning down close to Orphie, his expression softening. "How are you holding up, Miss Cates?" he drawled, the charm he normally dripped replaced by concern.

If I'd been able to catch Orphie's eye, I would have sent her a warning look. Gavin was like a snake with blue eyes, drawing you in before he shot out an attack. The conversation between him and Lindy Reece was front and center in my mind. Either he suspected Orphie of having something to do with Beaulieu's murder, or he was using Orphie to get more information about me, Beaulieu, and the whole ugly situation. Maybe both. No matter what, I was afraid this was all just a game to him. I easily envisioned him with a toothpick or blade of grass, ready to spin his six-shooter and take out Jesse James or some other old-time outlaw.

But Orphie didn't look my way. She remained focused on Gavin. "Doctor said I'll live," she said, managing a pained smile.

"About that." Gavin skirted around me, pulling up the chair that had been pushed into the corner.

She looked up at him, her eyes wide and expectant.

Oh Lord, she was enamored with him. With Gavin McClaine. The overzealous, pompous deputy. Good God, I'd thought Orphie had better taste than that.

He cleared his throat again. "I just talked to the doctor. They're still waitin' on the results from some of the tests, but it seems pretty clear that you ingested poison."

What little color Orphie had in her cheeks instantly vanished. "Poison?" she repeated, her voice scarcely more than a whisper.

"What?" I said, squeezing her hand, bolstered by Will's hand on my shoulder.

"There's more," Gavin said, grimacing. "The symptoms are consistent with a plant. Something called a sago palm . . ."

My temples pounded, drowning out the rest of his voice. The sago palm. "That's the same poison that killed Beaulieu," I said, my voice strained.

Will's hand tightened on my shoulder, just barely, but enough to bring me back to the moment.

Gavin nodded. "One and the same. I'm afraid this was an attempted murder." He looked back at Orphie and once again, a soft, reassuring smile graced his lips. "Thank the Lord it didn't work."

She pulled her hand away from mine and held it out to Gavin. I watched, shocked, as he placed his, palm down, in hers, their fingers wrapping around each other's hand. "Wh-who?" she managed.

Gavin broke his connection with Orphie long enough to shoot me a penetrating look. "I don't know yet, but believe me, I will find out, and whoever it is will be strung up by their heels."

I'd Googled the sago palm after the sheriff told me

about it, and found that symptoms can start quickly, or take up to twelve hours. That didn't narrow down the time frame much. I perched on the side of the bed, edging between my friend and the deputy. "Orphie, what did you eat today?"

"Or drink?" Gavin added.

Her eyes glazed, her lids drifting to half-mast. "Breakfast at Harlow's," she said. "I had c-coffee while I helped M-Midori organize patterns and sort through . . . through the Prêt-à-Porter rack."

She stopped, her breathing growing heavy. Labored. My gut clenched, worry invading every one of my pores. She had the same poison in her that had killed Beaulieu. I reminded myself that she wouldn't have been moved to an ordinary room if she was in danger. Then again, people relapsed. I squeezed her hand. "Come on, Orphie. You can fight this."

Her eyelids fluttered, then opened. "I—I went to S-Seven G-Gables," she muttered softly. "T-tea and s-scones."

My gaze snapped to Will's, then to Gavin's. "Why'd you go to the inn?" I asked, my mind racing through the possibilities. Hattie and Raylene would have made the tea and scones, but any one of the various suspects could have poisoned Orphie's food. They were all staying there, after all.

But Orphie's eyes drifted closed and she didn't answer. Panic set in. I pressed the nurse's call button, standing back when a woman dressed in teal scrubs rushed in and assessed Orphie. "She's all right," she announced after an agonizingly long exam. "Her body's fighting, but she needs rest."

Relief flooded me. She was going to be okay. She *had* to be okay. But she wouldn't be able to give us any more answers for the time being, which meant another visit to Seven Gables was in order.

After another minute, Will, Gavin, and I retreated to the hallway.

"So, Harlow," Gavin said after the pneumatic door closed again. "I have to ask, did you poison your friend?"

The energy around the three of us pulsated and Will surged forward. "What the hell is your problem, Mc-Claine?"

Gavin stepped back, but his jaw tightened, the veins in his neck pulsing. "You best watch yourself, Flores."

This time I put my hand on Will's shoulder, hoping he'd simmer down. His muscles bunched under my touch, but he stilled. "She didn't have anything to do with that guy's death."

Gavin folded his arms over his chest. "He was stealing her designs. I have to ask."

Will's eyes darted my way before zeroing in again on Gavin. "That hardly makes her a murderer."

"I agree," he said.

I'd been ready to fire off another rebuttal, but stopped, staring at Gavin. "You do?"

"If you're a murderer, I'm a rodeo star," he said. "But I wouldn't be doin' my job if I didn't pursue every avenue of investigation."

Will's fists were still clenched tight, but his shoulders loosened up. "So, what *do* you think?" he ground out.

"I think it could have been any one of the people at Buttons and Bows that morning," he began, "and I think there must be a connection between Beaulieu and Miss Cates."

His eyes clouded as he spoke Orphie's name. Did he have real feelings for Orphie? Maybe his flirting and flippant nature was merely a ploy or a defense mechanism he used to protect himself from getting hurt. After all, in high school, he'd been shy and awkward—and had been picked on. Those were not things easily overcome.

Interesting.

"Cassidy?"

I blinked, coming out of my thoughts as Will said my name again. "A connection. Right."

"Who would want both Orphie and Beaulieu dead, and why?"

The only thing that came to mind was the Maximilian book Orphie had taken.

I glanced at the closed door to Orphie's room, debating with myself. Did I tell them, or did I not? Someone had tried to kill Orphie. What if it had something to do with the book? I had to tell them. Her safety was more important than her secrets.

"There is something," I said, hoping it wouldn't color their opinion of Orphie. Gavin seemed smitten, even if he'd only known Orphie for as long as it took to be thrown from a mechanical bull.

Gavin folded his arms over his chest again and Will leaned against the hospital wall. "What is it, darlin'?" Will said.

I gulped down my reservations and just blurted it out. "Orphie came here because she sto— uh, she's in . . . possession . . . of one of Maximilian's design books and . . . some of her designs were based on what's in that book."

They stared at me as if I were crazy. Clearly they didn't understand. I gave them a frame of reference. "It would be like plagiarism. Like if a writer stole someone else's words and claimed he'd written them. Designs are personal. They're the creative work—and property—of the designer. You can't just steal them."

"Like Beaulieu was going to steal yours," Gavin said. And maybe Midori's. "Exactly."

"So if someone—like Beaulieu, for example," Gavin said, his expression turning grim, "knew that she had the book and had used designs that weren't hers, that would be a pretty decent motive."

I glared at him. That was *not* the takeaway from this story. "She came here because she feels guilty and needed my advice. She plans to mail the book back. Orphie is *not* a killer. And she's lying in there right this very minute because someone tried to do the same thing to her."

"Which raises the question," Will said. "Who would want to kill both Orphie and Beaulieu, and why?"

Gavin's jaw pulsed. He hesitated, finally saying, "You know her the best, Harlow. Could she have poisoned herself?"

I balked. "Of course not!"

He sighed, shaking his head. "Desperate people do crazy things, Harlow. You've seen that in action."

That was true. Since I'd been back in Bliss, I'd seen three murders, each committed by people desperate to hide the truth or protect some secret. Someone in Bliss was desperate right now to have killed Beaulieu and for attempting to kill Orphie. But there was no way I would believe she had done this to herself to redirect suspicion.

"Someone did this to her," I said, turning and pushing through the door and into the hospital room once again. I needed to ask her one question and to reassure myself that she was going to be okay.

She looked fragile lying in the sterile bed. Her eyelids fluttered open as Will and Gavin filed in behind me. "Orphie," I said, figuring it was best just to come right out with it. "Did Beaulieu know that you had Maximilian's book?"

Her fingers curled around the blanket, bunching the material in her fists. "Wh-what?"

I cupped my hand over hers, looking her square in the eye. "Someone killed Beaulieu and tried to kill you. We need to figure out why."

"The book . . . ?"

"He didn't know, did he?" In a trial, that question probably would have garnered an *objection, leading the witness* from the prosecution, but I knew Gavin wanted Orphie to be innocent. He kept quiet.

But instead of saying, *Of course he didn't know!* Orphie pulled her hand away from mine and looked down at the crumpled blanket.

My spine stiffened. "Orphie? He didn't know, did he?"

One of the men behind me shifted on his feet and I felt the tension in the air grow heavy.

She nodded, lifting her gaze back to mine, peering at me through her muddy eyelashes. "He knew," she said, her voice barely more than a whisper.

My heart sank. I thought about the night she'd shown

up on my porch, pounding on the door in the middle of the night. "Did you know he was going to be here? Is that why you came?" I asked, knowing the answer deep down.

As her fingers worked the blanket, Gavin sidestepped around me and leaned down to whisper in her ear. Her hands stilled, and then relaxed. "H-he sent me an ... an e-mail," she said.

She stopped and Gavin nodded to her.

I glanced at Will, lifting my eyebrows in surprise. Gavin and Orphie. They had a connection.

She cleared her throat and continued. "He didn't know about the book, but he said he knew that I'd stolen Maximilian's designs and he was going to tell everyone, there'd be a story about it in the newspaper, and I'd be ruined. Unless ..." Her voice trembled with emotion. "Unless I agreed to pay him. He knew about us being roommates in Manhattan. He said he'd suggested having you as part of the magazine article, and he could pull the plug on that just as easily as he'd made it happen."

This time she did meet my gaze. "I couldn't let him destroy *your* career over a stupid mistake *I'd* made."

"He stole ideas," I said, trying to understand. "He tried to steal my designs. He had sketches of Midori's designs. He was blackmailing you—"

"He has—*had* a reputation. He was *somebody*, and I'm nobody. I believed him, that he'd destroy any future I might have, and that he'd take you down, too. He knows—*knew* people. I couldn't let that happen, so I agreed to meet him here."

"Why?" Gavin asked. "To what end? Were you going to pay him?"

She nodded. "I was going to give him the book, b-but I couldn't."

She looked down at her hands again, ashamed. "But he died before I could pay him."

Gavin notched his cowboy hat back and looked her straight in the eye. "I need to ask, sweetheart, and I need a straight answer."

She lowered her chin in one nod.

"Did you kill Beaulieu?"

"I've done some things I'm not proud of," she said quietly, "but no, I didn't kill him. I didn't kill Beaulieu."

Chapter 24

The big question suddenly front and center in my mind was whether or not someone else knew about the Maximilian book in Orphie's possession. Was that why she'd been targeted? But that still didn't answer the question of why Beaulieu had been killed.

"My head hurts from thinking about this," I told Will as we walked up the flagstone path in front of my house. We stopped short at the base of the porch steps. "That was closed when we left," I whispered, seeing the door cracked open.

"Yes, it was."

I searched the yard for a weapon, zeroing in on a trowel tucked under a geranium plant by the steps. I grabbed it with one hand and grabbed Will's arm with my other hand, and together, we tiptoed into the house.

I stopped short at the sight, my breath stalling in my chest. Most of what I owned appeared to be on the floor. My dress forms lay on their sides, the outfits that had been on them disheveled and askew—including Mama's wedding dress. Magazines had been dumped from their rack, patterns were in a pile on the workroom table, and every cookbook from my collection was on the kitchen floor.

"Do you think they're gone?" I whispered.

Will snatched the trowel from my hand and skirted around me. Silent as a panther, he crept through the gathering room, into the dining room, quickly surveying the kitchen and utility room. He peeked out the back window before heading toward the stairs. He held one finger to his lips, pointing to himself and then to the stairs.

My temples throbbed, my head swimming with fear. What if the killer was upstairs? What if Will couldn't subdue him—or her—with a garden tool?

He disappeared around the bend at the landing. The house creaked, like all old houses. My muscles clenched with each sound. I moved forward, and then, like a beacon from a lighthouse, the floor lamp in the workroom flickered, finally turning on. Meemaw.

I crept forward, jumping at a movement to my right. Earl Grey scurried past me. "Oh, thank God you're okay!" I whispered as he disappeared into the kitchen.

In the workroom, the lamp clicked on and off. I paused in the threshold, gripping one of the French doors. "Meemaw?"

A series of sounds and movements went around the room like a trail of dominos triggering the actions. The light stopped flickering, illuminating the room. The curtains next to it billowed, even though the window was closed. They blew to the right, lightly dusting the last outfit hanging on the privacy screen. It fell to the floor, sliding across as if it were being pulled by an invisible string. Once it stopped, Meemaw's old Singer came to life, the presser foot clamping down and the motor bringing the needle up and down, up and down, up and down. It went faster and faster, the sewing machine bouncing across the table until it balanced on the edge.

"Meemaw, stop!" I dodged the mess on the floor, pushing the Singer back to the center of the table just before it crashed to the floor.

"Meemaw," I said, hoping she would calm down. The room fell quiet. "What happened here?" I asked, knowing she couldn't answer me.

The pipes in the ceiling were one of her go-to methods. If only we knew Morse code, it might have been effective. The pipes groaned and clanked, starting slowly, then growing as she became more agitated again.

"Loretta Mae Cassidy," I said, my voice as stern as I could make it. It was like scolding a precocious child— only worse. "This is not helping. Listen, how about you clank once for no, twice for yes?"

I'd seen that type of thing in movies. Maybe it would work now. It was worth a try. "Okay?"

Two clanks. She was game.

Excitement bubbled inside me. This could really work!

Now that I had her here, I backtracked to the murder itself. "Meemaw, did you see who murdered Beaulieu?"

One clank. No. Which was what I expected since he was most likely poisoned before he'd come to my shop.

I fast-forwarded to today. "Did you see who did this to Buttons and Bows?" I asked as I bent to pick up spools of thread, tossing them into a basket.

Two clanks. Yes! I knew she had to have seen them.

"Who? Who came in here?"

Silence. Because, of course, she couldn't answer that question with a yes or a no.

I kept getting ahead of myself. "Meemaw, can you tell me who did this?"

One clank.

"Why not? You said you saw who it was."

Two clanks.

What did she mean? "Did you recognize the person?"

One clank.

"Okay. Did you see a face?"

One clank.

I threw up my hands in frustration. "Then, Meemaw, I don't understand! You said you saw who did this but didn't see anything helpful?"

Two clanks.

I tried one more tactic. "Was it a woman?" This question seemed easy enough. Quinton had been the only man around that morning, aside from Beaulieu. If it wasn't a woman who'd ransacked the place, then Quinton was the likely culprit. If it *was* a woman, then I was still at square one.

Two clanks.

And a creak from behind me. Will was back from his search upstairs. When I turned, he was staring at me, his eyes darting around, but the pipes had gone quiet.

Will hadn't really seen Meemaw in action, and seeing it was a lot to take in. Gracie had sensed Loretta Mae's presence but hadn't put two and two together yet. One thing at a time.

"It's her? She's here?" he asked, his gaze on the ceiling.

So now seemed like the moment it would all become real for Will.

"Yes." I looked up at the ceiling, too. The chances were good that Meemaw had already vacated the pipes, and even if she were still there, I had no idea if she could see through walls. Or even if her senses worked that way. Maybe she hadn't even known it was happening, and by the time she realized something was going on, the culprit was already gone.

"Did you find anything upstairs?" I asked him.

His attention was split between his curiosity about Loretta Mae and the ransacking, but bless his heart, he rallied and focused on my question. "It's a mess."

"Orphie's book!" I'd forgotten to ask her if she'd actually mailed it yet, and now I worried that it was gone.

I hurried past Will and double-timed it up the stairs. He was right behind me. I turned left at the landing and went down the hall and past the table. The bowl of handmade felt beads was overturned and the drawers were pulled out, the contents riffled through. I glanced at my room as I passed. The dresser drawers had been yanked out, clothes strewn about, and the bed pushed out from the wall and the quilt pulled half off.

We continued down the hall, stopping at the guest room Orphie was using. Her suitcase had been up-ended, all her clothes scattered on the floor. I searched, quickly looking through the drawers, under the twin bed, and under the piles of her clothes. No book. "It's not here."

Will leaned back against the doorjamb. "Why is that book so valuable?"

I sank down on the bed, my thoughts racing. "It's got

his drawings, designs, and notes. Another designer could use it all to create a collection."

He came and sat down beside me, his presence just as comforting as the cocoon of warm air that Meemaw typically brought with her. "So either Orphie or Beaulieu had to have told someone that she had the book," he said.

I'd been thinking the very same thing. "But who?" I mused aloud. "And why would anyone else care?"

Chapter 25

"Don't touch anything," Deputy Gavin McClaine told me when I called him from the phone in my bedroom. "I'm on my way."

"Yes, sir," as I hung the receiver back in its cradle.

I turned in a circle, taking in the mess. "I can't clean it up yet."

I sidled up to Will, wrapping my arms around him. I tried to stay away from Will when we were at my house, what with Meemaw around all the time, but I could hear a vague clanking from downstairs, so she was busy at the moment. "Can't clean. Can't work in this mess."

He flashed a wicked grin. "I can think of a thing or two to keep us occupied."

I was wearing flats, so I stood on my tiptoes, bringing my lips to his. Ah yes, just as comforting as a blanket of—

Warm air. It encircled us, weaving through the safe gaps between our bodies. I felt pressure as the air seemed to grow denser. Meemaw was pushing us apart—

Or was she? The space between us grew cool, the warm air circling around our bodies and forcing us together until we were as close as we could be.

Meemaw! She wasn't trying to keep us apart; she was trying to force us together. That rascal. She wanted to expedite my relationship with Will.

And Will was all for it. He lowered his lips to my neck, his warm breath making my skin sizzle.

My thoughts turned fuzzy as his hand slid to my lower back and with the tiniest amount of pressure, he urged me even closer.

But in the back of my mind, I knew Meemaw was around, Orphie was in a hospital bed, Beaulieu was dead, and a murderer was loose in Bliss. I managed to gather my thoughts enough to utter Will's name.

"Hmmm?" he responded before finding my lips.

"Loretta Mae is—"

He drew his head back, a faint smile playing on his lips. "She's here?"

I nodded. "Do you feel that warm air?"

He hesitated, then nodded. "Thought your heater was faulty."

"Nope, that's Meemaw."

"It felt like it was pushing us together," he said, drawing me close again. "She knows what she wants."

"Yes, she does," I said, sinking in to him again. Even with the horrible things happening around us, being with Will made me feel as if everything would turn out all right.

"And didn't you say what Loretta Mae wanted, Loretta Mae got?"

"Mmm-hmm." That was her Cassidy charm. Sort of a

powerful catchall, and she was going strong with it at the moment.

"Looks to me like she wants us together."

"Mmm-hmm." There was no question about that.

"So there's no point in fighting it."

"There's not," I said, my voice a mere breath against his skin.

His lips traced along my jaw, nuzzling into the crevice of my neck again. My hands cupped his shoulders as my knees turned weak.

"Then maybe we should skip ahead and..." He trailed off, pulled away, and looked up at me.

"And what?" I asked, a sudden nervous pull low in my stomach.

His smoky blue eyes met mine, that half smile hovering on his lips as though he was up to no good. "I love you, Cassidy."

He backed me up against the wall, lowering his lips to mine, kissing me as if he wanted to burn this moment into his mind for always. "I want to be with you every day," he said, his voice low and deep in his throat.

My heart thundered in my chest. I thought I knew what was going on in his mind, but I couldn't be sure. He knew everything about me. He knew about the Cassidy charm. About Meemaw. About Gracie and her charm. He knew ... and he was still here.

Loretta Mae knew how to pick them.

His hands slid to either side of my face, his fingers threading through my hair as his kiss deepened. The air around us had turned normal. Meemaw was gone. Giving us our privacy, thankfully.

I lost my breath and if he hadn't been holding me, I would have collapsed to the floor. "I . . . I love you, too, Will." And I did. I hadn't realized it until the words left my lips and floated upward like rose petals on a soft breeze. "I love you, too."

Chapter 26

While we waited for the deputy to show, I called Seven Gables. I had a meeting scheduled with Lindy Reece in just a little while, but didn't want to ask Raylene or Hattie about Orphie's visit to the inn this morning in front of her.

Hattie answered the phone with a clipped "Seven Gables."

"Hattie, it's Harlow."

"Is the weddin' on or off?" she demanded.

"Far as I'm concerned, it's still on." She hemmed and hawed, but I got right to the point of my call. "My friend Orphie said she came by the inn this morning." I'd seen her drive off, in fact. I'd racked my brain, trying to remember who I'd seen and what they'd been doing. Esmeralda had had a cup, and Jeanette had been carrying a plate. Either one of them might have had the opportunity to doctor the food Orphie'd had. Lindy and Midori had been there, too, so truly, it could have been any of them.

"Yep, that's right, for tea and scones. That journalist had me set the table and answer the door, even, all formal-like."

So Lindy had arranged the meeting. "What about the others? The models or the designers, were they around while Orphie and Lindy talked?"

Hattie paused for just a second before responding, "I reckon so, Harlow, though I don't recall specifically. I think they were all in and out. They act like they own the place, wandering around at all hours, demanding special food and scented linens. Good grief, I'll be glad when they all go back to wherever they came from."

"Aren't all guests demanding like that?" I asked her. Seemed to me that if you owned a bed-and-breakfast, you'd best get used to having people around your house.

"To a degree, but not as bad as all these women. The man, at least, is quiet. He don't hardly say a word, and don't hardly show his face, but tell me this: Who needs blenders and mini choppers and all the M&Ms separated from the trail mix?"

I took a guess. "The models?"

"All the M&Ms removed from the trail mix," she said again, as if I hadn't really understood what she'd meant the first time. "Red, green, blue, yellow . . . every last one."

I couldn't help her understand the mentality of models who hardly ate or their eccentricities, so I didn't try.

A car pulled up outside, so I hung up with Hattie, shrugged at Will, and watched as Gavin opened the door and stood in the threshold of Buttons & Bows, legs spread, engineer boots planted heavily on the pecan flooring, hands on his hips. "Did I, or did I not, tell you not to touch anything?"

I folded my arms over my chest, possible responses circling in my mind.

I'm sorry! But Gavin wouldn't take my apology.

I didn't! But that wouldn't fly because the downstairs was entirely picked up, everything put right, not a spool of thread or bolt of fabric out of place. The busy noises Will and I had heard from upstairs had been Meemaw's cleanup efforts. I knew she could wreak havoc with the quick flick of her invisible wrist, but I hadn't known she could do the opposite and clean up.

Now I did.

My ghost of a great-grandmother did it! Definitely not something I could say.

So I kept quiet.

He knocked the rim of his cowboy hat back with his knuckles. "Ransacked, eh?" he finally asked, his voice tight, his lips tighter still.

"Yes."

"Anything missing?"

"The book. Maximilian's book," I said. I wasn't one hundred percent sure it had been stolen—again—but we definitely hadn't been able to find it among Orphie's things.

The three of us fell silent, not at all sure what the missing book meant. My thoughts were laced with the expression of love Will and I had just shared, and Gavin had arrived one second later, bursting into Buttons & Bows with guns metaphorically blazing.

"How's Orphie doing?" I asked.

"Hangin' in there," he said. He looked down as he shuffled his boots on the floor.

I forced my eyebrows to stay put. Orphie and Gavin.

I was getting used to the idea, and just like everyone else, they both deserved their slice of happiness. I'd just never imagined it would be with each other.

I spent the next thirty minutes showing Gavin the upstairs, which Meemaw hadn't cleaned up yet. He didn't unearth anything new to point him in the direction of the culprit. "I'll get someone in to dust for fingerprints," he said, but he sounded skeptical that it would yield the identity of whoever was behind this, so I just nodded.

Gavin left and not two minutes later, Gracie flounced into the shop looking more rested than I'd seen her in months. "I'm here to help," she announced. "Those dresses aren't going to finish themselves."

"Did you turn middle aged overnight?" I said with a laugh.

"That's what a good night's sleep does to me, I guess. I slept, like, eleven hours!"

I gave her a hug. "So glad, darlin'." I paused for a split second as I heard my mother's words come from my mouth. Bliss, right down to the Southern-speak, was part of me just as surely as I was part of it.

"Eleven hours," Gracie said, breaking away from me and throwing her arms around her dad.

"They did you some good," he said, ruffling her hair.

After Gracie was situated in the workroom, I glanced at my watch. Lindy had scheduled an interview with me. I had plenty of time to do that—find out more about Orphie's meeting at Seven Gables, and get back here to work on the final wedding preparations.

I grabbed my purse, the keys to the truck, and told Will my plan. Three little words still floated in the air between us, bolstering me up and filling me with hope.

Love. I'd wondered if I'd ever find it, and now I had. "Be careful," he said, brushing his lips over mine.

I needed to put everything right for Mama and Orphie, both, but I'd be extra careful. And with any luck, we'd be able to finish what we'd started upstairs.

Chapter 27

Even Madelyn Brighton's yelp in my ear sounded British. "That's huge, love!"

The distinct heat of a blush spread to my cheeks, and not even the air rushing through the open driver's-side window of my truck could cool me down. "I know. He's the one," I said.

She yelped again, louder this time, so I had to pull the phone away from my ear. "It's fate. You two are meant to be together. Next, he'll be asking you to marry him."

I could picture her grin, her brown, gold-flecked eyes sparkling, but her statement gave me pause. If Meemaw hadn't wanted us together, I wondered if we'd still have found each other. It was my one hesitation. How much magic was involved in my relationship with Will and was it really destiny, or was it otherworldly intervention?

"Harlow, you're soul mates. I know that just as surely as I know Billy and I are. Will and Bill. We each have our own Williams."

I had to laugh at that.

Madelyn's husband was a homegrown Texan who'd gone to Oxford, met Madelyn, and come back home with her. To say they were an atypical couple was an understatement. Billy, as she called him, was over six feet, wore wire-rimmed glasses, had pale, creamy skin, and looked like a walking scarecrow. Madelyn was pure Brit with a thick accent and quirky humor. She was a good six inches shorter than Billy, and the colors of their skin next to each other were like day and night. She had a fresh, Halle Berry haircut that clung to the lovely shape of her head, but she was full-figured instead of waif thin, and never went anywhere without her camera.

We'd become fast friends, in part because she was a self-proclaimed magic junkie with a penchant for all things supernatural or inexplicable. The Cassidys fell into those categories. She knew my family secrets, and like Will, she didn't care. In fact, she was enthralled by them and always wanted to see and know more.

"What about Gracie? You're like a family, you know. I guess you are family, quite literally," she said, "but, you know, if you and Will are to have a future, you'll *really* be family." She rattled on, barely taking the time to draw breath in between.

"I love her like a cousin. Or a daughter. Or both," I said with a laugh.

"Where are you off to?" Madelyn asked.

"I have an appointment with the *D Magazine* journalist."

"To talk about Beaulieu?"

"She wants to do an interview," I said.

"Right. And you're going to dig a little while you're there, are you not?"

My silence was answer enough for her.

With mysteries and magic, Madelyn was like a girl in a candy store. "What are you going to ask her? I'm free as a bird. I can join you! We're a pretty good team, you and I."

That we were. She knew exactly how my mind operated. I was going to do the interview, but more than anything, I wanted dirt on Beaulieu so I could put the pieces of the puzzle together. Madelyn had helped me before. She could definitely help me again. "Deal. Meet you at Seven Gables."

A few minutes later, I parked in front of the refurbished old house, thinking through my next steps as I waited for Madelyn to show up. My thoughts were scattered just as all the contents of my house had been a little while ago. I decided I'd go through the suspects one by one to eliminate the innocent and ultimately implicate someone in the murder. First up was Midori. As much as I hated the idea that the friendly Japanese-American designer could have anything to do with killing Beaulieu and poisoning Orphie, she was definitely at the top of the list.

I ticked off what I knew about her, which took all of twenty seconds. She came from Japan and her aesthetic was heavily influenced by Japanese kimonos, flowers, clean lines, and simplicity. She'd been featured in *D Magazine* before, along with Beaulieu; had made a name for herself in the fashion design world, appearing from nowhere with designs that were fresh and exciting; used authentic fabrics from Japan, as well as designing her own; and had loyal models.

"Why would she kill Beaulieu, and try to kill Orphie?" I said aloud, my voice hollow in the cab of the truck.

Professional jealousy was at the top of the list. If she somehow knew that Beaulieu had tried to steal her designs, she had a pretty good motive. But I couldn't think of a good reason why she'd have it in for Orphie. She was successful in her own right. Stealing Maximilian's book to copy his designs didn't make sense—if she even knew about it.

Next was Jeanette. She was a disgruntled employee, but was that enough of a motive? She'd told me that she'd overheard Beaulieu's conversations. Maybe she also read his e-mails and knew about him blackmailing Orphie for the book. She could have decided to make her own name in a cutthroat industry by stealing the book for her own use. "Maybe Beaulieu got wind of her plan and she killed him before he could fire her," I mused. It was possible, but I didn't know how likely the scenario was.

I considered Lindy next. Journalists were a dying breed, and she'd mentioned wanting that Pulitzer. But was she crazy enough to kill in order to make a story bigger? And what about Orphie? If Beaulieu had told her about the book and if she was motivated by a bigger story, would she have tried to eliminate Orphie to get the book thinking there might be something valuable in it?

It all seemed so unlikely, and yet someone had killed him, and had poisoned Orphie. I kept thinking. Meemaw's claim that whoever had searched 2112 Mockingbird Lane was a woman let me discount Quinton. My head spun as my thoughts moved to the four models. I couldn't begin to fathom motives for any of them to target Orphie, which was the problem. And which brought my attention back to the other three at the top of my list.

A horn beeped from behind me, and two seconds later, Madelyn fairly skipped down the sidewalk to the driver's-side window of Buttercup. I got out and we walked up the front path.

"Did you solve it all yet?" she asked, half joking, half hoping I hadn't because I knew she couldn't wait to dig in and help.

I laughed. "Not quite." I filled her in on all my ideas.

"All very circumstantial—if that, love. None of it proves anything, and you're right, there's no obvious connection to Orphie from any of them."

Exactly the conclusion I'd come to, so I had to keep digging until something turned up. I raised my hand to knock just as the front door opened. Lindy stood there, notepad in hand, her dark brown wavy hair a tad unruly and pulled back by a stretchy headband. "Right on time," she said. "Let's talk outside. Those sisters are batty."

Batty was an exaggeration, but I was sure Raylene and Hattie were ramped up right now over what was—or wasn't—happening with the wedding.

I introduced Lindy and Madelyn as we walked to the redwood picnic table the sisters had placed under a pecan tree in the front yard. Lindy slid in on one side of the table while Madelyn and I sat on the other side.

"I'm moving forward with the article," Lindy said as she flipped open her notebook.

I reined in my circling thoughts, focusing only on

Lindy as a possible killer. "The magazine's okay with it, even with Beaulieu dead?"

"There's an editorial meeting coming up, but if I wait, all my time will be for nothing. I've spent too many hours researching—" She stopped, tapping her pencil against her notepad, her attention shifting to some point over my shoulder. "I was there and I can bring something to the story that no one else can. Some depth and a greater interest level from which to frame your and Midori's stories. I have to say, though, that I'd feel a lot better about the chances the story will run if the murderer was caught. It feels like a dark cloud hanging over all of us right now, and the magazine won't want to be in the middle of that. Bad PR."

"Maybe you can write the story on spec and sell it somewhere else," Madelyn said.

That's just what Midori had suggested, and from the slight tic on one side of Lindy's mouth, I suspected that was exactly her plan. But then she shook her head. "Not unless *D* officially kills the story—or I come up with a completely different angle."

I realized how difficult making a living as a journalist had to be if you weren't on staff somewhere. Spending your time researching and writing a story that might never get to print.

"Someone tried to poison my friend Orphie," I said, hoping this one little sentence would open up the conversation. "The same way Beaulieu died."

I watched her carefully, looking for any sign she'd been the one to administer the poison. The tip of her pencil hovered above her paper, the corner of her mouth twitching again. It almost looked like a smile, but then it was gone and I wondered if I'd seen anything at all. "Tried to poison?" she asked.

"She's in the hospital."

"Doing well," Madelyn added. "Full recovery, the doctor said."

Lindy shook her head, her lips drawn together in a tight line. "Why would someone try to kill her?" she mused, finally dropping the lead to the paper and making a few notes. "Beaulieu, I can almost understand," she said, "but your friend? That doesn't make any sense."

She was far too blunt to be a native Southerner. "Why can you understand about Beaulieu?"

She scoffed. Not very impartial for a journalist, but at the moment, I liked that about her. Maybe she'd reveal something with one of her responses. "You met him. He was an ass."

Madelyn looked from Lindy to me. "I never met him. What was he like?"

I stopped myself from answering, vaguely wondering how much Lindy actually knew and how likely it was she was fishing for her own information. She was a journalist, after all, and for all I knew, I could become an unnamed source.

"It's reported that he stole from other designers," Lindy said.

Madelyn gaped. "Really?"

Lindy nodded. "A lot of others think so, but I'm not so sure. Even if he did, he certainly wouldn't be the first and he won't be the last."

I thought about Orphie and knew she was right.

"I've been following him for years, from his days in New York to his rise as a Dallas designer. There have been a few similarities to a few other people—certain design elements, for example—but out-and-out theft of ideas? I'd argue that he didn't actually do that. I've done a lot of research on it, actually. Intellectual property infringement is a big topic."

"But the sheriff found some of my designs on him when he died," I said.

She stared at me and I bit my lip, too late. She hadn't known that, and Hoss McClaine probably hadn't wanted me to tell anyone, least of all a reporter. Lindy tapped her pencil frenetically. "But that can't be right."

"It is. And here's one theory," I said, leaning forward on the picnic table. "Blackmail."

Lindy, with her dark eyes wide, and Madelyn with her grin growing bigger, both turned to me. "Really?" Madelyn said. "Who? How do you know?"

I couldn't—or wouldn't—breathe a word about Orphie coming here to make a blackmail payment to Beaulieu, and the conversations Jeanette overheard were hearsay, so I just shrugged. "Just a hunch."

A dazed look came over Madelyn and she seemed to look right past me. "The plot thickens," she said, her British accent making it sound very ominous.

Lindy wrote the word "blackmail" down on a fresh sheet in her notepad. "That makes perfect sense, actually. So whoever he was blackmailing could have killed him. The question is, who did he have dirt on?"

I answered carefully. "Seems like there are a few possibilities. The deputy's looking into it all."

"Fascinating," Lindy said, jotting something else

down in her book. "Something still doesn't make sense, but you're perceptive. Beaulieu always was the type to get as much as he could for the least amount of work."

That was a bold statement. "You seem to have known him pretty well," I said. "Do you have any other ideas? Anything else he might have been involved in?"

She tapped the eraser end against the picnic table again. "Not that I can think of, but if it's true and he really was stealing other people's designs, that's enough."

She stared beyond my shoulder again, lost in thought.

"What is it, Lindy?" I asked, not sure at all what I felt about her and how much to trust what she said.

"I've studied Beaulieu for a lot of years," she said, bringing her attention back to Madelyn and me. "There are similarities between his work and other designers, but isn't fashion sort of like a story plot? They've all been written before, just the characters change. A color-blocked dress is a color-blocked dress. If Midori does it first, then Beaulieu comes in and makes his own version, is that really creative theft, or is the idea of color blocking open for interpretation by any designer?"

It was a rhetorical question that didn't really need an answer, which was good because I didn't have one. Lindy's point was a good one. Diane von Furstenberg invented the wrap dress, but that didn't mean that no other designer could ever design one for fear of being derivative. No, the whole concept was now open for creative license. Taking an idea and making it your own was what designing was all about.

Which meant killing Beaulieu over stealing designs didn't make a whole lot of sense. It didn't make me feel less angry that he'd tried to steal some of mine, but I wouldn't murder over it. "But," I said, an idea taking shape in my head, "if someone had found out what he was doing with other people's designs, that person could have been blackmailing him."

"But why would he be the one dead, then?" Madelyn asked. "If he was being blackmailed, whoever was doing the blackmailing would be the one targeted."

"Things go wrong, though. If he were being blackmailed and tried to put an end to it, things could have turned ugly and the blackmailer could have decided to cut her losses. Or maybe Beaulieu discovered the blackmailer's identity," I suggested. "That would be a pretty good motive."

Lindy continued to scribble notes as we talked. Finally she looked up. "The same question still remains. Who was being blackmailed or doing the blackmail against Beaulieu?"

"What about Midori?" I asked, thinking aloud.

Lindy's gaze snapped from me to Madelyn and back. She clutched her pencil, looking as though she was forcing herself not to write. "What if Beaulieu had taken some of her designs? And what if she found out, turned the tables on him, demanding money for her silence?"

Madelyn piped up, continuing the hypothetical story. "He could have refused to pay up, she could have gone postal, and bam! Killed him."

My stomach seized. I had no idea how ethical Lindy was as a journalist. Lord almighty, I hoped I hadn't just thrown Midori under the bus. If she turned out to be innocent, she could still be tried in the courtroom of public opinion. Bad PR was tough to overcome.

It was a plausible scenario, though, so I went with it.

"How could she have done it?" I mused. "All the food and drinks from that morning have been tested. Everything was washed, so there's no way to know how he took it in." A vague memory tickled the back of my mind. He'd had the lemonade. I didn't know if he'd eaten any of the chèvre and crackers Nana had set out. But there was something else. He'd come into the shop after Lindy and Quinton, and after Midori. He'd looked around as if he were stuck in a junkyard instead of a designer's shop. He'd done something right as he'd come in, but what?

I racked my brain trying to remember, and then it hit me. He'd tossed something in the trash! "The garbage can."

"What?" The sharpness of Lindy's voice snapped the image from my mind. "What did you say?"

"The trash. Right after he came into my shop, he threw something away. A coffee cup." My skin pricked with goose bumps. "If the poison was delivered through the coffee, it happened before he got here. That would prove Orphie and I are innocent, and if we could figure out who was with him at the bourgeois coffee shop he mentioned, that would narrow it down."

I jumped up and raced back to my truck, both Lindy and Madelyn hot on my heels. Surely it couldn't still be there. Gavin, Hoss, and their team would have taken it as evidence. Or would they have? We'd all thought it had been a natural death at first, so there'd been no need to search the entire shop.

Madelyn voiced the very thought from behind me.

"Maybe they missed it. It's possible." I didn't think either the sheriff or the deputy was prone to shoddy police work, but I had to check out the possible lead.

I called Gavin as I turned the key and revved Buttercup to life. Lindy and Madelyn piled in next to me. "After Beaulieu died and your team came to Buttons and Bows, did you find a cup in the wastebasket by the door?" I asked the deputy.

It was a quick conversation. He consulted his notes and reported back to me. "No coffee cup, Harlow," he said, and he hung up.

Maybe I'd been too quick to dismiss Gavin and shoddy police work. A few minutes later, we were back at Buttons & Bows. I threw the truck into park and we all spilled out, dashing through the side gate, over the flagstone path, up the porch steps, bursting into the shop.

We stopped short just inside the door and gathered round the wastebasket as if we were the three Shakespearean witches circling their cauldron. We stared down at it. An empty spool of thread. Tissue. A few lopsided felt beads—rejects from my bead making with Orphie. A crumpled piece of paper from my design book.

No cup.

"Maybe you just thought you saw him throw something away," Lindy said.

No, I wasn't delusional. "I saw it." I replayed the scene in my mind. "He walked in after Midori. He threw the cup away, then started his tirade against small-town America." The answer suddenly came to me. "Oh no."

"What, love? You look like you've seen a . . . a ghost," Madelyn said. She hesitated, looking around in case Meemaw was actually present and I had seen her.

"No, no ghost. Someone broke in here and searched the shop and the upstairs." I whirled around on my boot heels. "What if that's what whoever broke in was after?"

Lindy jotted something in her notepad but shook her head. "Are you saying they came for the cup? But they searched the whole house?"

"Why would they do that?" Madelyn asked. "If they were after the cup, why keep looking?"

Maximilian's book no longer seemed like the most logical answer, but I didn't have a better one. If someone poisoned Beaulieu before he ever got to Bliss, they'd planned it, knowing he'd simply collapse sometime during the day. No exact time or place. Maybe it was just my bad luck that he'd died in my shop. Maybe it had nothing whatsoever to do with Orphie or the book.

But then what else were they searching for?

My head spun, my thoughts compressed like the tufts of wool pressed together to make the felt beads. "I don't know. I really don't know."

Chapter 28

Lindy had gone back to the inn, Madelyn had gone home to her husband, and I was on my own back at Buttons & Bows. Some people turned to yoga or alcohol or chocolate to relax their nerves and give them clarity. Not me. I turned to hand-sewing. I'd hoped a needle, thread, a leather thimble, a pile of beads and sequins, and Mama's wedding dress would do the trick, but so far understanding was eluding me.

No answers miraculously appeared before me. I still had a slew of ideas, none of which I could prove, and none of which seemed quite right. Not even Meemaw's warm presence could help direct my thoughts in what felt like the right direction. Some detail danced on the edges of my brain, but I couldn't get a handle on what it was, or what it might have to do with Beaulieu's murder or Orphie's poisoning.

There was a murderer on the loose in Bliss, and I was no closer to figuring out the truth than I'd been the day before. A car door slamming outside broke through the swirling thoughts in my head. A few minutes later, the sound of footsteps on the porch sent a jolt of fear through me. I threw down my handwork and hurried to the front door, checking the lock. Secure.

My heartbeat was frenzied, but I leaned my ear against the door, listening. The footsteps had stopped, but something scraped against the wood, and the door handle turned.

My breath caught in my throat. "Meemaw!" I whispered with a sharp hiss. I wasn't sure what she could do against an intruder, but surely between the two of us, we could fend off whoever was on the porch.

The door handle twisted again against the lock. Three quick, heavy raps came next, and I jumped back. "Meemaw!" I whispered again, my heart in my throat.

"Harlow! Open up."

I scooted to the side of the door, pulling the shade back to peer through the narrow window. Gavin stood there with his arm around Orphie.

"What in tarnation . . . !" I threw open the door and stood back while Gavin steered Orphie inside. Glancing out toward the empty street eased my mind. The night was calm and quiet and no murderers seemed to be lurking in the dark.

"I couldn't stay another minute in that hospital," Orphie said as Gavin helped her recline on the red velvet settee. Lounging on her side and with her black hair and drawn cheeks, she looked like Cleopatra.

"But did the doctor give the okay?"

Gavin spoke up. "He would have preferred her to spend the night, but I told him we'd keep a good eye on her. She needs rest, is all. Need anything, sweetheart?"

She shook her head, smiling up at him.

He sat on the love seat in the little sitting area, crossing one ankle over the opposite knee, his attention fully on her. These two were the epitome of love at first sight.

We spent a few minutes making small talk, making sure she was comfortable, each of us tiptoeing around what had happened. Finally I couldn't keep quiet about it a second longer. "Orphie, do you remember when everyone arrived here the other morning?"

She had one arm tucked underneath her body as she reclined on her side. With her free hand, she brushed her black curls away from her face. "Yes, of course I do. I was a bundle of nerves getting ready to meet Beaulieu."

It was the perfect opening. "When he came in, do you remember if he had a coffee cup?" I didn't think I'd imagined him having it, but I needed someone to corroborate what I'd seen.

She closed her eyes, as if she were trying to bring the moment to the front of her memory. Finally she shook her head. "I don't remember. I was getting my things together to take upstairs."

The sheer curtains rustled. Orphie jumped, straining to look over her shoulder. Gavin jerked, instantly on alert. "What the devil—?"

Meemaw! I silently cursed her for showing herself so blatantly. I'd just called her, wanting her help when I'd thought the pounding on the door was an intruder, but everything was fine now. "Probably just Earl Grey. My little teacup pig," I added when Gavin cocked an eyebrow up.

"Look," I said, drawing them back to Beaulieu and the missing coffee cup. "They stopped for coffee on their way from Dallas to Bliss. Any one of them could have put the poison in his coffee, right?"

I picked up Mama's wedding dress again, diving back into the beads and sequins adorning the dress. "But what do I have to do with any of it?" Orphie asked, her eyes wide as she looked at us both.

That was another question none of us had an answer to. Gavin, looking like a younger version of his dad, sat quietly, tapping his fingers in a rhythmic pattern against his knee. I knew he was listening to every word, processing every idea, and I also knew his priority had become trying to figure out exactly why Orphie had been targeted.

Chapter 29

I slept fitfully, my mind spinning around the different threads that had been tangling up every part of my life, and the lives of those around me. I was no closer to figuring out what had really happened to Beaulieu and Orphie, and that, more than anything, made me feel as if I were wearing a bonnet full of bees.

But morning was here. The sun shone through the slats of the blinds in my bedroom. A blanket of warmth, not uncomfortable from the early heat of the day, but cozy, eased around me like a layer of wool batting. I blinked away the foggy remnants of sleep, sitting up and rubbing my hands over my face. Today was the day. Tessa Cassidy and Hoss McClaine's wedding day.

"If Mama shows up," I said to myself.

I'd finished the last of the beading late into the night and dropped off Mama's wedding dress around midnight. She hadn't wanted me to come inside. "It's late, ladybug. I'll see you tomorrow."

It was as good a promise as she could give that she'd

show up at the church, so I'd left with a warning. "Will is picking you up at one o'clock, Mama. You best be ready to get hitched. Hoss'll be waiting." I had to have faith that she'd do what was good for her. Or at least what I was convinced was good for her.

Orphie had slept in the guest room, but now she was back on the settee, reclining, while Nana and I spent the next three hours over at Seven Gables helping Raylene and Hattie set up the backyard. They'd put up two tents the day before, had had the tables and chairs delivered, and had set up twinkling lights and ornamental branches to decorate the space. "Those models talk too much," Raylene said, stifling a yawn. "All night long. I thought they'd come to blows a few times."

"Quinton finally got them to simmer down."

"How'd he manage that?" I asked, grateful to not worry about Mama for a few minutes.

"That camera of his. He started taking pictures of them. They had this competition going of strikin' different kinds of poses, or somethin' like that. Seemed pretty silly to me, but those girls ate it up. Made 'em a little teary-eyed."

"Why?"

"Said it made 'em think of the guy that died. He always posed them in certain ways, and it brought up memories for 'em, or somethin'." Raylene shrugged. "I don't get it, really. Seventeen-year-old girls trying to look like they're all worldly. Don't they realize they'll grow up soon enough?"

"They're losing their childhoods," Hattie chimed in. "It's a shame."

We worked in silence for a few minutes, blowing up

helium balloons using the tank we'd rented, and tying the blue and silver metallic ovals to silver foil-wrapped baggies filled with sand.

"Do you think she'll show?" Nana asked as we placed the last of the balloons around the head tables.

"I gave Will permission to drag her there if he needs to."

"Which he won't do, honey."

"Probably not, but I told her yesterday that he'd do it, so maybe the threat will be enough."

She frowned, clearly not convinced. I felt the same way.

"We're all set," Raylene said, standing back to take in the backyard. It had been transformed. Misters and several enormous fans were situated around the perimeter of the tents to keep the area cool. The weather was supposed to cooperate and be a comfortable, if warm, eighty-two degrees, but things could change on a dime in Texas. If the wedding happened, we were prepared. And if it didn't, well, we could drown our sorrows in the misty tents.

I headed back home. Orphie was ready for the wedding, but dozing on the settee. I tiptoed to the workroom. Will was stopping by before he went to pick up Mama, and Midori would be here any minute with my maid of honor dress. Which meant I had a few minutes to puzzle things out. From the back window, I could see that Thelma Louise, grand dam of Nana's goat herd, had her chin resting on the fence that spanned between my grandparents' property and mine. The goats seemed to be present whenever I needed to think seriously about things. I'd come to believe they were a good-luck sign.

"I'm counting on you, Thelma Louise," I said softly. I turned, nearly bumping into Will with a *whomp!*

He caught me by the arms, keeping me upright.

"You're as quiet as a ghost," I said.

"As quiet as Loretta Mae?"

I laughed. It was so nice to be able to talk to him about Meemaw. It was like having the weight of all the Cassidy family secrets lifted from my shoulders. I had nothing to hide from him.

"What are you doing?" he asked.

I paused, my hand cupped under my chin. "Just thinking."

"About?" he prompted.

I didn't have a definitive answer for that. "I'm not quite sure," I said, my gaze traveling around the workroom. "There's something—"

My words froze in thin air as my gaze landed on the designers' garment bags and Midori's dresses, which hung from hooks on the wall by the French doors. Esmeralda's and Barbi's words about the hems being uneven and heavy came back to me. Hearing them talk about it when I'd first caught them trying on the clothes had stuck with me, but I couldn't pinpoint why. The fact was, not every designer was also a capable seamstress. But Midori was the whole package. She was as well rounded as they came, excelling at all aspects of fashion, from draping and tailoring to project management and business savvy. It wasn't easy to build a successful business, but she'd done it, and she'd done it well.

"Shut the doors, please, Will," I said over my shoulder, stepping back to get a full view of the dresses.

Once the French doors were closed, Will came to my

side, eyeing the dresses, a heavy frown on his face. "What do we see here?" he asked.

I stood back, taking in every aspect from head to foot. "We see beautiful dresses."

"Yeah, I'd agree with that. So why are we staring at them?"

My focus had trailed from the bodices with their buttons and frog closures to the hemlines. I tapped one of my hands against my thigh, thinking. If one of them had said something about the fit, I could have dismissed it. Two? That could still be chalked up to coincidence. But three ... and four? That meant something else altogether. That meant there really was something wrong with the hems.

Nothing that I could see with the naked eye, however.

Something Lindy had said rose to the top of my consciousness, kind of like cream floating on top of a cup of cocoa. "Midori uses the same models all the time."

Will leaned back against the table, arms folded over his chest. "I thought the other guy did, too."

"Right, but Lindy mentioned something. I hadn't paid any mind to it, but it's interesting."

"What?"

"Zoe and Madison."

"Cassidy, you're going to have to spell it out 'cause I don't know what you're talking about."

"They're old."

He stared at me as if goat antlers had sprung from my head. "What are they, in their late twenties? Early thirties? I have shirts older than that."

I tapped the toe of my pump, thinking. "Not old compared to you, me, or anyone else in the normal world, but old compared to other models. I look at Esmeralda and Barbi and they're babies. They're like Gracie—"

"They are *not* like Gracie."

"Agewise, they're like Gracie," I amended. "Beyond twenty, if a model hasn't made it, she probably won't."

"So the designers want children to model their clothes." He didn't shake his head, but from his tone, he might as well have.

"Unless they stay completely out of the sun, they'll start getting wrinkles in their twenties. And then there's gravity and skin elasticity and all that other stuff teenagers don't have to worry about. Perfect bodies, perfect skin, perfect hair. It all starts being a little less perfect the older a woman gets."

This time he did shake his head, clearly mystified by the realities of the modeling industry. "That completely depends on your perspective," he said, pulling me into an embrace. His hand slipped down to my hip and he drew me closer. "Curves and wrinkles, and whatever else life throws your way is perfectly fine with me."

I laughed. "You're easy."

"No, just in love."

I lost my breath. He'd said it again. It was real.

He continued on with the conversation rather than arguing the finer points of modeling, as if what he'd just said hadn't been monumental. "So the Dallas models haven't made it?"

I gulped, getting control of the emotions flouncing through me. "Midori's here in Dallas, not in New York, and she's good, but she's not like Stella McCartney or Donna Karan, so working for her steadily? No, they haven't made it."

Examining another designer's garments went against my nature, and until this moment, I hadn't felt a need to, as curious as I was about what the models had said. But my instincts had kicked in and were telling me to take a closer look. I held my hand out, letting my fingers dance gingerly over the fabric of the first dress. I wasn't Gracie, so no visions accosted me. No memories flooded my consciousness. No clues surfaced, as much as I wished they would.

Will continued to watch as I lifted the first of Midori's dresses off the hook, slipping the shoulders from the hanger. Having no clue what I was looking for, I simply ran my hand along the neckline, then down either side, and finally, draping the skirt over my arm, I felt along the hemline. The hem had to be almost two inches wide. Unusual, but another of Midori's signature couture elements. While other designers made invisible hems, she made a point of incorporating the hem into the overall look of the garment.

My hand stopped at a knot in the seam on one side. She'd used French seams, the finishing work on the dress impeccable. I flipped the seam so I could examine it. There was a gap, large enough for my index finger to fit in. Calling for a finger, actually. I obliged, digging mine into the hole and feeling around.

"Did you find something?" Will asked, peering at the hemline of the dress I was digging into.

I withdrew my finger and slipped the dress back on the hanger. "Not a thing."

"What are you looking for, Nancy?"

I cocked one eyebrow upward at him. "Nancy Drew's a little dated, don't you think?" There were a million and one fictional female detectives who'd be a better comparison. "How about Brenda Leigh Johnson?" I quipped. "From *The Closer*?"

"You can be whoever you want to be," he said. "What are you looking for?"

"I wish I knew. Midori was here when Beaulieu was murdered. She was with him on the road, so she could have put something into his coffee. Twice I heard the models say something about the fit of her clothes, and then there's the fact that her models are so much older than the average."

He seemed riveted. Waiting expectantly. As if I'd make some deductions just as brilliant as Brenda Leigh Johnson's and would suddenly reveal just who the guilty party was. Kyra Sedgwick made it look so easy.

If only.

"I keep coming back to why," I said. "Why would her clothes fit wrong? Why would she choose to work with older models?"

"Any answers?" he asked, his expression turning skeptical. Figuring out some elusive answers to a murder via a few custom-fit dresses did seem far-fetched.

I folded my arms, tapping the fingers of one hand in a steady rhythm against my forearm. "Nothing. Not a darn one."

I checked the clock again. Midori was going to be here in fifteen minutes, and then it would be time to get ready for the wedding. I turned back to the dresses, wondering what I was missing but stopping short when the bells on the front jingled faintly, barely audible from behind the closed French doors. I held my breath, but it wasn't Midori. Gracie came in, framed in the threshold of the door. Zinnia James was right behind her.

"For heaven's sake, Harlow Jane, hadn't you best get ready for the wedding?" Mrs. James said, Southernness dripping from her words like honey.

"Yes, ma'am. I will be in just a few minutes."

Mrs. James's iron gray hair was pulled back in a sophisticated do, and her tailored outfit conveyed just the right combination of power and grace. I'd made plenty of outfits for her over the past year, and I was quite sure that she'd realize all of her dreams throughout the next decade as a result.

"I found Gracie glued to the rocking chair on the porch," she said. "She won't hardly say a word to me." The look she gave Will could have been construed as a silent chastisement for raising such an impolite daughter, but the truth was that Zinnia James adored both Gracie and Will Flores and ushering her into the house was her way of showing concern.

"What's wrong?" I asked Gracie, noticing right off the bat that she wasn't wearing the sweetheart dress Jeanette and I had made for her. Instead she had on a plain eyelet sleeveless blouse and a flouncy off-the-rack skirt. The sweetheart dress appeared to be folded up in a plastic grocery bag, the top of the bag twisted and clutched in Gracie's hand.

She held out the plastic bag, her arm trembling. "I—I can't wear this. Too m-many—"

She broke off, enough wherewithal about her to sneak a look at Mrs. James.

"It's okay," I said. The circle of people who knew about the Cassidy charms was growing. It included Zinnia James, an old friend of my grandmother and related, directly and in a roundabout way, to the line of charmed girls herself. Bliss was like a soap opera, complete with relationship twists and turns to rival the TV show *Dallas*. And then some. I needed a family tree printed out just to keep all the little offshoots straight in my head.

"Darlin', I've told you before, I'd like you to consider me your grandmama. A girl can never have too many grandmothers, you know."

Gracie gulped, her chest noticeably heaving. "I c-can't w-wear it."

"But it's brand-new," I said. "There's no history associated with it." So far, Gracie's charm had only related to vintage garments. Maybe it was evolving, just as my own realization of my charms was.

I took the bag, withdrawing the dress from it and hanging it on a hook next to Midori's pieces, standing back for a moment to ponder. Nothing unusual jumped out at me about the dress. The cut was impeccable. The darts were expertly done. The hem was wide and straight.

Gracie's deer-in-the-headlights expression faded. She came up next to me. Her jaw tensed, right alongside her body, as if she were bracing herself for a whuppin' or some other horrible situation. But there was no whuppin' heading her way.

Except it was. She lifted her arm, opening and closing her hand as if she was gearing up for what she was about to do. And then, before I could stop her, *bam!* her arm shot out and she grabbed a wad of fabric from one of the dresses, squeezed her eyes shut, and stood stock-still.

"Baby—" Will started, but Mrs. James touched his arm and he broke off. A visible shudder passed through

Gracie. His own jaw tightened just as his daughter's had, his breathing becoming shallow and ragged as Gracie's eyes closed and she slipped into what seemed like a trance.

We watched her in silence as she released the first dress, shuffled to her left, and repeated the process with the next dress. Her actions were identical, right down to the way she stood, her heels planted firmly on the floor, as if roots had sprung from her soles and gripped her in place.

I felt Will's hand brush mine, and then he took it into his, squeezing. I didn't want to look away from Gracie, but I tore my gaze from her for a split second and snuck a look up at him. He stared straight ahead, his attention fully on his daughter. He'd grabbed my hand without realizing it, seeking something to ground him where he was. I knew the feeling. Another second on my own and I would have lunged to Gracie and ripped her away from the clothing that was filling her with such turmoil.

"She's okay," I said softly, hoping my voice would get through to him. There was one thing I knew for certain about Butch Cassidy's wish in Argentina so long ago. While it had posed problems for the Cassidy women over the years, none of us had ever suffered because of our charms. They were inherently good. Gracie might be struggling as she adjusted to her gift, but she wasn't in danger. Nothing bad would happen to her. I knew that as surely as I drew breath into my body.

Chapter 30

Gracie perched on the stool at the cutting table cradling a cup of sweet iced tea, the outside of the glass beading with condensation. "I kept seeing these flowers. Pink and purple and white," she said. "And then this weird river of white gooey cream. And that lady, the designer from Japan? She's walking through this field, picking the flowers and turning them upside down and shaking them."

Gracie's vision sounded much more like a nightmare than something that had really happened. And it had nothing to do with the dresses, unless Midori had been wearing each one while in a river of cream. Which seemed highly unlikely.

"What could it mean?" she asked, looking at me as if I would know the answer right off the bat.

"I wish I knew." I'd looked at the hems one more time, but I still had no idea why they'd be so uneven or what it was that bothered me about them. I hoped I'd have another chance to look, but that would have to wait.

I glanced behind me to where Beaulieu's garment bags hung. I didn't know why I hadn't thought of it before, but maybe they held a clue. I circled around the cutting table. As I approached the garment bags, my gaze hitched on two bolts of fabric Midori had brought with her. The ones she'd told me that she carried with her always, in case inspiration struck. "What if that's not the reason?" I mused.

Will and Gracie were by my side again, Gracie asking, "What if what?"

Fabric wound around a cylindrical piece of cardboard was heavy and unwieldy. It had struck me as odd that Midori would drag these around with her. I tried to put myself in her shoes. I had an armoire filled with fabric, as well as bolts lined up against the wall. Upstairs in the spare bedroom, the closet held even more fabric. Was there any that I'd deem so important that I'd haul it around with me wherever I went? My gut response was no, there wasn't any fabric *that* special to me.

I did a mental walk-through of everything I had ever owned, giving it another try. Again, I came up with the same response. No.

A crazy idea sparked in my mind. I crouched down and started to grab hold of one of the bolts, but Will intervened. "I'll get it."

I smiled my thanks, then patted my hand on the cutting table. "Right here, please."

He laid it down, the two open ends of the cylinder hanging off either side of the table. I poked my fingers inside, feeling around. For what, I didn't know, but there had to be something.

A momentary twinge of guilt slipped over me. I didn't

have anything other than a bit of odd behavior that pointed the finger at Midori. "I'm sure there's nothing here."

"If she had something to hide in there, she wouldn't just leave it sitting here, would she?" Gracie asked.

I'd thought the same thing, except . . . "Maybe, but then again, it was odd enough that she brought it with her. If she hauled it around with her to keep an eye on it, that would look suspicious. Just leaving it here would be the normal thing to do. It is a dressmaking shop, after all."

"Makes sense," Will said. "It would look strange for me to haul around blueprints everywhere I went, or project materials. If I were trying to hide something, I'd leave them where they were safe and where they'd blend in."

I crouched down and peered into the hollow of the cardboard. The light from the window made it easy to see right through to the other end. There were no obstructions. Nothing packed inside. Nothing out of the ordinary. So much for that idea.

Will picked up the bolt again, putting it back where it had been.

"I don't know what I thought I'd find," I said. I gestured wide with my hands, frustration settling over me. The answers to whatever had happened to Beaulieu just weren't coming.

The bells on the front door jingled and Midori walked in, my finished maid of honor dress draped over her arm in a pliable garment bag. Orphie roused herself on the settee, and Will, Gracie, Mrs. James, and I all froze. We'd put the bolt of fabric away just in time.

"Let's go, baby," Will said to Gracie. He grabbed the

sweetheart dress, brushed his lips against my cheek, and said, "Off to pick up your mom. See you at the church."

I thanked him, and moved aside as Midori came into the workroom. "I hope you like this," she said, hanging the garment bag on the hook next to her other dresses. She put down her bag.

Orphie came in and sat on the stool Gracie had just vacated. "May I?" she asked, reaching for the sketch-book peeking out of the bag.

"It's Jeanette's," Midori said, but she pulled it out and handed it to her. "Sorry to hear about your situation. Very scary ordeal," she said. "You are lucky."

Orphie smiled wanly. She opened the book, leafing through the pages as Midori turned back to me.

"Your work is beautiful," I said, running my hand down the side of a black, red, and cream color-blocked dress, and I chastised myself for even suspecting Midori could be up to anything illicit. She was a great designer, not a murderer. The design was simple, as most of Midori's things were, but it had a clean, classic cut that would compliment most figures. It reminded me of a few of Beaulieu's recent pieces, and just like that, my doubt about Midori resurfaced.

"Thank you." She unzipped the bag, showing me what she'd been working on for the last two days, her personal distraction from the murder investigation.

Slowly, the dress was revealed and I was speechless. It could have been a wedding gown itself, it was so meticulously crafted. The strapless bodice was entirely ruched, the skirt, which would hang to the floor, flared at the base and spread into a small gathered train in back, and just at the hipline, a good several inches below the waist, she'd put in what looked like a Western belt with two offset rhinestone ornaments that were reminiscent of buckles, but were situated near the hipbones rather than in the center. They added a whimsical flair to the design.

"Wow," Orphie said, looking up from the lookbook. "That is beautiful! And perfect for you, Harlow."

Midori smiled. "I think so."

It was stunning. But was it me? I didn't do strapless, and while I knew what to do to work with a woman's body, I didn't often do extremely fitted things for myself.

"It's very sexy," I said, letting my fingers dance over the fabric.

Midori angled her head, her sleek black hair falling over one eye as she studied the dress. "Just sexy enough."

"Agree," Orphie said, holding her arm up as if she were casting a vote.

Midori pulled the short train from the garment bag. "I am quite good with fitting. I have an eye for size and shape, but please try it on in case I need to make some last-second adjustments."

Last second. Oh boy. I checked the clock. The wedding was in fifty minutes and I hadn't even showered. "Okay," I said, "but I'll just be a minute." I raced upstairs and jumped in the shower. The phone rang just after I'd stepped under the hot water, but whoever it was would have to wait. I finished my shower in record time and then dried my hair, piling it up in an artfully messy bun. Maybe the dress would work. It *was* gorgeous.

I applied a touch of makeup, threw on a lightweight robe, and hightailed it back downstairs. Will was probably getting ready to go pick up Mama. Before too long, the wedding guests would be arriving at the church. Time was running out.

As I entered the workroom, Midori came right toward me. "Try on your dress. It's time for the wedding, yes?"

It was a strange feeling to slip behind the privacy screen to try something on. In truth, I'd never done it before, preferring to stay on the other side of the room, designing things for other people. I hung my robe on one of the hooks I'd provided for my customers and stepped into the dress, holding it up at the bodice with one arm as I emerged to have Midori zip up the back. "I told you, I have an eye for size and shape," she said. "It is perfect."

I stepped into the cream-colored pumps I'd brought down with me and moved to the mirror. The moment I saw my reflection, I caught my breath. True, the dress was nothing I'd ever have made for myself, and yet, just like the designs I created for other people, it was perfect on me. The bodice hugged my body, the skirt felt like air against the curves of my hips, the fabric flaring at the knees, giving me an hourglass shape.

"Lord almighty, you're a vision." Nana had come in through the kitchen's Dutch door and now gazed at me as if I were a princess. "It's your mama's weddin', but, darlin', you might could steal the show. At least to one man," she added, throwing in a wink.

"One man named Will Flores," Orphie said.

"You're both incorrigible," I said to them, but inside, I smiled. I wouldn't mind having Will think I'd stolen the show. His proclamation of love still stuck with me. Being on the other side of things was a strange sensation, and I suddenly knew what my customers felt as they tried on my creations. Renewed. Energized. Like a better version of themselves.

In typical Coleta Cassidy fashion, Nana changed the subject. "Harlow, your granddaddy's waitin'. It's time to go."

Orphie slowly rose from the settee. She was gussied up and ready for the wedding, but still pale and drawn. "Are you sure you're up for this?" I asked her.

"No way am I missing Will's face when he sees you," she said, smiling.

We'd also invited Midori, Jeanette, the four models, Lindy, and Quinton. We couldn't call ourselves Southerners if we didn't extend our hospitality to our guests, murder suspects or not. I knew Midori was coming, but the others hadn't RSVP'd, so I had no idea if they'd make it to the chapel and the reception, just to the reception, or not at all.

Midori had changed into a sheath dress made from another printed chirimen crepe, this one with a bright pink and teal background, lots of flowers, and whimsy that once again reminded me of an old-fashioned kimono. It was an odd combination of fabric and design, almost discordant, and yet it worked.

We hurried out to my granddaddy's SUV sitting in front of the house and raced to the chapel, barely getting there on time. By the time we arrived, most of the guests were there, seated in the pews, voices low and anxious as they waited. A local fiddle player played up-tempo bluegrass—not your typical wedding music, but what Mama had wanted.

Will was there, standing toward the front of the sanctuary near the altar, hands in his pockets, black slacks, a casual cotton button-down shirt and tie giving him a rugged dapper look. But none of that could hide the fact that he seemed stiff and uncomfortable.

It only took a second to realize why ... and to remember the missed phone call. Hoss wasn't standing up there with him. And Mama wasn't anywhere to be seen.

My heart sank. We'd both failed. There wasn't going to be a wedding.

Chapter 31

"I can't believe she didn't show up," I whispered to Nana and Granddaddy after I'd powwowed with Will. He stayed in the front of the church, a stoic sentry that we hoped would keep the speculation about the missing groom at bay. "What are we supposed to tell folks?"

My granddaddy Dalton rocked back on his heels, his arms folded over his chest. His lips were drawn into a thin line. "The truth."

But the truth was, none of us knew where she was. I peeked my head around the corner and smiled wanly at Will, lifting my hand in a subtle wave from the back of the church. It didn't do anything to calm my nerves, and I'm sure it didn't do anything to simmer down whatever uncertainty was circling inside Will.

We gave it another ten minutes, but Mama still didn't show. I called her house. No answer. All of her friends were sitting right here in the pews, so I was at a loss. Where could she be?

Nana and Granddaddy had their heads together, whispering, but I could only see the expression on Will's face, his jaw tight under his goatee, as he finally left his post and came into the vestibule at the back of the church. He stopped when he saw me, as if it were the first time. Looked me up and down, his eyes smoldering. And then he was next to me, taking my hand in his and drawing me close. "You're still gorgeous, Cassidy," he said, his voice low in my ear.

Everything around us faded away and for a few seconds I forgot Mama, the wedding that wasn't happening, and all the people in the church wondering what was going on. I forgot about Beaulieu, Orphie, Midori, and the fact that there was a murderer walking among us.

For a few seconds I couldn't think at all. My heart thundered in my chest, and I wanted nothing more than to have Will's arms around me so I could forget everything except that he loved me.

But Nana's and Granddaddy's whispers brought me back to reality. Will sensed it, too. He let me go and stepped back, swallowing the desire I was sure was coursing through him.

"You checked the greenhouse?" Nana asked him for the third time.

"The greenhouse, the neighbors, the whole house. Her car was there, but she wasn't."

Panic started to set in. Where was she? What had happened to Beaulieu and to Orphie zoomed to the front of my mind. What if something had happened to her?

But of course that wasn't logical. Orphie and Beaulieu were at least peripherally connected through Maximilian's book. Mama had nothing to do with that, so she wasn't in any danger. She was just running from her own fear of committing to Hoss. I was her excuse.

Gavin appeared in the vestibule, Orphie on his arm, looking pale but managing to keep up a brave face. "So your mama got cold feet, eh?" he said.

"Your dad, too," I shot back.

"He was just smart enough to stay away so he wouldn't be humiliated by your mother," he said.

Will's hand tightened, right along with his jaw. "He's the one that started this by thinking Harlow could be a killer."

Orphie cleared her throat, sounding weak, but it was enough to stop us from bickering.

"You've called him?"

"I have," Gavin said. "He's not picking up."

Granddaddy, Nana, and I looked at each other, communicating silently between us. "Mama's not answering. Hoss isn't picking up. They might could be—"

"Together," they said in unison.

Gavin lifted his chin indignantly. "No, I don't believe that. The sheriff isn't one to go kowtowing to some woman who's stood him up."

"She didn't stand him up," I said, hands on my hips. "They just had a misunderstanding."

"They're practically hitched, even if they aren't churched," Granddaddy said. "They love each other. I have every confidence they'll work out their differences."

Granddaddy straightened his bolo tie, held his chin up, and marched down the aisle. "Folks," he said, holding up his hand when he reached the front of the church. "Y'all know Tessa. She does things her own way, and her own way today means she's decided not to get hitched. All y'all are welcome to come on back to Seven Gables. Nothing says we can't have some good vittles and good company, even without the bride and groom."

The fiddle playing stopped and a low buzz went up around the sanctuary as the guests processed Granddaddy's statement and began filing out.

"We'll be along shortly," Gavin said. "We have a stop to make on the way."

I raised my eyebrows at them both.

"The book," Orphie said. "We're going to mail it back. Gavin's been holding it for safekeeping."

Together. Something was in the air. I couldn't say if it was love, but whatever was between Orphie and Gavin had them joined at the hip and was bringing out the nurturing side of the deputy.

I was glad for it if it made Orphie happy and set her back on the right path. Returning Maximilian's book was a step in the right direction.

They headed out and I gathered up the skirt of my gown in my hand, hurrying toward the door. "We have to hurry and get there before everyone else. Call Raylene and Hattie, please," I said to Will. I hadn't seen them at the church yet, so maybe we'd be able to intercept them before they left Seven Gables so they could turn right back around and get ready for an early reception.

I stopped short at the sidewalk. "I came with my grandparents," I said to Will.

"I'll drive." He grabbed my hand, but instead of heading toward his truck, he pulled me close, planting a kiss on my mouth. "Damn. What a waste of a good church," he said, a crooked half grin on his lips. "Some other time, Cassidy."

I gulped down the surprise bubbling inside me, but before I could respond—or even wonder at yet another reference to him and me in wedded bliss, he pulled me into motion, and off we went to host a reception for a wedding that hadn't happened.

Chapter 32

Will sped up to Seven Gables, pulling into the driveway. He threw it into park, and I jumped out, running as quickly as I could in my high heels. Up the drive, through the back gate, up the back porch steps, and in through the door into the kitchen.

"Raylene! Hattie!" I hollered through the house. I grabbed an apron and picked up the first tray. It would take who knew how many trips to haul them to the tents. Will grabbed two trays, and we backed out of the door, set the food on one of the tables under the tents, then raced back inside.

I was just bending over to pull one of the trays laden with fried chicken from the oven when I heard a sound from the front room. The creaks and noises were different than those at Buttons & Bows. Every old house seemed to have its own personality and quirks. Mine also had a ghost.

I closed the oven door as Will came back in. At the same moment, a woman's voice wafted into the kitchen, growing louder as its owner came closer. I whipped around, recognizing the voice instantly. "Mama!"

She appeared in the kitchen and I forgot all about the chicken and the wedding guests about to descend on the inn. "Tessa Cassidy," I demanded, "where the devil have you been?"

Mama didn't look distraught. Nor did she look as though she'd just missed her own wedding. In fact, she was wearing the dress I'd made for her, blinged-out boots, white cowboy hat with a tuft of tulle she must have affixed herself, and a good amount of makeup for her, which is to say she had on a dash of mascara and her lips were a shimmery coral.

Her cheeks matched her mouth, and from her Cheshire Cat grin, she looked as if she'd been up to no good and was mighty proud of it.

"Darlin', don't be sore."

I jammed my hands on my hips, perfectly aware of how ridiculous I looked in my designer gown, heels, and colorful, ruffled apron. But I didn't care. Mama had bailed on her nuptials, and she had some explaining to do.

"Don't be sore? Mama, you left us at the church without a word. We were worried sick." I lowered my voice to a harsh whisper for emphasis. "There's a murderer around here, remember? I thought . . ." I gulped down the fear that I'd kept tightly bottled up inside me. "I thought something had happened to you." I waved my arm up and down, gesturing to her dress. "And why in tarnation are you wearing that?"

"It's what a gal wears when she gets hitched," Hoss McClaine said as he sauntered into the kitchen.

From the corner of my eye, I spotted the plant sitting

in the center of the kitchen table and saw that it trembled and shook, its stalks stretching toward the ceiling before my eyes. When Mama was distraught, the plants around her withered. If things were really bad, they died. But the lavender wasn't wilting. It was growing and the colors of the buds were changing to a deep purple right before our eyes.

Hoss stretched his hand out to Will, who moved forward to shake it. "Sir."

I studied them both as my mind raced through the possibilities. "But you didn't get hitched," I said, my eyes narrowing. Mama wasn't one to wring her hands, and if I could base anything on the lavender, she wasn't upset. Still, her hands were clasped and twisting in front of her.

Hoss dropped his hand back to his side and Will came back to me, touching the small of my back. My mind processed. Wringing hands. Shaking hands. Mama's smile and her wedding outfit. Hoss hitched his thumbs into the front pockets of his brand-new black jeans. Something shiny caught the light from the window over the sink, drawing my eye. A ring.

A ring? My gaze flew to Mama's left hand. To her fourth finger. And, holy smokes, to the gold band firmly situated below the knuckle.

"What is that?" I asked without blinking. Without shifting my gaze. Without breathing. "Did you *elope*?"

"Darlin'," she said, moving close enough to put her hands on my shoulders. With my pumps on, I towered over her a good five inches, but she looked up at me, still my mother and still full of motherly authority. "Hoss was over when you brought the dress by. We were talkin' late last night, and well, one thing led to another and we just decided we wouldn't wait. We shouldn't wait."

"Got a hold of my cousin to officiate for us in Corsicana," Hoss said. "He performed the ceremony early this morning."

I stared at them, stunned into silence. They were married. Tessa Cassidy and Hoss McClaine had jumped the broom. They were husband and wife. And they'd done it on the down low, keeping us all in the dark, from me to Gavin and everyone in between.

"But why?" I finally asked. "Why not just wait for the ceremony?"

Hoss took hold of Mama's fidgety hand. "I wasn't gonna let her try and back out again, Harlow. Your mama's jittery, and dagnabbit, no way was I lettin' her get away."

I could understand where he was coming from, but still. "Ever hear of a phone? I know you both have one," I said. The irony of the conversation wasn't lost on me. When I'd been a rebellious teenager in Bliss, I'd been wrung out plenty of times by Hoss, and then hung out to dry by Mama directly after. My, how the tables had turned. Here I was, ready to read them both the riot act for not calling, for worrying us all, and for shirking a commitment they'd made.

But looking at the goofy, love-struck grins on their faces, I was sure my words would fall on deaf ears.

"You do know you're partly to blame," Mama said to me.

I sputtered, pressing my open palm to my chest. "Me? Just how do you figure that?"

She winked at me. "Darlin', you know your charm

works like a . . . well, like a charm. You made my dress, and sure enough, I felt something the second I put it on. What I wanted most was to live out my days with Hoss, and I had a moment of clarity. Now, that doesn't mean I didn't have some doubts, but I'm smart enough not to fight my destiny."

I gestured to my dress. "I was supposed to be the maid of honor. I might have liked to *see* you get married." I tried not to come across as too disgruntled. The truth was, I was happy for her and Hoss, both. They deserved the happiness they'd found with each other, with or without a church wedding in Bliss.

"Now, now, Harlow." Mama pulled away from her new husband, came to me, and placed her hands on my shoulders. "It's all right. Everyone will understand. We're here now."

I sighed. I *was* thrilled they'd come back for the reception instead of hightailing it to Choctaw Casino a short ways over the Oklahoma border. There was no more time for recrimination. Outside, car doors slammed. Voices, conversation, and laughter rang out as the wedding guests, now exclusively reception guests, followed the trail of helium balloons and traipsed up the driveway of Seven Gables toward the tents.

Raylene and Hattie burst into the kitchen like twin tornados, spinning into action. "Good grief! We just made it to the church, heard there wasn't a weddin', and had to turn back around," Raylene exclaimed. She laid eyes on Hoss and Mama, dropped her gaze to the ring on Mama's finger, blinked, but didn't pause to ask why or what for. We backed away as they flew into action, grabbing trays of food from nooks and crannies in the kitchen that I hadn't seen. "You get the cheesy biscuits and I'll get the barbecue chicken wings," Raylene told Hattie.

Esmeralda and Barbi came up next to us. I was struck by a vision of the two of them, both of them wearing jeans and T-shirts and looking like regular teenage girls. Nothing designer. Nothing fancy. Nothing that I could make for them, yet it was what they should be wearing. Clothes meant for girls rather than the grown-up ensembles they wore on the runway every week. "Go enjoy some fried chicken," I said, ushering them through the kitchen and out toward the tents.

For now, there was nothing else I could do. I took off my apron, tossing it aside as Gracie led the way outside. Will guided me with his hand on my lower back, and before long the murder was pushed to the back of my mind and all my thoughts went to celebrating Mama and Hoss's marriage.

Chapter 33

With the exception of Quinton, the photographer, who'd opted out of the wedding festivities, the out-of-towners stuck together in one corner of the bigger of the two tents set up. To a bunch of city slickers, the backyard barbecue wedding was surely a sight to behold, especially given that there'd been no ceremony to go with it.

Hoss McClaine was a tough man to read. With his iron gray soul patch, matching mustache, and black cowboy hat, he still looked more like the sheriff than the groom, but my perception of him might always be a trifle off. I saw him—and then I saw myself tipping a cow or climbing the town's water tower right before being caught and hauled off to have a little heart-to-heart with the man himself.

He was a quiet observer, and I knew for a fact that the fashion folk who'd descended upon Bliss a few short days ago and who were sticking together like a bunch of mud daubers in a nest had not escaped his notice. They'd not escaped my notice, either. One of them was likely a murderer, and while I'd thought it might be Midori, all I had were unfounded suspicions. They hung together like a pack, either not wanting to separate and possibly become the next victim, or not wanting to be singled out as not part of the group.

The models were still fast friends, but all I could see when I looked at them was the age difference. Were the Dallas women good influences on the impressionable New York girls? My gut was telling me that something was wrong with the fact that Zoe and Madison were still working for Midori.

"Beautiful dress," I said to Madison. It was a short cream-colored sheath with cutouts along the sides. Revealing, yet sophisticated. "Is it one of Beaulieu's?"

She shook her head, her mane of ginger locks floating around her shoulders like a cloud. "I thought so, too, but Jeanette made it," she said.

If I'd had any doubt as to Jeanette's talent, this proved the girl had it in spades.

"This one's Midori's," Zoe said, looking down at her own outfit.

"It's lovely," I said to Zoe. It was from Midori's collection the previous year, but the dropped waist and asymmetric hemline were always avant-garde and fashionable.

"Beaulieu has one just like it," Esmeralda said, shaking her head.

Barbi's head bobbed up and down. "Almost identical."

I did a mental headshake. Yet another design Beaulieu had stolen from Midori. How long before he would have reproduced some of mine?

Lindy broke away from the group, catching my eye so I'd follow. "So they skipped the ceremony and came to the reception, huh? Interesting. Maybe I'll do an article on most unusual Texas weddings. Don't think it would win me any awards, but it might be good for kicks."

A "whoop!" went up from the portable dance floor set up in the center of the bigger tent. The country band we'd brought in as entertainment had launched into Waylon Jennings's "Luckenbach, Texas." They sang the first lines, paused long enough for another "whoop!" to go up, and then everyone broke out singing the chorus. It was a country wedding anthem, celebrating the basics of love and the simplicity of country living, the Waylon and Willie way.

Mama led the guests in the singalong, Hoss standing to the side, just watching, a happy crook of a grin playing on his lips. He had the basics of love down, but good.

The twinkle lights flickered in time to the music. It couldn't be Meemaw, could it? I didn't think she could leave Buttons & Bows or the 2112 Mockingbird Lane property, but maybe I was wrong. She never had been able to sit out a party. Mama came by her eccentricities honestly. As the saying goes, the apple didn't fall too far from the tree.

My apple fell a little further out, but not out of reach. I might not be whooping it up on the dance floor, but I was hunting down a killer. We each had our own way of being unconventional.

Will and I stayed till the bitter end, finally seeing Mama and Hoss off to their first night of marriage, but Mama wasn't quite done working her own magic for the evening. She stopped at the passenger side of Hoss's truck and caught my eye before turning her back.

And then she tossed the bouquet.

Right to me.

Chapter 34

"You caught the bouquet!" Josie sat next to me in the dining room of Seven Gables, her five-month-old baby girl, Molly, in her lap. A tuft of dark, fluffy hair was pulled into a plastic barrette on the top of Molly's head, and she was dressed from head to toe in yellow ruffles. She looked up at me with enormous gray-blue eyes, her little lips drawn together in a bow.

"It was fixed," I said, typing as we talked. "She knew exactly where to throw it." Mama and Hoss had gone off on their four-day honeymoon and the guests had finally departed. Raylene and Hattie had taken care of the food cleanup and Madelyn's husband, Billy, Gavin, Nate, Josie's husband, Will, and a posse of other men had worked to clean everything else up.

When they were done, Orphie went off with Gavin, and Will eventually took Gracie home, shooting me a lingering glance that made me blush under my custom-fit dress. Josie kept me company until Molly couldn't keep her eyes open any longer.

"It means you'll be next," she said, ignoring my cynicism.

"Only if you believe in superstitions like that." Which, truth be told, I did. But I wasn't going to brood and wait expectantly for Will to propose. I had other things to occupy my mind, namely the murderer who was still at large.

A short while later, I was back at Buttons & Bows. Meemaw was by my side, her presence almost palpable tonight. I sat at my computer in the dining room, Googling random word combinations that I thought might offer me some revelation.

"What's Midori hiding?" I asked aloud, taking a break when searching fields of flowers and white rivers didn't giving me anything useful.

Meemaw didn't answer. A snack, I decided. I'd been so wrapped up in the events of the day that I'd hardly eaten. That didn't happen often, and my empty belly reminded me why.

I changed out of my maid of honor dress and into cotton shorts and a tank before warming up a bowlful of peach cobbler Raylene had sent home with me. Skipping straight to dessert seemed like a good idea at the moment. Who knew? Maybe the sugar would fuel my brain.

I added a scoop of Blue Bell vanilla ice cream before padding back to the computer. A new search for poppy fields was up on the computer. "Did you type that, Meemaw?" I asked aloud, but I already knew the answer. It couldn't have been anyone else.

"Poppies?" I clicked one of the links and started reading. Before long, my cobbler was long forgotten, the ice cream melted and streaming in creamy white rivulets down into the base of the bowl. I was reading about a different milky extraction—the air-dried stuff that came from the unripened opium poppy. The article went on to talk about the alkaloids in the plant, including morphine, codeine, and others I'd never heard of.

I grabbed for the phone and dialed. "Poppies," I said when Will answered.

"Little orange petals?" he said. "As in California's state flower?"

"Or, you know, the ones used to make opium."

That caught his attention. "I'm listening."

I forwarded him the article I'd just read and asked him to have Gracie take a look. "Is that what she saw in her vision?"

From my end of the phone, I heard him ask her the question. There was a lengthy pause while I assumed she looked at the pictures of the unripe capsules that looked like green balloons on the flower stalks, the fields of purple and lavender flowers, and a man patrolling another flower field, assault rifle cradled in his arms. Exactly what she'd described from her dream.

A rustle came over the line followed by Gracie's excited voice. "That's it! What's it mean?"

Will's voice followed, from the extension, I presumed. "You think that Beaulieu character was killed because of opium?"

"I think it's possible," I said slowly, new ideas formulating in my mind as we spoke. I thought again of the bolt of fabric Midori hauled around with her. It wasn't the fabric that was so valuable; it was something else hidden in it. That had to be it! "What if someone is smuggling this dried poppy drug to Midori, and then she—"

Oh Lord. Another piece of the puzzle came together in my head. Her signature wide hems! "What if she takes the stuff from there and the next step is to hide it in the hems of the dresses?" That would explain why they were uneven and why the fit was wrong. If she cut them to compensate for extra weight from whatever she might hide there, it wouldn't fit correctly until she'd added the packaged drugs to the dresses.

"How much can you fit into the hem of a dress?" Will asked, his voice skeptical.

It was a good question. "She'd have to be very exacting when she packaged it, and who knows how much it sells for an ounce, or however they measure it? By the gram?" I didn't know and I didn't care. I just wanted to see if it was true. Her bolt of fabric was still here, those silly hummingbirds playing hide-and-seek behind the flowers taunting me. *You can't find it.*

"We already know Beaulieu wasn't above blackmail." I described the copycat sketches I'd found in his book of Midori's work, including the close-up of the hem. But then something else struck me. Zoe had said Beaulieu had a dress just like the one Esmeralda was wearing. I'd seen that dress in one of Lindy's articles. An article she'd written several years ago. "He wasn't stealing design ideas from her," I said. "No, no, no! Will, *she* was stealing from *him*!"

I ran to the workroom and flipped through her lookbook, turning to the end pages. And there it was. Sketches of my designs from my Prêt-à-Porter rack. "She's the one who went through my designs."

"So Beaulieu was innocent?"

I considered this. Was he? "He had sketches of my designs on him," I said, trying to figure out why.

"So he did steal designs?"

My pulse ratcheted up. "Or he really did blackmail people, just like Jeanette has said all along. Maybe he had sketches of my designs to use against her."

"So you think he found out about the opium, assuming you're right?" Will said.

"If he did, and he confronted her, that's a pretty good motive to get rid of him, right? She could have put the sago palm stuff in his coffee when they stopped on their way up here She wouldn't have known when he'd die, just that he would."

I shook my head, remembering how distraught she'd been after we'd found him dead. She was either an Academy Award–caliber actress or she'd been genuinely horrified by what she'd done. "I have to go," I said. No way was I going to bother Hoss and my mother on their honeymoon. Which meant I had to call Gavin and tell him my theory, and then I was going to unwind that entire bolt of fabric to see if, like the hummingbirds, opium was hiding behind the flowers.

Chapter 35

I manhandled the bolt of fabric, laying it out on the cutting table, thinking about how to unroll it. It might be hiding something addictive and dangerous, but it was still expensive, gorgeous fabric and I couldn't, in good conscience, unwind it and let it sit in a huge heap.

Lucky for me, I had no shortage of fabric in Buttons & Bows. Thanks to Meemaw, everything had been put to right after the ransacking and I knew just where a few tall, cylindrical bolts of fabric were stashed. I raced up the stairs, past the pictures that elbowed their way up the wall. Old, discolored photographs of Butch Cassidy and his Hole-in-the-Wall Gang, one of a solemn-faced Butch and an equally contemplative Texana Harlow, my great-great-great-grandmother, as well as other family portraits from generations gone by, made me pause every now and then to take stock of where I'd come from.

Now was not one of those times.

I hightailed it past the photos and into my bedroom. With the exception of the attic, Meemaw had kept a tidy

house when the farmhouse was hers. I did the same—
one way in which the apple fell right next to the tree—
and I had great intentions to clean out the space she'd
used to store anything she didn't want to part with but
didn't want front and center in her life anymore. Given
that she'd been a seamstress, that meant she had squir-
reled away more than the average person's share of fabrics, notions, and other miscellany.

Hence me naming my shop Buttons & Bows. It was
my homage to her.

Loretta Mae had been a spry eighty-something-year-
old (she claimed to have been born any number of years
and no one quite knew the truth), but the dark attic
space through the door off the master bedroom was
something she'd never tackled.

I plunged through the door, weaving around stacks of
boxes, flying past the shelving stacked with Mason jars
of buttons, snaps, closures, and ribbon. I'd moved half of
Meemaw's collection down to the shelving unit on the
south wall of the workroom, but there were plenty more
to go through.

Someday.

I spied the rolls of fabric leaning up against an old
wooden rocking horse. The dim light gave enough illumi-
nation to make out which bolt had the least amount of
fabric. There was one bright floral tapestry that was fairly
sparse. It would do. I grabbed it, tucking it under one arm
and maneuvering back through the attic to the bedroom,
managing to hit the wall going back downstairs only twice.

Outside, tires screeched, doors slammed, and a second
later, the heavy thud of footsteps pounded against the
wooden planks of the porch.

My stomach catapulted to my throat and all I could think of were drug cartels, AK-47s, and me, dead in my shop. Earl Grey dashed around my feet, his quiet oink echoing in my ears. I whirled around as the bells hanging from the door jingled, swinging the cumbersome tail end of the bolt and narrowly missing the floor lamp next to the sofa. Will rushed through first, Gavin close on his heels. Orphie brought up the rear, moving slowly and looking pale.

"Cassidy, what the devil are you doing?" Will demanded, skidding to a stop and staring at me.

"What am I doing? What in tarnation are you doing? You scared me half to death!"

He stared me down. "You call me, have me look up opium plants, deduce that these highly illegal and addictive flowers are the ones Gracie saw in her vis—"

"Will!" I cut him off before he could finish that sentence and reveal the Cassidy charms—and that they extended to Gracie—to the deputy.

He shot a terse glance at Gavin before saying, "You can't catch murderers by yourself."

"I don't want to catch murderers by myself. That's why I called you."

"This is serious, Harlow. One man is dead, and Orphie was poisoned."

As if on cue, she sank down on the couch in the front room. The toll of the wedding and reception had snuck up on her. Like the doctor said, she needed rest.

"I know it's serious, Will," I said, maintaining my grip on the tall bolt of tapestry.

Gavin stepped between us, holding his arms out as if he were officiating a boxing match. "Let's just simmer down, why don't we," he said, more of a statement than a question.

"I don't need to simmer down. I'm fine," I said, wishing my roiling stomach would cooperate with my words. He was one hundred percent right. There was a murderer in Bliss, and everything was pointing at it being Midori. Midori, the woman who'd made me the most beautiful dress I owned. Midori, the woman who'd helped me make Gracie her sweetheart dress. Midori, the woman who I'd spent hours and hours with and was supposed to share the spotlight with in *D Magazine*.

Now I really did feel sick to my stomach, and there was no hope of simmering down.

Chapter 36

Something nagged at me, but I couldn't put my finger on it. It smoldered in the back of my brain while Gavin took charge of my workroom. I'd explained my plan of unrolling Midori's special fabric and rerolling it onto the bolt I'd found in the attic. "To search for opium," he'd said dryly. Not a question, but a disbelieving statement.

"Exactly."

He'd pushed back his cowboy hat, scratching his head. "It's a harebrained idea."

"So harebrained it might actually be true," Will had argued.

I checked on Orphie, making sure she was still okay. Her cheeks were hollow, her olive skin pale and carrying a faint patina. "Tell me if you find anything," she said, letting her eyes drift closed.

I passed the message on to Gavin. He raised one eyebrow at me. "If who finds anything?"

Oh, brother. "If *you* find anything, Deputy McClaine," I said. "If *you* find anything."

Mollified, he went back to work. He had called in a fellow deputy, a woman dressed in the same beige uniform he usually wore, minus the off-white cowboy hat, and Madelyn, who walked around the room, snapping official photographs of the event. The deputies pulled on thin latex gloves and slowly unrolled Midori's fabric, carefully winding it around the second bolt, readjusting every few minutes as it slipped off-center.

"I could help," I said, impatient at how slowly they were moving.

Gavin didn't bother to look up at me. "We got it," he said.

"But I know how to roll fabric. It'll be easier if—"

"Harlow," he said, this time looking up at me with narrowed eyes, "I said we got it."

Another ten minutes passed before they finally reached the end of the roll. Will put his hand on my shoulder as I started forward. "Cassidy, let him do his job."

"I just want to see," I said, but I stopped. Gavin would only shoo me away, and I didn't want him to kick me out altogether, which he certainly could do if he chose to.

Another agonizing minute passed. Part of me didn't want them to find any opium or seeds or, or whatever might be being smuggled in. The nagging feeling that I'd missed something started up again. Seeds. What was it about seeds that picked at my brain?

"Seeds," I murmured. "Seeds, seeds, seeds." As if saying it aloud would somehow provide me with the elusive answer.

"Seeds from the poppy?" Will asked.

I shook my head. "No, that's not it." I wandered out

to the gathering room, turning in a circle as I thought. I closed my eyes for a minute, remembering the day everyone had descended on Bliss, and on Buttons & Bows. They appeared before my dark eyelids like ghosts, more visible than Loretta Mae ever was. But Meemaw made me feel, whereas the people in my mind were just vacant images that weren't providing me with any answers.

Bang!

The sound came from the kitchen. "What the—"

Bang! Bang!

Will and I looked at each other and then, as if we'd communicated telepathically, we both took off for the kitchen. I don't know what he thought, but I was sure it was Meemaw.

We stopped short in the entrance of the kitchen, staring. The cupboard doors were being flung open and then slammed shut by an invisible force. Drawers slid open before banging closed again.

Will stumbled back a step, staring. "Loretta Mae?"

One cupboard banged open and closed in rapid succession. Her response. But she didn't stop at flinging cupboards. The air in the room began to spin, forming a cyclone right there in the kitchen. The particles seemed to grow heavy, laden with moisture. The cyclone concentrated in the center and right before our eyes, it began to take the shape of a figure.

My breath caught in my throat and I couldn't move. Couldn't swallow or blink or move. My great-grandmother was finally going to appear before me in a corporeal form! Her legs formed first, a bluish tint on the bottom, a subdued red on top. I smiled to myself. Meemaw's eternal clothing was what she'd loved wearing in life.

Blue jeans and a plaid snap-front blouse. Nothing could be more fitting.

"Holy mother of—" Will raked one hand through his hair and then looked at me. "It's really her?"

"It's really her," I said. I reached a hand out toward the figure, watching in awe as it took shape, looking more and more like Loretta Mae. Her wavy ginger locks framed her head, and a rosy glow splashed across her cheeks, visible even though her form was still blurred around the edges and wispy.

Gavin's voice bellowed from the workroom. "What the devil is goin' on out there?"

Instantly the banging stopped and Meemaw's figure grew still, her form rippling and growing fainter.

"Nothing, Deputy," I said hurriedly.

"Yeah," Will added, looking as though he'd seen a ghost. Which theoretically he had. "Not a damn thing."

I held my breath, waiting to be sure he didn't come out to investigate. The low sound of voices from the workroom told me they'd gone back to the fabric. I turned back to Meemaw. "Don't go!"

She didn't. She got back to work, her ghostly form floating around the kitchen, swooshing in between Will and me, leaving a cloudy trail as it wound through the kitchen. One of the drawers near the stove slowly opened and closed. There was no banging at the end of each motion. She didn't want to cause a commotion, which was good, but I had no idea what she was trying to tell me.

"What is it, Meemaw?" I asked aloud, walking toward her, wishing more than anything that she'd stay still, appear to me completely solid and tangible, but she didn't.

A soft moan, sounding like the word "Looooookkkk," came from the delicate form. Her rippling arm lifted, pointing to the drawer in question. Beneath my feet, the linoleum was suddenly cold. She dragged the drawer open and closed again until I stepped closer.

As I reached for it to hold it open, a memory flashed. Standing right here in the kitchen, Nana cleaning up. A baggie with some ground seeds. She'd put them in the—

"Oh my . . . oh no. No." I grabbed the drawer and looked inside. Right there, tucked in between the cumin and the cinnamon, was a snack-sized baggie with seeds like nothing I'd ever seen before.

"Is this . . . it's the . . . ?" I looked up at my great-grandmother's ghost. "Meemaw, is this what killed Beaulieu?"

Her head moved slowly, but distinctly, in a nod. I didn't dare touch it, instead hollering for Gavin, realizing too late that calling the deputy meant Meemaw would have to vanish.

It happened in the same moment. Gavin traipsed from the workroom into the kitchen, holding his cowboy hat by the rim. At the same moment, Meemaw's ghostly form popped like a bubble, splitting into a thousand tiny pieces and disappearing into thin air. Gavin didn't seem to notice, instead shaking his head at me. "I have to give it to you, Harlow," he said. "I thought you were one fry short of a Happy Meal when you started talkin' 'bout opium. Plumb crazy, but darn it if you weren't right on the money."

"You found something?" Will asked, sounding just as amazed.

"Oh yeah, we found something all right. Packaged

and lined up all nice and neat where the material attaches to the cardboard. Very clever, I must say."

"What's the theory, then?" Will asked. "Beaulieu found out about the drugs, confronted her—"

"You mean tried to blackmail her like he did me?" Orphie interjected, coming through the dining room and stopping at the threshold of the kitchen, holding on to the wall at the entrance.

Will nodded and finished with "And she killed him?"

"It might coulda gone down just like that," Gavin said.

The seeds! I pointed to the drawer, pushing down my disappointment at finally getting a glimpse of Meemaw after all this time only to have her vanish again. Soon. Hopefully I'd see her again before too long. "Look at those." I'd seen Nana put the baggie away, not realizing at the time what it was. "Could that be the poison?"

Orphie gasped, a jolt of energy making her surge forward. Gavin sidestepped, blocking her, and then catching her when she stumbled back. He guided her to the table. "It's evidence, baby. You can't touch it."

Baby? Wow, they had progressed quickly.

Her face contorted as she dragged her arm up, pointing at the drawer. "Somebody poisoned me with . . . with . . . that."

I stared at her. She was all bowed up, as Granddaddy would say, and more than that, she was the wild card in the whole deck. The unknown. If Midori had killed Beaulieu, and it seemed plausible that she had, had she also been behind what had happened to Orphie? It was the only logical conclusion, but we still didn't know why.

Chapter 37

Seven Gables. It was fitting to break the news about Midori here given that seven sets of eyes were staring at me. The four models, Jeanette, Lindy, and Quinton stood in the parlor and I was the sole focus of their attention.

"Arrested?" Jeanette shook her head, one side of her mouth quirking in disbelief.

"Opium?" Lindy stared, wide eyed. "So he was right," she muttered under her breath.

The attention shifted to her. "Beaulieu?" Quinton asked. He was a man of few words, but when he spoke, he cut right to the chase.

Lindy nodded, propping her black-framed glasses on the top of her head. I responded by straightening my own and pushing them up the bridge of my nose to sit more firmly. "He said her designs were off, and there had to be a reason why. His words," she said, "not mine."

I turned to the models. "You each commented on it. How the fit was wrong."

Esmeralda was the first to speak up. "Totally wrong. The hemlines were, like, totally messed up and—"

"Wide," Barbi finished. "Really, really wide. And they hung wrong."

Lindy had pulled out her trusty pencil and notepad and was tapping the eraser end against her cheek. "So let me get this straight. Someone would cultivate the poppies for the drug and smuggle it in the imported fabric. Midori would then collect it, sew it into the hems of her runway designs, and then what?"

I remembered something Midori herself had said to me. "She donates her clothes right off the models," I said. "That had to be her method of distribution. She gets a tax break and gets rid of the drugs all at once." I dug my cell phone from my purse and texted Deputy Gavin Mc-Claine. There were still missing pieces, but one by one, they were coming together.

Only her words as Gavin had arrested her still echoed in my head. She'd flatly denied having anything to do with Beaulieu's murder, and with Orphie being poisoned.

I'd watched her being handcuffed and dragged away, fighting the whole time, tears staining her cheeks, her gaze meeting mine before Gavin placed his open palm on her head and guided her into his squad car. "I did not kill him," she said to me before the car door slammed. "Please, listen to me. I did not kill him."

I wanted to believe her.

I braced myself to dig a little deeper, thinking maybe I'd missed something.

But blackmail was a powerful motive, and if Beaulieu knew about her opium scheme, she had every reason to want to eliminate him from the picture.

Lindy set three glasses on the coffee table before sinking down onto the Victorian golden couch in the Seven Gables parlor, taking the pitcher of tea from Jeanette, and pouring. She sipped as Jeanette sat opposite us, laying her sketchbook on the table next to her glass. Her eyes were wide, still looking dumbstruck by everything that had happened. "And then there was one," Lindy said. She frowned. "Sorry. Bad joke."

But she was right. Beaulieu was dead. Midori was cooling her heels in the Bliss County Jail while awaiting a court appearance. And I was the only designer left.

"Not the way either of them expected it to turn out," I said, turning off my cell phone and setting it on the couch next to my leg.

She gave a dry laugh. "No, I imagine not."

"The article," Jeanette started. "Are you still writing it?"

Lindy nodded. "I'm taking a different angle. New York fashion designer comes home to Texas and makes a name for herself and her town. It'll showcase more of your fall collection," she said to me.

I made myself smile. I didn't want to be ungrateful, but the truth was, Beaulieu was dead and Midori was heading to prison. Not the way I wanted things to end up and certainly not how I wanted to end up as the sole focus of Lindy's article. I'd rather have shared the spotlight with both designers, but I couldn't change the choices either one had made—or the result.

"Michel always thought he'd end up on top," Lindy said. "And Midori? I still can't believe she could have killed him."

"But I told you," Jeanette said. "Who knows how many other people he had dirt on?"

"But here's the thing," Lindy said, looking at some invisible spot over my shoulder. "People thought he was stealing from other designers, but he always denied that. I started investigating that."

I thought about the garments and sketches I'd seen since the designers had descended on Bliss. A few of Beaulieu's resembled Midori's. He'd had drawings of some of my designs in his pocket when he died. Madison's—or was it Zoe's?—dress at the wedding had similarities to Midori's, too.

My eyes strayed to the coffee table, to the sketchbook lying there, and something tugged at my memory. It was the one Midori had had with her the day before when she'd come to Buttons & Bows with my maid of honor dress. Jeanette's, she'd said. The same one that had a page torn out.

My breath caught in my throat. Midori's words as she'd been led away repeated in my head. *I did not kill him.* What if she'd been telling the truth? She was guilty as sin with the opium smuggling, but did her crimes actually extend to murder?

"What if . . . ," I started, but I trailed off, still making sense of this new idea. I was relieved to hear the distant sounds of someone bustling about in the kitchen. The creaks and groans of the old Victorian were disconcerting. The sounds couldn't be attributed to Meemaw, and every noise felt like nails on a chalkboard as I tried to untangle the mess of threads surrounding all that had happened.

Lindy and Jeanette waited, Lindy tapping her pencil eraser and Jeanette's foot swinging back and forth in a frenzied motion. "What if what?" Lindy asked.

I thought about the time frame of Beaulieu's designs compared to Midori's. "What if it wasn't Beaulieu who was copying Midori?" I said slowly, wondering if it was possible. "What if Midori had copied his designs?"

Lindy smiled, nodding. "Possible."

She had questioned the very idea that Beaulieu was the one stealing intellectual property. To her, I was definitely on the right track.

But Jeanette balked. "But you saw the dresses. They're too close to not be stolen designs."

"You said you and Midori just met recently, right?" I asked her.

Jeanette reached for her sketchbook and iced tea. "That's right."

Lindy's chin snapped up. "No, that's not right. I interviewed you both almost a year and a half ago for an article on Japanese fabrics when you were interning for her. And again about a month ago when I started investigating this article."

Jeanette's foot started moving faster than the wheel on a freight train. "Met her again, I guess. I didn't know her well back then. You know how interns are treated," she said, offering a self-deprecating smile.

One by one, small, seemingly insignificant details I'd overlooked began to take on greater importance. It was Jeanette's dress that Madison had been wearing, and that I'd mistaken for Beaulieu's work. I'd assumed that Beaulieu was stealing from Midori, but now something Meemaw said came back to me. Whenever I'd tell her about trouble at school and what different girls would say behind my back, she'd say, "There's a lot of jealousy, ladybug, and quite often, what you hear and think is actually the opposite of the truth." What if Midori and Jeanette had both been the ones stealing ideas from Beaulieu, instead of the other way around?

"You said you overheard his conversations about blackmail," I said to Jeanette.

I leaned forward, elbows on my knees, my hands cupped under my chin. "The page of my designs he had on him when he died ... it was from your sketchbook, wasn't it? Was he blackmailing you?"

She sputtered, shaking her head and saying, "No! Of course not!" but her shaking foot gave away her agitation.

"You did everything for him, didn't you?" I'd been shocked by how she'd hurriedly stopped picking up the things spilled from her purse to take the magazine from Beaulieu's hand. How he'd ordered her to fetch him water. "When you stopped for coffee on your way to Bliss, did you get it for him?"

She scoffed. "Of course. He didn't want to step foot in a bourgeois coffee shop. I was his assistant. That's what I did."

The baggie of spices Nana had found and tucked away in my kitchen. I suddenly realized that they'd probably fallen from Jeanette's bag when she spilled the contents. The murder weapon.

I continued to rearrange the ideas in my head, placing Jeanette at the center of everything instead of Midori. "He'd turned his blackmail to you, hadn't he?" I asked her.

"You'd been taking his abuse. Being his assistant was far worse than interning for Midori. Did you know about her drug smuggling? Did you tell Beaulieu? Try to play his game and get the upper hand?"

A red splotch spread up her neck, turning her cheeks ruddy. Her knuckles turned white as they gripped her glass, and her lips thinned. "I don't know what you're talking about," she spit. "He was blackmailing her, but it had nothing to do with me."

Lindy cocked her head to one side, as if she could hear every detail of what was transpiring better that way, filing it away for the article I was sure she planned to write.

"You copied one of his designs," I said, thinking again of Madison's dress. "Did he find out? Was he blackmailing you, too?"

She seemed to realize that she had no way out, and she also knew the police weren't here at the moment. Anything she said now she could deny later. "He turned the tables on me," she snapped. "Trying to blackmail a blackmailer isn't so easy. He said he'd ruin me."

Just as he'd told Orphie.

And just like that, my brain hitched. Not only had she killed Beaulieu, putting poison in the coffee she'd gotten for him on the way into Bliss; she'd also tried to kill my friend. This was the one thing I had no answer to. "Why did you poison Orphie?"

Her eyes skittered around the room, settling once or twice on Lindy before straying again. That was all it took for me to realize the truth. "Lindy invited Orphie here for tea to flesh out her interviews, but the poison wasn't meant for her, was it?"

Lindy's eyes narrowed from behind her heavy-framed glasses. She glared at Jeanette. "You intended to poison me?"

"The cups were switched," she said tightly. "I asked

Raylene which cup was for which of you, and when she had her back turned, I put in a little of the powder. But those stupid sisters switched them somehow. You drank the wrong one." She shrugged. "After it happened, though, I thought it might give me another chance to look for Maximilian's book."

"Which you knew about because—"

"I knew everything Beaulieu had his hands in," she said flippantly.

"And you wanted it to help you with the creative part of designing." She'd told me that was her weakness. I'd seen her tailoring and sewing skill with Gracie's sweetheart dress. It was the conceptualization she struggled with.

Lindy clamped her hand to her throat, staring at Jeanette as if she couldn't believe what she was hearing. There was no remorse. No sense that she regretted killing Beaulieu, attempting to kill Lindy, and accidentally poisoning Orphie.

I gripped my own glass of tea in my hand, the beads of condensation dampening my skin. From the kitchen, I could hear the faint sound of Raylene's west Texas drawl mixing with Hattie's. I willed them to come to the door, hear what was going on, and call Gavin. But they didn't come and their voices faded away as Jeanette spoke again.

"Have some tea," Jeanette said, nodding toward the glass I held. "You look a little peaked."

I *felt* pale and drawn and, frankly, more than a little frazzled. I'd already raised the glass to my lips, but stopped suddenly. Had she managed to sprinkle some of that poison powder into our tea?

"Oh God, you poisoned it, didn't you?" Every bit of color drained from Lindy's face. "Stupid. How could I have been so stupid?"

From the corner of my eye, I saw a movement at the registration desk. Either Raylene or Hattie. My skin grew cold and clammy, the breath leaving my body as I realized another truth. "It was you," I said to Jeanette, my voice barely more than a breath. "You ransacked my shop to find Maximilian's book."

She sat there, still as a trapped lioness ready to pounce, but I kept going, slamming the glass of tea down on the table, the amber liquid sloshing over the edges. "Is this poisoned, too?"

"You should just leave well enough alone," she said. "I like you, Harlow, but I like being free more."

I stood, skirting away from the old-fashioned furniture and backing away. Lindy looked too pale to move. If the tea was poisoned, was it working on her already, or was she just stunned into immobility?

Jeanette's hands clenched by her sides, she grew completely still, and I knew she was going to pounce. She did, moving with speed I wouldn't have imagined she had. But she didn't fling herself toward me. She bolted for the door, barreling through it, careening down the porch steps and across the flagstone pathway, and hurling herself into one of the cars parked along the curbside.

I was on her heels, but stopped short as she fired up the engine. The tires squealed against the asphalt, and she tore off. An urgent call to the sheriff's department was all I could do. Dixie picked up.

"Harlow, honey, Raylene Lewis already done called. Said she was overhearin' a conversation between you and the deceased's assistant and that it sounded like the murder was being discussed. One of our deputy sheriffs was on her way when she just intercepted the suspect. Backup's on the way and they're fixin' to bring the woman in."

"Send an ambulance," I said, praying that Lindy would be okay.

I collapsed on the porch steps of Seven Gables to wait for help, all the adrenaline that had coursed through me during the confrontation with Jeanette seeping away. Midori was still guilty of plenty, but at least she wouldn't be accused of murder. And once again, Bliss was safe.

Chapter 38

"Is the reporter going to be okay?" Gracie asked.

I pulled her in for a hug. "She is. She didn't ingest enough to . . . to . . ."

"To kill her like Beaulieu," Gracie finished. She trembled. "It could have been you."

I gave her another squeeze before letting her go. "But it wasn't. And you . . . you are a crime solver extraordinaire. Without your visions, we wouldn't have figured out Midori's smuggling scheme."

Earl Grey squealed in her arms and she laughed, releasing him. He scampered away to the workroom window. On the other side, several of Nana's La Mancha and Nubian goats milled about. Thelma Louise, however, had her nose pressed up to the glass.

"But you have the real knack," she said. "Jeanette? Wow. Just wow."

Will nodded his agreement. "I don't think anyone even suspected her."

Gracie's head bobbed up and down. "She's cray-

cray. Blackmail and poison and dressmaking. It's like Project Runway behind bars," she said. "But are they sure?"

"Sure about what?"

"Is Deputy McClaine sure Midori had nothing to do with it?"

"Nothing to do with the murder," Will said, "but she's plenty guilty."

Gracie had on the sweetheart dress—which I still couldn't believe. "No visions?" I asked her.

She shook her head. "I realized something. Once I see the vision the first time, I can control it. I can close my eyes and sort of, like, summon it up, or I can . . . not."

"She doesn't know how or why, but it's a start," Will said. He looked as though a burden had been lifted, and I knew that was just what he felt. I felt it, too. Gracie had been plagued with images since before any of us knew her relation to Butch Cassidy or that she was charmed. But now she was figuring out how to control the charm rather than having the charm control her.

"Where's the bouquet?" she asked just as Orphie and Gavin came in from the porch.

Orphie went straight for the antique armoire that stood against the back wall of the gathering room. Inside, I'd hung the bouquet upside down so it would dry. I planned on making a potpourri from the petals. "It's not what I imagine you carrying down the aisle," she said.

Will reached in and took it off the hook. "Me, either."

I laughed, ignoring the implication that he'd imagined me carrying any kind of bouquet. "I think I'd go for a more natural arrangement, but you know Mama and her flowers. Go big, or go home."

"And would you have the cowboy hat with the veil like she did?"

"Mmm, I think not," I said. There was no harm in playing along. Love was step one on the possible path to marriage, and if Loretta Mae got what she wanted, Will and I would be there before too long.

Orphie joined Gavin on the paisley love seat, laying her hand on his knee. It had taken her a while to garner up the courage, but she'd finally done it. Mailing Maximilian's book back was a step in the right direction for her, phase one of getting her life back on track. What would happen between her and the deputy was anyone's guess. She was heading back to Missouri in a few days, but long-distance love was not impossible. "We'll enjoy the time we have together," she told me when I'd asked. "I've got nothing but time."

Nothing but time, just like Will and me.

Gracie scooted off in search of Earl Grey as her dad launched another question at me. "Day or night?"

"Day or night what?"

"Wedding."

"Night," I said, "with lots of twinkling lights."

"Veil or cowboy hat?"

"Ah, tiara!" I said, laughing. "On my wedding day, I know I'll feel like a princess."

"So no bluegrass and barbecue?" he said with a chuckle.

I grinned at him, pushing my slipping glasses back into place. "I guess I'll cross that bridge when I get there."

"No, Cassidy," he said, pulling me close, his voice playful. "*We'll* cross that particular bridge together."

Make Your Own Felt Beads

Try making these fun, easy felt beads! You need just a few grams of carded wool or wool roving and some warm, soapy water. Combine them with more traditional beads, like glass, metal, or ceramic, to make fun, whimsical and one-of-a-kind jewelry.

Instructions

1. Fill a bowl with warm water and add a small amount of liquid dish soap.

2. Gather up a tuft of the wool roving, approximately 4 to 5 inches long. This amount will result in a small, cherry-sized bead. Once you get the hang of it, make beads in all different sizes. For size consistency, weigh each tuft of wool before beading.

3. Roll up the tufts, tightly, until they're shaped like a ball.

4. Submerge the ball of wool into the soapy water, then add a small amount of dish soap.

5. Roll the ball between your palms, coating it with the soap. Do not apply pressure or compress the ball. If you do, you'll wind up with a matted, unshapely form rather than a nice, round bead.

6. The ball of wool will begin to shrink slightly, hardening as you continue to roll it between your palms.

7. The completed bead will be firm, but soft enough that you will be able to poke a hole through it. Rinse the excess soap from the bead and allow it to dry, pushing a darning needling through the center to create the hole.

Cassidy Family Tree

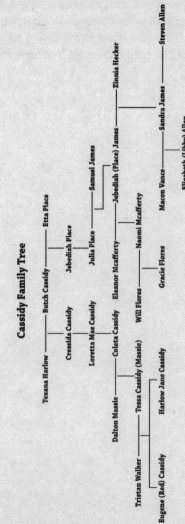

Watch for Harlow's adventure
in the next book in the
Magical Dressmaking series,

A KILLING NOTION

Coming from Obsidian in April!

"A weekend getaway, Cassidy. You. Me. The hill country."
Will Flores leaned against the archway between the dining area and the kitchen of 2112 Mockingbird Lane, his
arms folded over his chest, a cream-colored straw cowboy
hat on his head. He looked like a cross between Toby
Keith, with his bandanna biker look, and Tim McGraw,
goateed and lean. "The place is called Biscuit Hill. You're
going to love it."

"Do they have homemade scones?" I asked. No bed-and-breakfast would be complete without sweet biscuits,
British style.

"I'm sure they do."

"With Devon cream? If you're going to have scones,
you have to have clotted cream to go with them. Or
lemon curd. Lemon curd could work, too."

He stifled a grin. "I'll call and make a special request
for lemon curd and cl—?"

"Clotted cream," I finished.

He pushed off the wall and ambled over to the sink, where I'd been rinsing our dinner dishes.

"Your chicken-fried steak is mighty tasty," he said, taking up the dish towel and drying my hands.

"Secret recipe." We'd grown into an easy rhythm with each other since I'd moved back home to Bliss and Meemaw had done her matchmaking from beyond the grave. Dinner together a few times a week, a shared teacup pig, which Will and Gracie had given me for Christmas, and even comfortable silence when I was working on a project and Will, on my sofa, was drawing sketches to remodel an historic building in Bliss all got me thinking more and more how we belonged together.

"Biscuit Hill sounds lovely. But being alone with you for the weekend," I said with a wink, "sounds even better."

He took the towel from my hands and tossed it on the counter beside me; then he placed his arms on either side of me, moving in close and lowering his lips to mine. I started to wrap my arms around his neck, but stopped as the bells in the front room jingled, announcing someone's arrival.

"Dad! Harlow!" Gracie's voice bellowed, echoing in through the rooms as if she were shouting into a megaphone.

I didn't know how Meemaw could affect Gracie's voice, but I had a feeling she was magnifying it somehow. The power of a Cassidy ghost. Communication with Loretta Mae was sketchy, at best, but it was getting easier. Until she went and threw a wrench in things by adding a new supernatural skill.

"In the kitchen," Will said, pulling away from me and dropping his arms to his sides. The warmth that had seeped into the space between us chilled. It was more than just the space created when Will stepped back. Meemaw, I knew, was reacting to something.

The second I saw Gracie's face, I knew that was the reason. Will and I moved forward at the same time. "What's wrong?" I asked as Will clutched her shoulders and said, "What happened? Are you okay?"

She half nodded, half shook her head. "Shane," she said, breaking down into a sob.

Will's spine stiffened and he went into what I was beginning to recognize as full-protective-Dad mode. "If he hurt you—"

"Daddy, no. He didn't. He wouldn't!"

"What is it, Gracie?" I asked.

Her anxiety flooded the room, weighing down the air and pressing down on us. "The sheriff said they think someone tampered with Mr. Montgomery's car, and . . . and . . . and they think maybe it was Shane. Just because he works at Bubba's, they say he'd know how. They think he might could have caused the accident that killed his dad."

Will and I both stared at Gracie. Death wasn't anything new to either one of us. We'd each seen our share and helped solve a mystery or two right here in Bliss. But Gracie's young boyfriend being accused of murdering his father? That was too close to home.

"Harlow," she said, dragging the back of her hand under her nose. "You have to help him."

"Whoa." Will held his hands out to her, palm first, the message clear. *Simmer down and knock that thought right out of your head.* "Harlow isn't going to get involved in this. The sheriff has it under control, Gracie."

Her mouth dropped open and her head jutted forward. "No, they don't. Not if they think Shane had anything to do with it. Daddy, he couldn't possibly kill anybody. Certainly not his father."

Will's jaw pulsed and his eyes narrowed. "I hope not."

"Innocent before proven guilty," I said, stepping closer to Will. He looked like a panther ready to attack, and I was grateful Shane wasn't anywhere near Buttons & Bows because he'd get the brunt of that force.

"He's innocent," Gracie said again, but this time, instead of looking at her dad, she looked at me. Tears pooled in her eyes and her lower lip quivered again. She was barely holding it together.

"I'm sure he is, darlin'," I said, taking her hand. "The sheriff"—who just also happened to be my new stepdaddy— "is a fair man. He's got to look at all sides of a situation before he can know what happened."

"What about his son? The deputy? You don't like him much, Harlow. What if he thinks Shane's guilty?"

"I like Gavin McClaine just fine." More, even, since he was carrying on a real, albeit long-distance, relationship with my good friend Orphie Cates. The deputy sheriff had grown up with a chip on his shoulder, but love at first sight with Orphie had dug away at it. He still got my craw, but not quite as often as he had in the past. "But more important than that, he's good at his job. He and Hoss both believe in justice. They're not going to do anything that would falsely accuse an innocent person."

I hadn't really thought about it so succinctly before, but now that the words had left my mouth, I knew it was true.

Gracie didn't look like she believed me, so I gave her

hand another squeeze. "Let them do their jobs," I said. "You just be a friend to Shane right now. He's going to need that more than anything.

Gracie shook her head, her dark hair swinging into her face with the motion. "No, Harlow, you have to help him. You've done it before, solved a murder." Tears pooled in her eyes, one slipping down and streaking her cheek. "Please," she said, her voice quiet and pleading.

I looked squarely at Gracie, nodding, then turned to Will. "Biscuit Hill is going to have to wait."

Melissa Bourbon

Deadly Patterns
A Magical Dressmaking Mystery

Bliss, Texas, is gearing up for its annual Winter
Wonderland spectacular and Harlow is planning the main
event: a holiday fashion show being held at an old
Victorian mansion. But when someone is found dead on
the mansion's grounds, it's up to Harlow to catch the
killer—before she becomes a suspect herself.

**"Harlow Jane Cassidy is a
tailor-made amateur sleuth."
—Wendy Lyn Watson**

Also available in the series
A Fitting End
Pleating for Mercy

Available wherever books are sold or at
penguin.com

facebook.com/TheCrimeSceneBooks

OM0081